THE

SIMON BRETT is the auth[or] ... as the Charles Paris a[nd] ... president of the Detec[tion] ...

JAN BURKE is the author of the Irene Kelly novels, which include the Edgar® Award-winning *Bones*.

DOROTHY CANNELL is an Agatha Award winner and author of *The Importance of Being Ernestine*.

MARAGARET COEL is the bestselling author of the Wind River mysteries.

DEBORAH CROMBIE is an Edgar® and Agatha Award nominee and author of the Duncan Kincaid/Gemma James series.

EILEEN DREYER (and her evil alter ego, Kathleen Korbell) have published between them over twenty-five novels, including *With a Vengeance*.

CAROLYN HART is the author of the Agatha Award-winning Death on Demand series and the Henrie O series, and the recent novel *Letter from Home*.

EDWARD MARSTON has written plays, short stories, and more than thirty historical mysteries.

FRANCINE MATHEWS writes spy thrillers and, as Stephanie Barron, pens the Jane Austen mysteries.

SHARAN NEWMAN is the author of the medieval *Catherine Levendeur* series.

ALEXANDRA RIPLEY writes historical novels, including "You Know What."

WALTER SATTERTHWAIT was raised by wolverines in New Mexico and is an Agatha Award-nominee.

SARAH SMITH is the author of *The Vanished Child* and other novels set at the turn of the twentieth century.

CAROLYN WHEAT is the recipient of the Agatha, Anthony, Macavity, and Shamus awards for her work.

> **"The 14 writers here...know the period well... disguises and mistaken identities abound."**
> *-Booklist*

The Sunken Sailor

INTRODUCTION BY
Anne Perry

EDITED BY
Elizabeth Foxwell

BERKLEY PRIME CRIME, NEW YORK

THE BERKLEY PUBLISHING GROUP
Published by the Penguin Group
Penguin Group (USA) Inc.
375 Hudson Street, New York, New York 10014, USA
Penguin Group (Canada), 10 Alcorn Avenue, Toronto, Ontario M4V 3B2, Canada
(a division of Pearson Penguin Canada Inc.)
Penguin Books Ltd., 80 Strand, London WC2R 0RL, England
Penguin Group Ireland, 25 St. Stephen's Green, Dublin 2, Ireland (a division of Penguin Books Ltd.)
Penguin Group (Australia), 250 Camberwell Road, Camberwell, Victoria 3124, Australia
(a division of Pearson Australia Group Pty. Ltd.)
Penguin Books India Pvt. Ltd., 11 Community Centre, Panchsheel Park, New Delhi—110 017, India
Penguin Group (NZ), Cnr. Airborne and Rosedale Roads, Albany, Auckland 1310, New Zealand
(a division of Pearson New Zealand Ltd.)
Penguin Books (South Africa) (Pty.) Ltd., 24 Sturdee Avenue, Rosebank, Johannesburg 2196,
South Africa

Penguin Books Ltd., Registered Offices: 80 Strand, London WC2R 0RL, England

This is a work of fiction. Names, characters, places, and incidents either are the product of the author's imagination or are used fictitiously, and any resemblance to actual persons, living or dead, business establishments, events, or locales is entirely coincidental.

THE SUNKEN SAILOR

A Berkley Prime Crime Book / published by arrangement with Malice Domestic, Ltd.

PRINTING HISTORY
Berkley Prime Crime hardcover edition / April 2004
A Berkley Prime Crime mass-market edition / March 2005

Copyright © 2004 by Malice Domestic, Ltd.
Individual Stories: "Introduction: Charting the Course for the Sunken Sailor" Copyright © 2004 by Anne Perry; "Chapter One: A Murder Is Announced." Copyright © 2004 by Simon Brett; "Chapter Two: Sir Gerard in Charge." Copyright © 2004 by Sharan Newman; "Chapter Three: An Inspector Calls." Copyright © 2004 by Francine Mathews; "Chapter Four: Sea Shanties—And State Secrets." Copyright © 2004 by Walter Satterthwait; "Chapter Five: The Woman in the Tutti-Frutti Hat." Copyright © 2004 by Margaret Coel; "Chapter Six: Revelations at The Three Horseshoes." Copyright © 2004 by Carolyn Hart; "Chapter Seven: The Other C.B." Copyright © 2004 Carolyn Wheat; "Chapter Eight: What the Butler Saw." Copyright © 2004 by Cannell & Company; "Chapter Nine: Blackmail!" Copyright © 2004 by Deborah Crombie; "Chapter Ten: Journey into Fear." Copyright © 2004 by the Estate of Alexandra Ripley; "Chapter Eleven: The Lady Investigates." Copyright © 2004 by Eileen Dreyer; "Chapter Twelve: The Phoenix Rises." Copyright © 2004 by Jan Burke; "Chapter Thirteen: Peril at Castle Crawsbey." Copyright © 2004 by Sarah Smith; "Chapter Fourteen: Bon Voyage." Copyright © 2004 by Edward Marston.

ISBN: 0-425-20202-X

Berkley Prime Crime Books are published by The Berkley Publishing Group,
a division of Penguin Group (USA) Inc.,
375 Hudson Street, New York, New York 10014.
The name BERKLEY PRIME CRIME and the BERKLEY PRIME CRIME design are trademarks belonging to Penguin Group (USA) Inc.

PRINTED IN THE UNITED STATES OF AMERICA
10 9 8 7 6 5 4 3 2 1

CONTENTS

The Sunken Sailor
DRAMATIS PERSONAE

REGGIE ARBUTHNOT—A chief inspector with a sea shanty problem

DAISY NÉE DIGBY, DOWAGER DUCHESS OF FAUGHSTRAYNE ("FESTON")—former chorus girl turned aristocrat

DUDLEY, DUKE OF FAUGHSTRAYNE—the Dowager Duchess's son, missing in South America

CONSUELA, DUCHESS OF FAUGHSTRAYNE—the Dowager Duchess's purported daughter-in-law

LADY AMELIA CRAWSBEY—the Dowager Duchess's daughter, keeping more than one fellow on a string

RODERICK BENFLEET—pesky country solicitor

COUNTESS KATERINA BORONSKAYA—an impoverished Russian emigré—or is she?

ADMIRAL CORNELIUS BRANDON—the victim, an American sailor

CECILY BARBARA BRANDON—the admiral's brash daughter

WHITCHELL BRANDON—the admiral's tactless son

EDWIN COOPER—grouchy cabbie

ENRIQUE DA SILVA—flashy foreigner

DR. SQUIFFY FROBISHER—a golf-mad pathologist with a seafaring past

SIR GERARD "GERRY" HAWKSMOOR—wounded WWI veteran, dashing amateur sleuth, and all-around meddler

JEAVONS—the imperturbable butler

MRS. LOUISA LEDBED—a London charlady with a secret life

LEWIS—a clumsy new servant who swears in Spanish

MAISIE—the short-lived upstairs maid

ARCHIBALD "ARCHIE" NETTLE—a strapping if dim local constable with an eye for the ladies and unusual reading tastes

"THE PHOENIX"—a person or persons unknown

INTRODUCTION:

Charting the Course for
The Sunken Sailor

by Anne Perry

THE authors and the editor of this serial novel would like to
begin by acknowledging the debt they owe to the Detection
Club of Great Britain, and its collective mystery novel *The
Floating Admiral*. Of course the resemblances are obvious—
The Sunken Sailor is also a novel whose chapters are all written
by different authors, each one receiving the manuscript com-
pleted up to his or her own section and picking the tale up
from there, writing a chapter, then passing it on.

I have written a chapter in a round robin mystery done in
this fashion, and it is the most enormous fun! Although
mine was for a different group.

And speaking of groups, what is Malice Domestic? Well,
it is not a club with a specific membership; it is, loosely,
anyone who writes, edits, or reads crime stories where the
killer and the victim have a personal relationship so that the
murder is in the broadest sense "domestic." This is as opposed
to a police procedural (although of course police procedurals

can be domestic as well), underworld or organized crime stories, or a "caper." Frequently the detective is an amateur, and involved for personal rather than professional reasons.

As you can see, this is a very broad category and, in my opinion, all the better for it. It is also very often, in a sense, "juicier" in that all kinds of passions are enclosed in a hothouse and left until they reach a critical point. A recipe for such a dish might read something like:

Take one country house or other closed environment.

Add a family with intense and conflicting relationships (preferably of long standing—old wrongs, old loves, etc.), one or more newcomer, and intruders of various sorts, seasoned to taste.

Mix well with private and public gatherings, dinners, secret rendezvous, quarrels, etc. Allow to marinate overnight.

Heat over a crisis, any will do—marriage, divorce, birth, death (natural or unnatural), disputed will, financial disaster, return of a prodigal, family reunion, long hot summer, long cold winter!

Keep increasing heat until mixture explodes—with as much gory and imaginative fallout as possible.

Serve in a dish constructed out of a specialist background of any type you like—as long as it is interesting—from any country, any period of time.

Garnish to taste with humour, romance, and vivid description.

The result will be enjoyed by anyone whose tastebuds are open to entertainment of a sharp, compassionate, and funny nature—i.e., a spot of domestic malice.

There are certain rules for writing a round robin mystery novel. The obvious ones are that you observe the integrity of the story insofar as you do not contradict any of the facts stated by your earlier colleagues (there is nothing whatsoever about not turning them inside out, backside foremost, and standing them on their heads!). You may bamboozle the reader as much as you like; in fact you should, the more thoroughly the better, but you must not tell an outright lie. That is cheating. There used to be rules about butlers and identical twins, but I think they have been relaxed, if done with sufficient skill. Pretty well anything can work, if you twist it into a clever enough shape!

This particular story of *The Sunken Sailor* begins with the classic ingredients, and there is always something pleasing about that. One feels a certain comfortable familiarity in a country house-party England between the wars. It is very fitting to bizarre crime. It comes complete with a Duchess, a castle sinking into genteel decay, mysterious and beautiful foreigners of uncertain origin, mysterious and sinister foreign gentlemen of even more uncertain origin, a tortured war hero (preferably also with a title), a missing heir (in the jungles of Brazil, naturally!), a beautiful daughter, an American who claims to be something he is not, and of course a grotesque and unnatural death. And of course a butler! It is all very right and proper, exactly what one wishes for a first-class evening by the fire with crumpets, or on the beach with lemonade, or whatever is your circumstance of choice.

From then on the pace picks up, rather like dancing to Ravel's "Bolero," getting faster and wilder with every turn. You couldn't stop even if you wanted to! But of course you don't want to. Heaven help anyone who is uncivilized enough to interrupt you!

Nothing is as it seems. We proceed at an even more hectic pace, changing styles as we move from one writer to the next, but never losing the plot, simply watching it metamorphose into something utterly different and which you had never thought of. But then who, watching a caterpillar, would imagine a butterfly, if you didn't already know?

Nothing is what it seems, but in the end everything is what it should be. Perhaps the only rule that matters is that it should be vastly entertaining, that you should fly through the pages, trying to predict what will happen next and always being surprised, one minute holding your breath with suspense, the next laughing aloud.

Perhaps writing round robin mystery stories will be the next really sophisticated house party game?

This is how it should be done!

Enjoy it.

ONE

A Murder is Announced

by Simon Brett

THERE were so many subjects off-limits that conversation in the presence of the Dowager Duchess of Faughstrayne was always a rather tense business, as the guests at that weekend house-party at Castle Crawsbey soon found out. Though a full five years had elapsed since the death of her husband, reference to him was still considered ill-advised, threatening as it might a crack of unseemly emotion in the Dowager Duchess's granite demeanour.

Nor was mention of her son any less hazardous an undertaking. The current Duke, whenever his name did come up, was firmly asserted to be "in South America," in a manner which implied that the subject was then closed. Supplementary questions as to what His Grace might be doing in that vast and challenging continent were met by the glassy, violet-eyed stare that had been perfected over centuries by the Dowager Duchess's ancestors.

In The Three Horseshoes, Public House of Market

Winsome, the nearest village to Castle Crawsbey, there were as many theories as to the Duke of Faughstrayne's current activities as there were pipe-clenching, beer-swilling locals to voice them. He was asserted to be conducting archaeological research into the lives of the Inca kings. He had "gone native," married a sloe-eyed Venezuelan beauty, and produced a half-caste heir to the Faughstrayne title. He had fallen among drug-traffickers and was being held prisoner in a remote Patagonian fastness. He had tumbled from a raft into the swelling Amazon and been consumed by ferocious piranha fish.

All of these conjectures bore exactly the same relationship to reality as most of the conversation in The Three Horseshoes. About the activities of the Duke's sister, Lady Amelia, there was considerably less speculation. She was not away in foreign parts; indeed she was a permanent fixture at Castle Crawsbey, under the firm maternal thumb of the Dowager Duchess. And though it might be expected that any high-spirited, handsome young lady in her mid-twenties would fret under such subjugation, Lady Amelia's breeding and education had been such that discontent—or indeed any other emotion—could never be read in the distinguished lineaments of her perfect face.

Sir Gerard Hawksmoor covertly watched the young woman in her shimmering white evening dress, chatting with genteel animation to that weekend's houseguests. As a concession to the languorously hot July weather, the Dowager Duchess had given her butler, Jeavons, the order to serve pre-prandial drinks on the South Terrace of Castle Crawsbey. Tall glazed doors opened out onto this area from the Library, whose leather-bound riches had remained unopened by generations of the Faughstrayne dynasty.

Sir Gerard Hawksmoor was a family friend, much decorated for gallantry during the Great War. But the horrors he had witnessed during those hostilities, along with the deaths of many of his close comrades, had left their permanent marks on the young man. Injuries received precluded the possibility of his ever again knocking up a breezy century in a cricket match at Lord's; a slight limp and the occasional wince registering on his pale face showed that he never passed an hour free of pain.

But his enforced station on the sidelines of active life gave Sir Gerard Hawksmoor a unique observation point from which to monitor the ambitions, follies, and hypocrisies of his fellow men and women. Though his body might be maimed, suffering seemed only to have sharpened the piercing acuity of his mind, whose analytical and deductive powers had more than once been enlisted by baffled senior investigators at Scotland Yard.

Sir Gerard Hawksmoor observed the throng and sipped at a glass of lemonade. Other wounded soldiers might have resorted to stronger drinks to ease their pains and blot out their memories, but he had witnessed too often the dangers of excess, and resolutely refused the offer of any stimulant that might blunt the razor-sharpness of his mental processes.

All that remained of Castle Crawsbey's Norman origins were the foundations, on which the twelfth Duke of Faughstrayne, enriched by mines in the Americas, had built a palace of eighteenth-century classical proportions and splendour. From the South Terrace of this magnificent edifice, the visitor's eye was led pleasingly through a formally symmetrical garden centred on an ornamental fountain, over rolling lawns and the hidden interruption of one of those cunning walls-in-a-ditch known as a "ha-ha," to rolling fields where impossibly white sheep cropped the rich green grass of Rutfordshire.

The fountain itself was worthy of note. It had been added by the fifteenth Duke, as a memorial to the minimal role he had played in the great events of the Battle of Trafalgar, and its theme was unmistakably maritime. At the centre a fanciful sea serpent coiled itself around the mast of a stricken vessel; from the creature's cruel mouth cascades of watery venom spouted upwards, splashing down in a neat circle on the surface of the round pond below. This falling water seemed to have no effect on the plump carp, koi, and orfe, which swam idly in and out of the stems of water lilies, immune to any turbulence.

A circular parapet, some three feet high, surrounded the pond, and along the top of this the fifteenth Duke had added specially-commissioned statues of sea-faring heroes. All guests could recognise the tridented figure of Neptune; Nelson's missing arm and eye made him easy to spot; most could also put a name to the pugnacious statuette of Sir Francis Drake; but for many, the identities of Jason, leader of the Argonauts, Magellan, and Sir Martin Frobisher had to be explained.

In more than a century since its creation, the statuary had lost its gloss. Some of the figures were chipped and stood uneasy on their pediments: Neptune's trident was down to two prongs, and all of the stone was blotched with moss and lichen. The green depths of the fishpond would also have benefited from a thorough scouring, and the sharp edges of the surrounding ornamental garden were fuzzy with weeds. A similar genteel neglect was evident on the frontage of Castle Crawsbey itself. Patches of fungoid damp had spread, crenellations crumbled, and wooden window frames were swollen or splitting.

Fortunately, in July the weekend guests would not be made so aware of the inadequacy of the house's one, ancient heating boiler, but other vagaries of the internal plumbing would be in evidence, whatever the season. Regular visitors were accustomed to the long wait before a brown trickle emerged from the water taps, the capriciousness with which the flow would turn in an instant from scalding hot to icy cold, and the thundering, as of Titans banging swords on shields in preparation for battle, which might suddenly erupt from the pipes in the stillest watches of the night.

The maintenance of tradition is an expensive business, and Castle Crawsbey had long ago lost the tradition of maintenance. A huge injection of cash was required to restore the home to its former stately glory.

It was not the first time that Sir Gerard Hawksmoor had had these thoughts as he looked down at the crumbling balustrade which divided the South Terrace from the gardens. He observed that two of the houseguests had drifted away from the knot of drinkers in the direction of the fountain, and seemed there to be engaged in disputatious conversation. One of the men Sir Gerard had known for a long time.

Roderick Benfleet was the Dowager Duchess's legal adviser, a humble country solicitor based in Market Winsome, who for some reason had been preferred by the late Duke over better-known London professionals. Benfleet was young and ambitious but not quite the genuine article. A twang in his voice betrayed the fact that he had not attended one of the best public schools, and he looked ill at ease in a dinner suit that might even have been bought "off the peg."

To the gentleman with whom the solicitor seemed to be arguing Sir Gerard had only been introduced that afternoon. His name was Mr. Da Silva and, even without that clue, the flashiness of his dress would instantly have marked him out as a foreigner, the jewels of his shirt studs and cuff links were much larger than those any English gentleman would wear, and across the crisp white of his shirt-front was draped a preposterous purple sash, insignia no doubt of a meaningless order from some Ruritanian kingdom.

Another betrayal—as if any were needed—of Mr. Da Silva's origins and lack of breeding was the fact that he used his hands when he spoke. But what prompted the emphatic gestures with which the foreigner was responding to Roderick Benfleet's unheard words down by the fountain, Sir Gerard Hawksmoor could not know. And further speculation on the matter was prevented by the approach of the Dowager Duchess, leading forward a guest for introduction.

The newcomer was a large-limbed man in his fifties, whose ruddy complexion suggested that the country seat of the Dukes of Faughstrayne was not part of his usual social circuit. He was dressed in a perfectly respectable dinner suit, but it did not fit him with the exactness that the care of the right Savile Row tailor would have ensured.

"Sir Gerard Hawksmoor," intoned the Dowager Duchess. "May I introduce Admiral Cornelius Brandon?"

The anomaly of an admiral appearing in an ordinary dinner suit rather than in his dress uniform was quickly explained. So too was the unlikely physical appearance of such a high-ranking officer. The moment he opened his mouth, Admiral Cornelius Brandon revealed himself to be an American.

"Good evening, sir," he said. "I must apologise for what

I'm wearing. The Castle Crawsbey manservant who unpacked my trunk spilled a bottle of coconut oil pomade all over my uniform."

The Dowager Duchess coughed. "As I mentioned, Jeavons has rebuked the boy Lewis very severely and organised for the garments to be cleaned."

"That's all very well, but meanwhile I'm stuck in this." The Admiral flapped the arms of his dinner suit contemptuously.

"I can assure you that the late Duke's clothes were all made by the finest tailors in London, and it's fortunate that you have very much the same build as he did."

"Fortunate, Duchess? I don't see there's anything fortunate about it. If that boy hadn't spilled the pomade, we wouldn't have gotten into this situation and we wouldn't have needed to be fortunate."

The Dowager Duchess ducked her head, an action that puzzled Sir Gerard. Still a handsome blonde, she had always been a British woman of the old school, unafraid of the recalcitrant Jack-in-office, rioting native, or rabid Labrador. And yet here she was, the elegant Dowager Duchess of Faughstrayne, meekly kowtowing to a mere colonial with the words, "It was, I agree, a most regrettable lapse."

"Yes, it sure was," the Admiral snarled, showing that lack of respect for the British aristocracy endemic amongst a certain type of American.

The Dowager Duchess coloured and went off to play hostess with other of her guests, leaving Sir Gerard Hawksmoor to ponder on the nature of the hold this brash sailor might exercise over a representative of one of the country's oldest families.

There was a silence between the two men. The Briton

racked his brains for something uncontentious to say. He had no wish to get into an argument about the merits of Republicanism.

The fact that his fellow guest was American explained so much, though. An Admiral in the United States Navy did not carry anything like the same status as an Admiral in the British Navy. Sir Gerard shared the common belief of his countrymen that in foreign countries ranks and titles were scattered around with a liberality verging on the profligate. He had the same view of academic qualifications. Though aware that the United States possessed universities of which it was inordinately proud, he knew that none of them could approach the tradition and gravitas bestowed by an education at Oxford or Cambridge. Anything the Americans did, he knew, would be bound to be essentially lightweight.

But Sir Gerard Hawksmoor was far too well brought up to draw attention to his own superiority (and also he knew that most foreigners would recognise it instinctively), so he said to the American, with frank and open bonhomie, "I'm afraid standards of efficiency amongst servants are not what they were in our parents' generation."

"Still are back in the old U.S. of A.," the Admiral countered combatively. "We have a culture of service back home. You serve a person because they're paying you for that service, not because they've got some fancy title like 'the Dowager Duchess of Faughstrayne.'"

The Admiral spoke the word exactly as it was spelt— "for-strain." Sir Gerard Hawksmoor chuckled lightly. "It's pronounced 'fes-ton,'" he said.

"Why?"

What a remarkable question, thought Sir Gerard, as he replied, "Because it is."

"Forstrain—Feston, I ain't too bothered about that. What does bother me, though, is incompetence. And spilling that pomade was incompetence. I tell you, if that boy Lewis was serving on one of my ships in the South Atlantic, he'd wish he'd been born with alligator hide instead of skin!"

Sir Gerard Hawksmoor decided it was time for a diplomatically neutral question. "So I dare say you've traveled through all the Seven Seas, Admiral?"

"Don't call me 'Admiral.' Call me 'Ceebee.'"

"Ceebee?"

"Yes, that's my initials. 'C. B.' Cornelius Brandon. Pretty damn famous name in naval circles, though it probably wouldn't mean too much to a civilian like you."

Sir Gerard Hawksmoor didn't think this was the appropriate moment to allude to his own military experiences, so he let the Admiral continue.

"Everyone calls me 'Ceebee.'"

"Right. Very well then. So have you traveled through all the Seven Seas, Ceebee?"

"Done my share. Recent years, a lot it's been patrolling the Caribbean, Honduras, coast of Brazil, that direction. Volatile people down that way. Need the calming influence of an American naval presence."

"I'm sure they do. So, Ceebee, where are you stationed at the moment?"

The Admiral coloured. "Between postings," he said gruffly, in a manner that didn't encourage further questioning.

There was no time for any, as it happened, for at that moment from the library irrupted a young man with red hair, a snub nose and so many freckles that it looked as though a chocolate scatter-bomb had exploded in his face. He was dressed in sportive flannels, a striped blazer, and a boater with matching band. The garb might have passed muster during the Henley Regatta, though even there the livery would have been recognised as the invention of an imaginative tailor (no English boat club would have descended to a combination of colours quite so strident). But, whatever the merits of the ensemble, it was entirely unsuitable for pre-prandial drinks at Castle Crawsbey.

Though most faces on the South Terrace were clouded with disapproval, the boy's appearance had the opposite effect on the ancient mariner who insisted on being called "Ceebee." A broad beam split his weather-beaten cheeks and, with a cry of "Ain't you just the goods, Whitchell!", he shook the youth ecstatically by the hand.

"Sure thing, Pop," said the boy, helpfully identifying his relationship to Ceebee for Sir Gerard.

"This here's some Lord or other—I didn't get your name, chum."

"Sir Gerard Hawksmoor" was gracefully supplied.

"Meet my boy, Whitchell." The face glowed even redder with pride. "Whitchell Brandon. You bear that name in mind, Mister Sir Gerard, because you're going to hear a whole lot about it in the future."

"In what connection?" the Englishman asked politely.

"That I can't be sure," Ceebee replied, "but you take my word for it, whatever my boy Whitchell turns his hand to, he'll be the real lollapalooza."

"Good for him," said Sir Gerard.

"Now, Whitchell, have you been talking to your lady friend?" And the emphasis he put on the word left no doubt that the subject of his enquiry was the daughter of the house.

"Well, I said a few words, Pop, this and that, nothing

much, though. Kinda difficult to get her on her own, but when I do . . ." Whitchell Brandon sniggered and winked. "Oh boy, that'll be the fox in the henhouse!"

His father chuckled in complicit appreciation, then turned at a cough belind him as discreet as the noise of the *Times* being ironed. Ceebee found himself staring into the pallidly impassive eyes of the Castle Crawsbey butler, Jeavons.

"Yeah, what do you want, buddy boy?"

"I thought the young gentleman would wish to know, sir, that the dinner gong will be sounding in five minutes."

"Would you wish to know that, Whitchell?"

"Don't bother me none, Pop."

The butler's next cough was rather more assertive, as if to remove an exceptionally intransigent wrinkle from the surface of the *Times*. "I think Her Grace would be less than happy to have a guest at her dinner table inappropriately dressed."

The American father and son looked at each other, assessing how far they should pursue their egalitarian stance. Had the Boston Tea Party been for nothing?

Whitchell's look was purely interrogative; he was going to let his father make the decision.

After a tense moment, Ceebee climbed down from the potential confrontation. "You go get your dinner suit on, boy."

"Right, Pop."

"After all, if you're gonna be spending any amount of time with the English," the father called after the retreating stripes, "you're gonna have to learn their funny little ways."

As Ceebee turned back, he noticed Mr. Da Silva returning from the gardens and, with an abrupt "Pardon me," went off to greet the flamboyant stranger.

His movement had a strange effect on a watching lady of

whose presence Sir Gerard had only had seconds before becoming aware. She was tall, with dark hair beginning to make concessions to grey. Her white, bare-shouldered dress was from another age; the tiara, the brooches, and the jewelled necklace from which depended an order centred on an emerald fish seemed excessive for a country evening. Sir Gerard Hawksmoor had not yet experienced the pleasure of introduction, but he had no problem in identifying the lady. It was his invariable custom, on arrival for a visit to Castle Crawsbey, to have a quiet word with the butler, Jeavons, who would mark his card as to the weekend's guest list. The lady Sir Gerard was looking at was undoubtedly Countess Katerina Boronskaya, a Russian forced from her native home by proletarian unpleasantnesses in that country, and now reduced to drifting from country house to country house throughout Europe, dependent on the goodwill and charity of her many cousins.

But it was not the woman's identity which at that moment concerned Sir Gerard; it was the expression on her face. She had been crossing the South Terrace towards them, but at the sight of the Admiral's back-view, she had frozen to the spot, all colour draining instantly from her noble face. The expression was more than one of shock; it was sheer terror.

Only when Ceebee turned towards her did relief flood her body and tension ease away from her powdered shoulders. Then, moving off to greet some other distant relative, Countess Katerina Boronskaya was lost in the crowd.

Sir Gerard Hawksmoor made a mental note of the incident, but did not at that moment focus on it the analytical powers of his mind. Instead, he moved toward the terrace's balustrade to ease his back and leg. Still gave him a lot of gyp when he stood too long in one position. But at least he was standing, which was more than he'd been able to do for a year after the big show finished. He remembered hearing the nurses talking one night after lights out, when they thought he was asleep. "Never walk again, poor blighter. Lots of things he'll never do again. What a waste." And it was at that moment that he'd made the resolution to prove them wrong.

With an effort of will, Sir Gerard expelled the past from his mind and focused on the present. There was one obvious explanation for the recent exchange between Brandons Senior and Junior. The boy was being set up to marry Lady Amelia. It would not be the first time that American dollars had been enlisted to shore up British breeding, not to mention a dilapidating country estate. The theory would certainly explain the Dowager Duchess's uncharacteristic deference to Ceebee.

"Sir Gerard." The natural unpleasantness of Roderick Benfleet's voice was heightened by the anxiety with which he spoke. The man looked flustered, and even a little guilty. As Hawksmoor turned towards him, the solicitor eased a finger around the inside of his ill-fitting collar.

"What is it, Benfleet?"

"Some rather disturbing news, Sir Gerard."

"Oh?"

"About the Duke."

"What?" Excitement sparkled in the former soldier's eyes. "Has there been a sighting of him? Is he back from South America?"

"That, I would think, is most unlikely. I received a letter from a friend living out in Buenos Aires, in which he wrote—"

But there Roderick Benfleet had to stop. The dinner

gong had sounded. With a muttered "We must talk later," the solicitor joined the throng flooding back through the Library doors towards the Great Dining Room.

Sir Gerard Hawksmoor shrugged. The Dowager Duchess's unalterable seating plan would rule out the possibility of further discourse with Benfleet until after dinner.

Wincing a little at the pain from his back, Hawksmoor followed the crowd into the Library.

THAT night's dinner was unexceptional. Sir Gerard Hawksmoor survived it as he had many others of the kind. His expectations from an English country house dinner party were extremely low, and those expectations were met. The Castle Crawsbey kitchen staff followed the abiding principle of British cuisine: that it is impossible to cook anything—especially vegetables—for too long. And, as for conversation, the social usages of the upper classes ensured that nothing said at the table was indecorous, contentious or—worst form of all—interesting. Sir Gerard therefore resorted to the defense of something inbred, cultivated by attendance at the right schools, and modified by the attentions of a piece of shrapnel during the Great War—his stiff upper lip.

There was only one moment of note during the dinner. Lady Amelia was sitting directly opposite Sir Gerard, though the breadth of the dinner table made discourse impossible. At her right-hand side, possibly supporting his earlier conjecture, the Dowager Duchess's seating plan had placed young Whitchell Brandon, now in correct evening dress, though with a bow tie that used far more material than an English gentleman's ever would.

Lady Amelia did not appear to be at ease with her Amer-

ican companion, reacting with frigid disdain to most of his
bluff conversational sallies, and deliberately focusing her
attention on the gentleman on her left, a minor aristocrat
boasting as little wit as chin.

And when the incident happened, the spilling from a jug
of some Cumberland sauce on to the front of her white dress,
Lady Amelia seemed relieved rather than appalled by the
interruption to her dinner. Almost gaily, without a word to
the unfortunate swarthy-looking servant who had spilled
the sauce, or to either of the gentlemen beside her, she had
hurried away from the table to change her garments.

It was left to Jeavons to rebuke the offender, hissing
imprecations as he hustled the boy away to kitchen, in
whose privacy no doubt the volume and vigour of the butler's dressing-down would considerably increase.

Sir Gerard Hawksmoor found the incident remarkable
for two reasons. First, was there more than one clumsy
young servant at Castle Crawsbey? Or had the same perpetrator, identified by the Dowager Duchess as "Lewis," been
guilty of the Cumberland sauce on Lady Amelia's frontage
and the coconut oil pomade on Ceebee's dress uniform?
These questions raised the tantalising corollary that the two
accidents might be linked, or might have been deliberately
arranged to cause diversions.

But it was not the moment, Sir Gerard decided, to pursue such speculation.

Nor to pursue the even more titillating detail—that
the clumsy servant's instinctive reaction, on seeing the
Cumberland sauce in mid-spill, had been to utter the word,
"Caramba!"

* * *

THE rest of the evening passed, like so many before, with brandy, billiards, and further conversational banality. Of Roderick Benfleet there was no sign. Whatever secret the solicitor had to impart to Hawksmoor, its revelation would have to wait for another day. At a relatively early hour, the houseguests started to yawn, say their good-nights, and go upstairs to face the unpredictable caprices of the Castle Crawsbey plumbing and predictable lumpiness of the Castle Crawsbey mattresses.

Before the Great War, Sir Gerard Hawksmoor had slept every night like the proverbial baby; since his military experiences, oblivion had become an elusive goal.

Accepting this fact with characteristic pragmatism, the former soldier rarely approached his bed before two o'clock in the morning. Rather than spending hours of restless wakefulness, he preferred to use the time in reading, particularly on his favourite subject, the ancient topography of Salisbury Plain.

Given the fact that among the unopened tomes in Castle Crawsbey was a fine collection on that very topic, it was no surprise therefore that the striking of midnight from the house's many clocks found Sir Gerard entering the empty Library. He paused by the door, surprised by a sound. Not far away, possibly in the garden, someone was whistling lightly. The tune was the old sea shanty, "What Shall We Do With The Drunken Sailor?"

When Sir Gerard switched on a light in the relevant Library alcove, the invisible whistling stopped abruptly in mid-note. Hawksmoor shrugged, put curiosity as to the whistler's identity from his mind, and settled down to an absorbing study of Stonehenge made by a seventeenth-century divine and amateur archaeologist.

Though the tall windows of the Castle Crawsbey Library were well provided with curtains to protect the fine leather bindings from the deleterious effects of sunlight, these had not been closed that evening. Sir Gerard wondered whether this was a deliberate response to the warmth of the July night, or a lapse of housekeeping. If the latter, it would be in keeping with other examples of slapdashness he had observed around the estate, symptoms perhaps of insufficient or inadequate staffing, whose causes could well be financial. The Dowager Duchess of Faughstrayne would not be the only aristocrat who had recently found the values of her stocks and bonds to be down to cat's meat prices.

But Sir Gerard Hawksmoor had more important matters to consider than the state of the Castle Crawsbey exchequer. After a quick glance towards the gardens, which revealed a still summer night washed in azure moonlight, he turned with relish to the seventeenth-century divine's explanation as to how the huge "bluestones" of Stonehenge had been transported from the Prescelly Mountains in Wales.

Sir Gerard was so caught up in his book that he was unaware of the passage of time, and might still have been reading at dawn, had he not been rudely interrupted by the sudden sound from the garden of a female scream.

He sprang to his feet and moved towards the window. He caught momentary sight of two figures down near the fountain, a woman in white and a man in a dark dinner suit. But in an instant they flickered out of sight behind a tall hedge.

Sir Gerard Hawksmoor pushed through the library doors, and hurried across the South Terrace to the place whence the scream had come. There was now no one in sight, and the night was ominous in its silence.

He sniffed and caught a distinctive whiff of tobacco

smoke. Not from a cigarette, nor from the best kind of cigar. Instantly he recognised the smoke as coming from a cheap cheroot of the kind favoured by the dock-workers of Rio de Janeiro. But the significance of that clue would have to await investigation until after he had inspected the fountain.

Something had changed. As he approached the structure, Sir Gerard became aware of a strange asymmetry. The six maritime guardians of the pool had been reduced to five. Jason, Magellan, Nelson, Drake, and Frobisher proudly stood their ground, but there was a gap where Neptune should have been brandishing his trident (or, to be strictly accurate, as it had a prong missing, his bident).

Sir Gerard Hawksmoor looked over the parapet into the pool below. As anticipated, he saw the statue of Neptune lying full-length beneath the water. What he had not anticipated, however, was that around the waist of the sea-god would be tied the purple sash of Mr. Da Silva's spurious decoration.

Nor that the sash had been used for the purpose of tying someone to the statue. Beneath Neptune's mass, nosed at by mildly curious carp, koi, and orfe, lay the very dead body of Admiral Cornelius Brandon, or, as he preferred to be called, "Ceebee."

Well, thought Sir Gerard Hawksmoor, prompted by the tune he had so recently heard, what shall we do with the Sunken Sailor?

TWO

Sir Gerard in Charge

by Sharan Newman

SIR Gerard did what any gentleman would do in such a situation. He returned to the Library and rang for the butler.

Jeavons arrived shortly after. The only sign on his part that he had been wakened was that he had regrettably misaligned the buttons on his waistcoat. In view of the seriousness of the situation, Sir Gerard did not mention it.

"Ah, Jeavons," he said. "I'm sorry to bother you so late, but it appears that Admiral Brandon has met with some misadventure at the koi pond. Would you be so good as to telephone the police? Ask for Sergeant—I mean Constable—Nettle. Then you might send some servants to guard the pond until he arrives."

Jeavons paled but remained steady. "Are you implying, sir, that the Admiral's misadventure has been fatal?"

"Unless he can breathe underwater, I fear so," Sir Gerard answered. "By the look of it, this was not an accident. Now,

I shall return to the site to guard the body until your men come."

"Yes, sir," Jeavons said. "Should I inform the Duchess?"

"Good gracious no! At this hour?" Sir Gerard was horrified. "There's no need to rouse any of the house party. They will all need a good night's rest before facing the news tomorrow."

Jeavons gave a discreet cough. "I believe that not all of the party have retired yet, sir."

"Really?" It hadn't occurred to Sir Gerard that the servants would keep tabs on who among the guests had gone to their beds, or someone else's, but it did make sense that they would need to know who was accounted for before they could lock up the house for the night.

"Very well," he said. "Which of them are still about?"

"I would have to check with the footmen," Jeavons answered. "But I believe that Señor Da Silva went out to smoke a cigar in the garden an hour or so ago and I know that the Countess sent her maid to the kitchen earlier to ask for a hot drink, but when the maid returned, she wasn't in her room."

"Wasn't the maid alarmed by this?" Sir Gerard asked.

"No, sir. She says the Countess often takes a walk if she wakes up in the night. I understand the poor woman is subject to nightmares relating to her experiences in her home country."

"Ah." Sir Gerard did not delve into that. He was all too familiar with the horrors of the past returning in dreams. "Anyone else?"

"Apparently the admiral," Jeavons said. "Although I regret to say that I wasn't aware that he had left his room."

"Well, one can't be everywhere," Hawksmoor assured him. "Perhaps you should go now and ring for the constable."

* * *

STANDING guard by a body in the middle of the night is a tedious business, as Sir Gerard knew well. He considered bringing his book but reflected that the allure of Stonehenge might cause him to become so immersed in his reading that his senses, normally acute, might miss a sound in the night.

So, taking a torch from the desk in the Library, Sir Gerard made his way back to the pond, there to await the arrival of the police.

He had only been there a few moments when he heard the sound of high heels tapping on the path.

"Gerry, what are you doing here?"

Lady Amelia came into the clearing around the pond and stopped in shock when she saw Hawksmoor. She was clad in a stunning rose-colored silk dressing gown that shimmered in the light from the torch. On her feet she wore matching mules with fetching pink pompoms.

Sir Gerard rose at once, moving so as to hide the bulk of the fallen statue.

"I came out to have a smoke and think," he replied before he remembered that he had left his cigarettes by the chair in the Library.

Fortunately, Lady Amelia didn't question his response. She looked around furtively, then gave him a nervous smile.

"I couldn't sleep," she told him. "Something in the air, I think. Perhaps a storm is brewing."

"The night seems unusually heavy," Sir Gerard agreed, wondering why she would go for a stroll in such unsuitable footwear.

She raised her hand to cover her eyes and he noticed that

she hadn't bothered to remove her makeup or jewelry before retiring.

"Could you turn off the torch?" she asked. "I can't see a thing."

That had been Sir Gerard's intent but he could not refuse a request from a lady. He switched off the torch.

His fears were well grounded. As soon as her eyes had adjusted to the darkness she exclaimed in chagrin.

"Dear me, Neptune has finally toppled! I told Mother that he was unsteady on his pins. Good thing it happened at night or someone might have been hurt. I do hope it hasn't traumatized the poor fish."

"I'm sure they are unharmed," Sir Gerard tried to keep her from coming closer to examine the damage but his confounded game leg prevented him from doing so swiftly enough.

"Gracious!" Lady Amelia seemed perplexed. "Why would someone have put a belt on the statue? It's not as if he had any other clothing to hold up."

She leaned closer. "There's something white floating on the surface. I thought you said the fish weren't harmed."

"Please, Amelia." Sir Gerard took her arm and endeavoured to steer her from the pond, but she was inexorable.

"Why, it looks almost like a human hand," she began. "Oh my God! Who is it?"

She fell back on her pink mules and collapsed into Sir Gerard's arms. Fortunately he had trained his upper body to compensate for the strength that his lower limbs had lost and so was able to keep them both from going over.

At that moment, they were both caught in the glare of a bicycle lantern.

"Hello?" An uncertain male voice spoke from the

darkness. "I was told that there had been an accident here?"

Sir Gerard quickly released Lady Amelia.

"Archibald!" she cried. "Oh, Archie, something dreadful has happened!"

Sir Gerard stepped forward at once.

"Constable Nettle," he said. "Good to see you again, although I'm sorry the conditions aren't more pleasant."

He turned to Lady Amelia, who had pulled herself together after her startling outburst.

"I took the liberty of asking Jeavons to call in the police, rather than having the Duchess wakened," he explained.

"Ah, of course," she replied. "Well done. Mother is not as strong as she likes to think and I would have her spared such a shock as I just received."

The constable put the lantern down on the edge of the pond, thus revealing his pleasant face with light blue eyes and a thatch of black hair. There was a scar on his right temple where a piece of mortar had just missed putting out the light in that eye forever. Sir Gerard reflected that there were few men between the ages of thirty and fifty who lacked such reminders of the Great War. Nettle had got off lucky.

"Perhaps you should go back to your room now," he suggested to Lady Amelia. "Jeavons could have a warm drink sent up."

"I'll certainly have something soon," Lady Amelia said. "Probably a stiff brandy. But first I want to know who the unfortunate person is lying under King Neptune."

Sir Gerard took back his control of the situation.

"That's what you were called about, Constable Nettle," he said. "I heard a splash not forty-five minutes ago. When I came out to investigate, this is what I found."

He turned on his torch again and shone it on the body

lying beneath the statue. The Admiral's arm, still in its borrowed jacket, floated freely on the surface.

"His name was Cornelius Brandon, or 'Ceebee,'" Sir Gerard explained. "He and his son are guests at Castle Crawsbey. They arrived only today from America, or so I understand."

He looked to Lady Amelia for confirmation.

"Yes," she said. "He's taking his son on a tour of Europe and started with England. So that's who it is. Mother will be very put out about this."

A thought struck her. "Should I have someone inform Whitchell?"

"The son," Hawksmoor explained to the constable. "I would suggest that it wait until morning. By then the body can be raised and the pathologist summoned. Do you agree, Nettle?"

"Yes sir, Major—I mean, Sir Gerard," Nettle answered. "No point in dragging the poor lad out for a sight like this. Much better that we get the body cleaned up a bit before he sees it. How old is he?"

"Twenty-six," answered Lady Amelia. "Although his manners are those of a much younger boy. They don't seem to train their children well in America."

"Is there a Mrs. Brandon?" Nettle asked.

Lady Amelia paused. "Actually, I don't know for certain. If there is, she isn't traveling with her husband and son."

"Then that can wait for the morning as well," Nettle decided. "If I may use your telephone, I'll rouse the pathologist. Is there anyone who can assist with the body?"

"Jeavons was going to send the footmen," Sir Gerard answered. "Perhaps he forgot."

Lady Amelia put her hand on the constable's arm. He reacted as if she had held a hot poker.

"I shall be happy to show you to the telephone," she said to him, looking up into his eyes. "Then I'll find out what happened to the footmen."

Sir Gerard felt a stirring of disquiet. Although they had both grown up in the area, he had not before been aware that Lady Amelia and Constable Nettle knew each other. Any familiarity between them would be much more displeasing to the Dowager Duchess than the annoyance of a body in the fish pond.

WHEN they had left, he turned his mind back to the immediate problem. Nettle had not inquired how the body had managed to get in the pond. Perhaps he preferred to wait for an official decree of murder. But there was no doubt in Sir Gerard's mind that this was no accident. He had made as detailed an examination as possible without moving the statue. The sash had been tied in a knot at the back. While it was possible for the Admiral to have done this himself, it was unlikely. What reason could he have had? And yet, it was even more odd that he would have allowed someone else to tie him.

Could he have already been dead or unconscious when he entered the pond?

Lady Amelia had said that the statue wasn't firmly balanced. Perhaps the murderer had intended merely to embarrass the Admiral by tying him to the God of the Sea and leaving him there until morning. The murderer might have been unaware that the statue was unstable. Then Ceebee could have caused his own demise by tipping the statue off its base as he struggled to free himself. It seemed a bizarre practical joke, but Hawksmoor was of the opinion that

Americans enjoyed more physical and cruel humour than those of better breeding.

It was at this point that the footmen finally showed up, led by Jeavons. Cautioning them to touch nothing until Nettle returned, Sir Gerard went back to the Library to retrieve his cigarettes and think over the events of the past hour.

He heard the muffled voices of Constable Nettle and Lady Amelia as they passed the Library door. A moment later he looked through the French doors and saw the Constable cross the lawn, heading back down to the pond. There seemed no point in his joining the crew as nothing could be done until the pathologist arrived.

He was settled down to his book again when Lady Amelia poked her head in the door.

"The pathologist says that he can't be here before morning," she told him. "The constable has gone down to see if the footmen can stay all night or if he has to bring up more help from the village."

Hawksmoor half rose to offer his help, but the stab of pain in his hip reminded him that his talents would be better used by staying in and applying his acute analytical skills to the problem.

HE was doomed to interruption, however, for, just after the Great Clock in the hall had tolled one, the Library door opened again and Countess Boronskaya came in.

Sir Gerard rose at once, wincing.

She gasped and pulled the lace edges of her peacock-blue dressing gown together, but not before Sir Gerard had received a glimpse of her well-rounded bosom. He was touched to see that the left one was graced by a small tattoo of the double eagle insignia of the Romanovs. Such loyalty to her slain ruler! Her dark hair fell across her shoulders and she brushed it back nervously.

"Please accept my apologies," she said in her rich accent. "I thought no one would be here at this time of night. I shall go."

"Not on my account," Sir Gerard replied. "May I offer you a glass of brandy? A cigarette?"

"No, thank you," she answered, but entered all the same. "I find sleep difficult and wished to find a book to make the night less tedious."

"I believe there is a matched set of Dickens in this corner." Sir Gerard went over to help her make a selection.

"I fear my English is not equal to Dickens," she confessed with a smile. "Perhaps something less literary or a novel in French?"

He remembered that to most Russian aristocrats French was the second language. He forbore mentioning that she might have been taught the tongue of a people who had not recently eliminated their monarch. Of course that had not been the Countess's choice, but that of her parents. Certainly, the dramatic emotionalism shown by most Russians was more in keeping with the French temperament.

"I doubt the former dukes of Faughstrayne were inclined towards French novels," he laughed.

"Perhaps then you could indulge me with a few moments of conversation?" she asked. "My difficulty in sleeping seems to be shared by many in this house. I have heard voices and footsteps since I retired for the night."

"And you didn't investigate?" he asked.

She shrugged.

"I did not feel comfortable doing so," she said. "I wait . . .

waited until all was quiet. But now that I have found you, you will tell me, yes?"

"If I can," Sir Gerard said cautiously.

He returned to his reading chair and she sat herself across from him on a faded overstuffed sofa that was starting to lose some of its horse hair. He schooled his expression to pleasant interest but his mind was clicking away like an aeroplane revving its engine.

She had already given herself away by not admitting that she had been out of her room shortly before the Admiral died. If he was careful, he might learn more.

"Well, I believe that Mr. Da Silva was in the garden for a time, smoking," he began.

"Ah yes, those dreadful cigars of his," Countess Boronskaya said. "I do not understand why he does not smoke better ones now that he can pay for them."

"He has recently come into money?" Sir Gerard raised his eyebrows to show that this was asked not for vulgar reasons, but to better understand the character of Da Silva.

"So I understand," she answered. "Something to do with a silver mine in Argentina, I believe. I know very little about him."

"And Lady Amelia came down for a few moments," he continued.

The Countess smiled. "Such a lovely young woman! Still so untouched by tragedy!"

Her dark eyes were wistful, and Sir Gerard had to resist an impulse to pat her hand in sympathy. He drew himself up straighter in his chair.

"As to the others, I may not be able to help you." He smiled. "Probably just the servants going about their business."

"Of course." She nodded. "I did think I heard that 'admiral,' as he calls himself, at one point. I suppose he was then on his way to bed."

"Admiral Brandon?" Sir Gerard sat bolt upright. "When was this?"

"I don't know; perhaps some time just before midnight," she said. "He is one I certainly do not wish to meet."

"Really?" he said. "I confess that his manner did not endear him to me, either. But why do you say, 'as he calls himself'? Don't you believe that he is really an admiral?"

She made a sound that, in a common person, would be considered a snort.

"Sir Gerard, I traveled in the United States after the war and I have met many of their generals and admirals."

Hawksmoor found himself wondering under what conditions she had met them and was shocked to have entertained such an unworthy thought about a woman of her obvious refinement.

"And you feel that Admiral Brandon is not of their caliber?" he asked.

She shook her head definitely. "For one to become a high officer in the American navy, one must go to their school, Annapolis, they call it. I do not know what they learn there, but I know that they do not speak English as Admiral Brandon does. He speaks worse than I do. Also, he does not stand or move in the way an officer does, although he walks like a man who spends much time on a boat. I fear that he is one of two things."

"And they are?" he coaxed when she paused.

"Either an adventurer who takes advantage of the kindness of the Duchess or"— she looked directly at him—"one of those men of which America has all too many, the man who has made his money in trade and now wishes to appear of a higher station than he was born to."

Sir Gerard could tell that in her view the latter was the more offensive explanation.

"It does make his behaviour and that of his son more understandable," he said.

"His, at least." The Countess made a moue with her lips. "The son, I fear, is a good representative of the typical 'college man' of America. They appear to rejoice in their loutishness."

She was lost in thought for a moment, then smiled at Sir Gerard.

"But it is equally ill-mannered of me to gossip so about my fellow guests," she said. "Shall we discuss something more pleasant?"

Unfortunately, they soon found that they had not read the same books, nor did they enjoy the same music. Politics was out of the question, as was religion. Sir Gerard had the vague impression that Russians were only one step removed from papacy. That left only the weather.

When they had agreed several times that the night was unusually warm, Countess Boronskaya rose and announced that she thought she could now sleep.

Sir Gerard rose and bade her good night. When she had left, he found that the wonders of the Stonehenge bluestones had paled and he, too, made his way to his room.

As he was a frequent visitor, Jeavons had thoughtfully prepared a chamber on the ground floor so that he would not have to face the grand staircase. Sir Gerard was grateful for that tonight as the unwonted exercise had brought about severe cramping in his game leg and lower back. He was wishing that he had brought his invaluable manservant, Percy, who knew how to iron out the kinks in his shell-wracked body. But Percy had expressed a desire to visit an ailing aunt in Orkney and Hawksmoor hadn't had the heart to forbid it.

Cursing the plumbing at the castle that deprived him of even the comfort of a warm bath, Hawksmoor made his ablutions in the basin and lay down.

But sleep eluded him. He sorted all the impressions of the evening and found more questions than answers. The more he tried to sleep, the more he found the flotsam and jetsam of the death of Ceebee floating to the surface of his mind.

Who had been the woman who screamed? He had glimpsed a white dress and yet, by the time he saw them, neither Lady Amelia nor the Countess was wearing one. He had assumed that the scream was associated with the death of Admiral Brandon. If so, did that mean a woman was involved? Or had the sound merely been the screech of an owl going about its predatory business?

And what of the whistler? While the scream might have been other than human, no bird that he knew of trilled "What Do You Do With the Drunken Sailor." Had it been one of the guests, one of the servants, or even a heretofore-unknown trespasser at Castle Crawsbey?

The last would certainly be preferable. One never wanted to suggest that one's hostess would invite a murderer as a house guest. It might be possible. If Mr. Da Silva had left his gaudy sash on a bench in the garden, an intruder could have appropriated it for his own use.

Then another piece of the puzzle drifted through his brain. Why had Jeavons referred to the man as Señor Da Silva? He had been introduced as "Mister." Did Jeavons know something more about the man? Could he be connected to the missing Duke?

He suddenly remembered that the solicitor, Benfleet, had been about to tell him something when they had been interrupted by the call to dinner. He had said something about Buenos Aires. Wasn't that in Argentina? Hawksmoor rose and went to his suitcase, where he found his Baedeker. He never traveled without the invaluable guidebook, even if he had no plans to leave England.

Yes, his geography classes in school had paid off. It was most definitely in Argentina. Curiouser and curiouser, he quoted to himself.

Before returning to bed, he made a note to find Benfleet and ask about the letter from Argentina.

At last he began to doze off. As he slipped into the welcoming arms of Morpheus, he was aware of one more query knocking on his brain. But he firmly told it to call again in the morning and went to sleep.

HE had meant to position himself at the bottom of the staircase the next morning to scrutinize the faces of the household as they descended but was awakened only by a tremendous clap of thunder at eight. He barely had time to comb his hair, shave, perform his muscle strengthening exercises, and dress before the breakfast gong sounded.

One look at those gathered at the table and he knew that they had all been told of the death of Admiral Brandon. The conversation barely paused when he entered.

"You knew last night, didn't you?" the Countess accused.

"Good morning," Sir Gerard said. He went over to the sideboard and selected toast, eggs, and prunes. He had lost his fondness for kidneys during the war.

"It's said you found the body," Mr. Da Silva spoke as he

was seating himself. "You should have told us. Imagine my shock at waking to find a policeman stationed at my door!"

"I felt that they were the logical ones to inform first," Sir Gerard replied. "Yes, Countess, I did know that Admiral Brandon was dead when I spoke with you but I knew that the information would not help you to a restful slumber."

He looked out the window. "Since it appears that we shall soon have a storm that will effectively blot out any possible clues as to the assailant's identity, I'm convinced that my decision was the correct one."

"And so it was, Gerry," Lady Amelia said heartily. "As you can see, Mother was so prostrated by the news that she was unable to come down."

His gaze swept the table. Yes, only Mr. Da Silva, Countess Boronskaya, and Lady Amelia were present.

"I presume that someone has informed Mr. Whitchell Brandon of his father's demise." He looked at Lady Amelia, who nodded.

"Archie—that is, Constable Nettle, called Roderick Benfleet. He came down quite early," she told him. "He's with Whitchell now. He first spoke with Mother, of course."

"And the pathologist, has he arrived?" Hawksmoor asked as he cut the crusts from his toast and arranged his eggs on the bread.

"I don't know," she answered. "Constable Nettle has been here all night. The pathologist may have reported directly to him."

At that point the door opened and Roderick Benfleet sidled in. He seemed very uncomfortable but Lady Amelia invited him to sit down and share the breakfast.

"How is Whitchell?" she inquired.

"Quite stunned, as one might expect," Benfleet told

them, dishing himself eggs, rashers, kidneys, and ham. "For a time all he could say was 'Gosh!' and 'I'll be blowed!' I'm not sure he fully realizes what has happened. He asked to be left alone and I, of course, respected that. I took the liberty of asking Jeavons to have someone bring him up a tray."

He looked at Lady Amelia like a puppy expecting the rolled-up newspaper but she only nodded agreement.

"Excellent idea," she said.

He exhaled in relief and began applying himself to the contents of his plate.

"Did the young Mr. Brandon mention anyone else in the family whom we should wire?" Sir Gerard asked.

"He said something about a sister," Benfleet answered when he had swallowed his kidneys. "But she's some sort of explorer and is out in the jungle somewhere. He doesn't know how to reach her."

"Well, there will certainly have to be an investigation," Lady Amelia said. "I hope that, by the time it's over, she can be found so that Whitchell will have someone to help him make arrangements for the burial."

"Investigation?" Mr. Da Silva dropped his fork. "I understood that the Admiral fell in the pond and drowned. Very sad, of course, especially for a man of the sea to meet his end in that way. But surely the pathologist's report will be enough."

Hawksmoor realised that the guests had not been told the full story. He looked at Lady Amelia, who shook her head a fraction. She must have had orders from her friend, the constable. He wished he knew the nature of their friendship. Archie Nettle had been a fine sergeant and a good soldier but he was hardly the sort to be accepted into the social circles Lady Amelia traveled in.

He drew his mind back to the immediate problem.

"I fear that the death of a high-ranking officer of the American navy may entail more than that," he said smoothly. "No doubt the embassy will want a full report of the events leading up to the . . . um . . . accident."

"I don't wish to speak ill of the dead," said Mr. Da Silva, preparing to do so. "But the man was drinking whiskey neat before dinner, had several glasses of wine during, and a large snifter of brandy afterwards. I noted this especially because I was astonished at his capacity. I suspect that the report will show that the poor man simply lost his balance due to drunkenness."

Sir Gerard shrugged. "The Admiral didn't seem to me to be adversely affected by alcohol," he said. "Seafaring men become accustomed to their grog ration, you know."

"Would you care to make a wager on that?" Da Silva grinned, showing several gleaming gold caps.

"Certainly not!" Hawksmoor said.

The Countess intervened. "I don't consider the cause of a man's death to be the subject of a wager. Perhaps you should confine your gambling instincts to the tables at Monte Carlo, Mr. Da Silva."

To Sir Gerard's surprise, Mr. Da Silva coloured angrily.

"I will not be lectured at by a woman like you," he growled. "You are nothing but a parasite."

Sir Gerard and Benfleet were on their feet in an instant.

"How dare you insult a lady!" Hawksmoor challenged.

"Really, Mr. Da Silva!" Benfleet remonstrated.

Da Silva looked at them both in contempt.

"Really, Katerina," he sneered. "Is this the best you can do for champions, a cripple and a boy in a bad suit? They aren't worth my trouble."

He stood, crumpling his serviette in his right hand and dropping it to the table.

"Lady Amelia." He bowed to her. "I believe my business here is finished. I shall leave at once."

"Much as I should like that, Mr. Da Silva," Lady Amelia answered, "I'm afraid that the police would not take kindly to your departure."

"The police!" Now Da Silva turned pale.

Sir Gerard wondered what colour would appear next. Mr. Da Silva was a positive chameleon! He hastened to explain. "They were of course called in when the body was found," he told the table. "It's possible that they may want to question all of us."

Lady Amelia gave a slight nod.

"Of course one must be certain that Admiral Brandon's death was truly an accident," the Countess said gravely but calmly. "Even influenced by liquor, it is strange that the poor man could not have got himself out from the pond."

"You're not suggesting m-murder!" Roderick Benfleet found it hard to maintain his carefully cultivated accent under stress.

"I only say that I'm sure the police will have questions." She looked directly at Mr. Da Silva.

"In that case, they will find me in my room, packing," Mr. Da Silva retorted. "Good morning."

When he had left the four remaining tried to act as if no social breach had occurred.

"More kidneys, Roderick?" Lady Amelia asked.

"A bit more toast, if you don't mind," Benfleet answered, enunciating carefully.

"I apologize," Countess Boronskaya said after a moment.

"I have encountered Mr. Da Silva before and, while I do not care for him, I have always been able to be civil to him until now."

"We're all unsettled by last night's events," Hawksmoor assured her. "I found nothing reproachable in *your* behaviour."

She smiled her thanks as she rose from the table.

"I shall also be in my room, if needed," she told them. "I may lie down for a few moments. I did not sleep well last night."

Lady Amelia got up next. "If the two of you have all you wish, I shall send one of the footmen down to see if the men guarding the pond would like some sustenance."

"I should go, too," Benfleet said as he brushed the crumbs of toast from his jacket. "Her Grace wanted me to retrieve some papers for her from my office."

Hawksmoor had wanted to ask him about the letter from Buenos Aires but this didn't seem an appropriate time. He finished his breakfast in welcome solitude, taking the time to mull over the sudden anger and nasty insinuations of Mr. Da Silva. He concluded that even in his own Latin culture, the man could not be considered a gentleman. So why had he been invited to Castle Crawsbey? It was clear that he would have to have a private talk with the Dowager Duchess soon.

But first he wanted to see the scene of the crime in daylight. He hoped that he could get there before the body was raised, as there was something he particularly wanted to check while it was *in situ*.

* * *

HIS arrival was greeted with enthusiasm by Constable Nettle.

"I've been on the phone to my superiors, Major," he said with a salute. "They'd be grateful if you could stay on the spot. With this storm brewing, we need to get the body up and to the morgue at once. The coroner has just shown up at last."

"Sir Gerard will suffice, Constable," Hawksmoor reminded him. "The war is over now."

Except in dreams, he thought.

"Now, where would you like me to start?" he added.

"I've done some preliminary examination of the area and not come up with much," the constable said. "There are a few cigarette ends of two different brands."

He led Sir Gerard to the spot where he had laid out his finds.

"We also found a few beads but no clue as to what they came from." He indicated several round beads, about as large as early peas and of a bright blue colour. "Could they have come from one of the ladies' necklaces?"

"I don't recognize them," Hawksmoor said, picking one up. "They don't seem to be of the sort anyone here would wear. I wonder what they are made from."

"Couldn't say for sure, sir," Constable Nettle told him. "But it's an interesting shade, almost turquoise, don't you think?"

Sir Gerard murmured something noncommittal and turned to the last piece in the collection.

"It looks like a feather from a shuttlecock," he said. "See how it's been shaved at the end to fit into something else."

"Of course," Nettle said. "I couldn't imagine any bird

around here having such bright red feathers. It may have been dropped by someone heading off for a game of badminton days ago."

"Possibly." Hawksmoor didn't want to tell Nettle what he really thought it was. The idea was too preposterous.

"Now, I'd like to have a look at the corpse before it leaves the water," he told the constable. "Is your man finished with the preliminary examination?"

"I am, Gerry." The pathologist straightened up from his task and Hawksmoor realized that it was his old friend from his hunting days, Squiffy Frobisher. "Though what there is to examine from this point of view beyond a pruny hand is more than I can guess."

"Squiffy! Good to see you!" Sir Gerard shook his hand. "You're quite right. Actually, I wanted another look at the sash that is holding the body to the statue."

"Oh yes, ugly purple thing," Frobisher said. "With silly gold fringe. Can't imagine what it is."

"I believe it belongs to a man named Da Silva," Sir Gerard told him. "But that's not what interests me."

He bent over to examine it and smiled.

"Just as I suspected," he told them, pointing to the sash. "Whoever tied this knew his business. This is a reef knot, used by sailors to hold objects firmly on a tossing sea."

"But what does that mean?" Frobisher asked. "We're miles from the sea."

"But not, perhaps, miles from sailors," Sir Gerard said enigmatically. "I must return to the house. Carry on with your work."

Under the constable's direction, ropes had been wound about the statue, between it and the body, and a winch attached to an overhanging tree. Now the men began to pull together on the other end and Neptune began to rise with his burden.

As he did, Hawksmoor could have sworn he heard someone whistling another line from the shanty.

Aye, aye UP she rises, Aye, aye UP she rises, ear-lye in the morning.

He turned quickly but there was no one to be seen.

THREE

An Inspector Calls

by Francine Mathews

DETECTIVE Chief Inspector Reggie Arbuthnot stared at the scrap of soiled paper tied to one of his milk bottles with pink ribbon—belonging, no doubt, to the carter's youngest daughter—then bent, with much grunting and creaking of vertebrae, to retrieve the milk from his front stoop. He had slept badly and risen two hours later than was his custom. It was now nearly nine o'clock, and the strength of the July sun suggested that his milk would be unpleasantly warm. Not for the first time did Arbuthnot wish for the brisk efficiency of Mrs. Ledbed, the ancient char whom he had left behind in London upon his removal to Rutfordshire. Mrs. Ledbed would have nothing to do with "the country," as she darkly called the hinterland surrounding Winsome-Under-Ware, nor with the dubious workings of Mortmain Cottage, the charming little thatched affair to which Arbuthnot had repaired three months before. Though he missed neither her caustic tongue nor her indifferent

housekeeping, it occurred to him now, as he sniffed despair-
ingly at the bottles, that Mrs. Ledbed would never have
allowed his milk to sour.

The sun shone weakly through the leaded casements of
Mortmain Cottage but the day promised to be sultry. As
Arbuthnot worked at the pink ribbon wrapped tenaciously
about the bottle's rim, thunder muttered in the distance. The
storm would come from the north, blowing its way through
Market Winsome, Winsome St. John, High Winsome, and
Winsome-Under-Ware before ending ignobly in Winsome-le-
Hatch, the southernmost of the villages strung like beads
along the river.

He had been disposed, upon first learning of his appointment to the Ware Valley, to regard the transfer as a political
snub. He was, after all, much older than the nervy young
men who had survived the battlefields of Ypres to return,
with an air of perpetual weariness, to the ranks of Scotland
Yard. A job of work in Winsome-Under-Ware—even when
exalted by so grand a term as Chief Inspector, Criminal Investigation Division—would never be more than a sinecure, a
prelude to retirement. There was little beyond hay wains and
sheep pasture to excite the interest, barring The Three Horseshoes in neighbouring Market Winsome and the ducal seat of
Castle Crawsbey some three miles distant. He had turned
aside the good wishes and smug blandishments of superiors
and colleagues alike, and retreated to Rutfordshire as though
going to his doom.

Three months, however, had worked a change upon
Arbuthnot's disgruntled brow. He had arrived in Winsome-
Under-Ware with the primroses, and the beauty of the place
had more than compensated for the loss of a London summer.
There would be excellent grouse hunting with the passage of

a few months, and Arbuthnot was the keenest of guns. The villages—each distinct, and yet so interwoven as to reveal a stunning complexity of commerce, rumour, and innuendo— offered their own pleasures. The Chief Inspector was a rotund figure, easy in his speech; he liked his bitter plentiful and often; and he had formed swift alliance with some of the deepest drinkers in the Valley. What he did not know about the inhabitants of Winsome-Under-Ware, Winsome St. John, and Winsome-le-Hatch was not worth knowing. And then there was the ducal seat crumbling gently into dust, on the edge of Market Winsome itself.

The scrap of paper, once extricated from its ribbon, revealed itself as a brief note scrawled in pencil.

Sir, Not wishing to disturb you before breakfast but think- ing as it was necessary you should know that a Naval gen- tleman met his end last night at the Castle. I have sent this message by Ned Chapman the milk carter so as to arrive early.

"Blast you, Archie Nettle," Arbuthnot muttered to him- self. "What sort of hash have you made of things this time, I wonder?"

Dr. Frobisher has been and says as the Admiral is dead, which leastways we knew, but Circumstances being Suspi- cious, I thought it best to conduct a thorough examination of the Ground. Respectfully awaiting your arrival and hoping as I did no harm, I remain, Archibald Nettle, Constable, Market Winsome.

P.S.: Her Grace is that Put Out.

Reggie Arbuthnot sighed heavily and crumpled the offending note in his fist. Archie Nettle was a fine sheep-shearer and a Don Juan among the local lasses, who favoured his dark good looks, but he was the absolute devil when it came to mucking up a crime scene. Why hadn't the Chief Inspector been summoned the very moment the body was discovered? What sort of end, exactly, had the naval gentleman met? And what constituted the Ground? Arbuthnot would have to bustle if he intended to speak to Squiffy Frobisher before the latter quitted Castle Crawsbey. The pathologist was generally admitted to prefer a round of golf to a round of patients in the surgery, and Arbuthnot was damned if he would tramp over the local links in pursuit of his medical examiner. As he ruminated on these and like details, the thunderstorm burst overhead with all the dramatic effect of the best London stage. Arbuthnot gazed heavenward with an expression of ill-humour. What evidence Archie Nettle had left undisturbed would be sluiced into the ducal ditches in a matter of minutes. The Chief Inspector would have his work cut out for him.

"FOR God's sake, Gerry," the Dowager Duchess snapped impatiently, "sit down. You make one think of cadavers— stiff as a board and grim-faced into the bargain. I suppose you'll claim it's due to the dicky leg, or hip, or whatever it is you brought home from the war—but really, Gerry, the war has been over for years, hasn't it? And still you persist in looking like something the mortuary forgot. It's no wonder Amelia refuses to marry you. There's never the least suggestion of blood in your veins."

Sir Gerard Hawksmoor sank with difficulty into one of

the charming little gilt chairs the Dowager Duchess had scattered about the boudoir. The room reflected the gifts and foibles of its mistress: the furniture, of highest quality and excellent taste, bore the marks of shabby treatment. Late dahlias fired a vase on the dressing table next to open jars of cold cream in which cigarettes had guttered. Shoes were kicked carelessly under tables and the Dowager Duchess's prized cat had ravaged the silk upholstery of the tufted ottoman—rather, Sir Gerard reflected, as Her Grace's claws had just ravaged him.

She stood by the tall windows that gave out onto the South Terrace, the long sweep of ill-tended herbaceous borders, and the Neptune Fountain so lately denuded of its principal god—a slim, elegant figure, though clearly past her first youth. Her hips were narrow, her faded gold hair fashionably bobbed, and her clothes excellent. The castle might crumble at her feet, Sir Gerard thought, but Daisy Digby would never appear less than exquisitely dressed. Daisy Digby! In his father's generation it had been a name worth toasting—and even as Daisy, Duchess of Faughstrayne, she could still stop conversation dead. Daisy Digby must be over fifty now—her daughter, Amelia, was twenty-six—but she had been forced into widowhood too soon. There had been rumours, of course, when the nineteenth Duke slipped his mortal coil: of an entanglement on His Grace's part with a grasping, unsuitable upstart of a woman; a hunting accident in some remote corner of the Castle Crawsbey grounds; even of Daisy, standing over the late Duke with a fowling piece in her hands. Who knew what sad histories were stifled in these ancient walls, or shrouded in Daisy Digby's violet eyes? She had survived all rumour, however, and carried on in her elegant, commanding fashion—but she never remarried, choosing instead to remain buried in remotest Rutfordshire. It was, Sir Gerard reflected, rather like the endurance of a protracted penance—one in which she had chained her daughter, who watched helplessly as her matchless twenties slipped irretrievably over the weir-gates of the River Ware. Lady Amelia, despite her determined conversation and air of serenity, was desperate enough to escape Castle Crawsbey that she might do anything—marry the first raw American boy who presented himself at the dinner table, or even the handsome local constable. But never, it appeared, her child-hood sweetheart Gerry Hawksmoor, so brutally changed by the trenches of the Somme.

"I shall have to talk to them, I suppose?" the Dowager Duchess said wearily.

"The police? Certainly." Sir Gerard roused himself from his brown study. "The Admiral died in exceedingly odd cir-cumstances, Your Grace. You know that he was lashed to Neptune with Mr. Da Silva's purple sash?"

"The Order of the Apothecary." The Dowager Duchess tapped some ash from her black-lacquered cigarette holder. "A Maltese affair, I believe, though nothing to do with the Knights. You were saying?"

"It might help if I could intercede, Your Grace. With the Chief Inspector."

"Playing detective again, Gerry?" Her amused glance was as scathing as a boy's first blooding in the hunt. "Are you even acquainted with the man?"

"Distantly. We met once or twice at Scotland Yard."

"This does sound ominous. And all for an American bounder who had no idea how to dress. Appalling." She glanced delicately at her manicured fingernails. A gout of ash drifted like thistledown to the carpet. "Did you hear the way the Admiral spoke to me last night, Gerry? Have you ever heard anyone address me in such a way?"

"Never, Your Grace. And yet you bore the insult with such—equanimity. May I ask why you invited the Admiral to Castle Crawsbey?"

She shrugged. "He offered a letter of introduction from a mutual friend—Letty Bracenose, the scandal writer—and I couldn't refuse. It doesn't do to refuse Letty, or one finds oneself smeared all over the *Daily Yell*."

"The woman's a veritable blackmailer, and her friends are worse. You knew nothing, then, about Admiral Brandon?"

The Dowager Duchess's eyes glinted. "Nothing at all— other than the fact that he's worth a most un-naval fortune. Something to do with gold mines in Minas Gerais. That gauche young man—his son, Whitchell—is swotting up engineering at Cambridge. Or so Amelia says. The boy rowed at Henley this year. Quite the naval family."

"And the son dresses no better than his father. Does Amelia think Whitchell has—how did Your Grace put it?— 'Blood in his veins?'"

"Poor Gerry. He has money, which is worse. He'll inherit the lot, you know, when the old man—" She stopped short, glanced away from his agonized face, and inhaled deeply of her cigarette.

"How convenient for all of us if the wretched boy were to hang for his father's murder!"

The Dowager Duchess went suddenly rigid, her gaze fixed on the scene unfolding below. "They've come, Gerry— a whole bloody picnic party of coppers, scrounging in the grass. Oh, God—I can't bear it!"

It was a picture, Sir Gerard reflected, vastly reminiscent of the late Duke's death five years before: a shrouded body, a diligent party of men sweeping the lawn for clues, and a woman standing watchful by an upstairs window—only this time, Sir Gerard recognized the portly figure in the Homburg hat who had placed himself at a slight remove from the evidence collectors.

Reggie Arbuthnot.

The Homburg shielded his balding head from the determined rain that poured in sheets across the ill-tended lawn and ruffled the waters of the Neptune Fountain. Next to the Chief Inspector was Squiffy Frobisher, a pipe stem clamped firmly in his massive jaws.

"Your Grace," Sir Gerard said in the Dowager Duchess's ear, "we haven't much time. It is imperative that I warn you. Constable Nettle found three items by the Neptune pool that you must be prepared to explain. Two blue beads, the size of peas and carved undoubtedly from South American turquoise, and the red-feathered shaft of a tribal dart, such as might be blown from a wooden pipe. I attempted to suggest it was torn from a shuttlecock."

"Nobody plays badminton these days, you fool." The Dowager Duchess grasped his arm painfully. "Bloody hell, Gerry! How many times have I told Amelia not to shoot at the guests from her bedroom window?"

"A curious case," Squiffy Frobisher mused around the stem of his pipe. He stood bareheaded in the rain, indifferent to the wet that had darkened the blanket thrown over the Admiral's corpse. He lifted one corner, and revealed the dead face with its startled expression and still-ruddy complexion. "No contusions on the body—it was buffered, I think, by the fountain's water as it sank. There's a good four feet in that basin."

Arbuthnot cast a glance over his shoulder at the koi pond. "When was the corpse discovered, Squiffy?"

"A bit after one o'clock in the morning, near as I can make out. Your constable was called about that time. Here are the contents of the Admiral's pockets, by the way." The pathologist tipped a few coins, a cigarette lighter and case, a small gold key, and a pocket comb into Arbuthnot's palm. The cigarette case bore the initials C. B., he noted, but the lighter was unengraved. It was small and delicate—the sort of item a lady might carry, rather than a seafaring man.

"Can you put a guess as to time of death, Squiffy?"

Frobisher's eyes narrowed behind a veil of blue smoke. "Not and remain an honest man, Reggie, as you very well know. Rigor has hardly come on—but there's no surprise in that; the fellow was left floating in a bathtub on a warm July night. He was last seen bidding Her Grace good-night from the door of the billiard room at half-past ten; he was discovered *in flagrante aqua* at roughly an hour past midnight. I imagine he met his death some time in between."

Arbuthnot grunted sourly. "But how did he meet his death, Squiffy? Any water in the lungs?"

"None that I could discover. The postmortem may prove definitive on that point. But it is my belief," Frobisher enunciated as though under oath in the coroner's box, "that our Admiral was already dead when he entered the water."

"No pistol wounds to the head. No marks of strangulation about the neck. No evidence of wrists or ankles bound prior to death."

Frobisher considered the corpse's ruddy face. "Surfeit of dinner, perhaps? Leading to stroke—or coronary?"

"Say the fellow keeled over near the fish pond," Arbuthnot said thoughtfully, "why lash him to Neptune with a borrowed sash?"

"To incriminate the sash's owner, naturally."

"It belongs to one of Her Grace's guests, I understand?"

"The foreign fellow—Da Silva. He's sitting in the back of a cream-coloured Daimler, waiting for permission to hie himself back to London. Doesn't like the scent of constabulary, I gather. Shifty-looking fellow, by all accounts, and more money than sense, from his appearance."

"Whom else has Her Grace got in keeping, Squiffy?"

"Lady Amelia, of course, and the pet solicitor—Benfleet, you know the name, keeps lodgings in Market Winsome. Then there's the Deceased's son, a callow youth by all accounts, though I've not had the pleasure of his acquaintance. A faded Russian countess who claims blood relations whenever her exchequer is in arrears." The pathologist hesitated. "And Sir Gerard, of course."

"Sir Gerard Hawksmoor?" Reggie Arbuthnot's craggy eyebrows shot up into his hairline.

"He rather took command of the situation last night, I'm afraid."

"The Major would do that." Arbuthnot shook his head regretfully. "Poor bugger. I understand, now, why Nettle failed to give me a ring—why you weren't called until daybreak—and why most of the guests were allowed to slumber undisturbed while a wealth of evidence sat rotting in the garden. A proper muck-up! But there—the poor lad's not quite right in his head."

"Shattered nerves, insomnia, hallucinations, and a dangerous dependence upon morphia for the relief of pain," Squiffy Frobisher summed up neatly.

"Still posing as the Great White Hope of Scotland Yard, is he?"

"When he's not wandering naked in the moonlight through Winsome St. John."

Arbuthnot sighed and adjusted his Homburg fretfully on his head. "Nothing you can do for Sir Gerard, I suppose?"

"I keep tabs on the amount of morphia he consumes." Frobisher extracted his pipe and tapped the bowl gently against the foot of resurrected Neptune. "I counsel his manservant not to leave the guns about. And I never put much credence in anything Sir Gerard says. He's a walking wreck."

"But harmless. This Da Silva fellow, now—the foreigner," Arbuthnot persisted. "Why should any of Her Grace's guests wish to throw suspicion on the man? What's his game, Squiffy—and what's he doing at Castle Crawsbey?"

"That's your job, Reggie—putting the wind up any bright lads who run afoul of murder." Frobisher grinned. "I'm almost tempted to stay and watch. But I think I'll get in a bit of practice on my short game."

"In this rain?"

"It's clearing."

"Before it does," Arbuthnot retorted, "get the Admiral down to your surgery, there's a good fellow. I want a thorough postmortem before the inquest. Have you any date in mind?"

"As tomorrow's Sunday—most unsuitable for a coroner's inquiry—I thought perhaps Monday would do. It's certainly the soonest a panel could be assembled."

"Very well."

Frobisher hesitated, his cheerful looks evaporating at the prospect of several hours' tussle with the Admiral's corpse. "Should I keep an eye out for anything in particular, Chief Inspector?"

"What you want, Squiffy," Arbuthnot told him heavily, "is the telltale mark of a swift-acting poison."

BEFORE the war, Sir Gerard Hawksmoor had been known as a man so light on his feet that he could creep through bedrooms in the still of the night without arousing cuckolded husbands. Many were the grateful ladies who, at an unnamed hour close to dawn, had settled into slumber serene in the knowledge that Gerry Hawksmoor should never be discovered. But a mortar shell lodged in the wall of a trench had changed all that forever. As he made his difficult way down the length of Castle Crawsbey's upper corridor, he was painfully aware of the shuffling sound of his shoes on the threadbare drugget. Pray God that no one—housemaid or police constable—was within range of hearing!

He hesitated at the door of Lady Amelia's bedroom. He knew that she intended to spend much of the morning hanging over Constable Nettle. An air of stillness beyond the threshold suggested that Lady Amelia's maid had already tidied the room. He might enter with impunity.

He dragged his game leg through the doorway and allowed his eyes to adjust to the blaze of light within.

The prospect from Lady Amelia's room was excellent. The apartment had originally been intended to serve as the Duchess's, should the present Duke ever return from his curious adventures in South America and present a suitable wife to Castle Crawsbey's intimates; but neither Duke nor Duchess being in evidence, Lady Amelia had claimed the suite of rooms as her own. Double sets of French windows gave out onto a wide balcony which overlooked the rolling progression of South Terrace, formal gardens, and lawns punctuated by the Neptune Fountain. A perfect vantage point, Sir Gerard thought grimly, for the shooting of any number of missiles at perambulating guests.

But he was not concerned with the Peruvian blow-pipe sent as a gift to Lady Amelia in the Duke's last Christmas package—he had confided that worry to the Dowager Duchess. His mission, at present, was far more delicate. He moved to Lady Amelia's large wardrobe, and threw open the doors.

The scent of lilies-of-the-valley nearly overpowered him. Her scent! Bound up in her tawny hair! With a groan he fell to his knees on the closet floor and buried his face in the hem of a simple cotton frock—and then recollected, in an instant, both the danger and the purpose of his position. He groped in darkness for the hamper containing Lady Amelia's dirty linen. He felt within—his fingers trembled upon a silken scrap of fabric—passed over a prodding length of whalebone—and came to rest in the slippery folds of an evening gown. He held it aloft—but it was not the white silk sheath that Lady Amelia had worn the previous evening. He rummaged further among the soiled clothes, finally tipped over the hamper entirely, and surveyed the contents as they sprawled haphazardly across the wardrobe's floor. Then he glanced upward, studying the ranks of hangers. A faint chill of apprehension curled in his stomach. The white silk gown was nowhere to be seen. Had Lady Amelia spirited the thing away in the night? A vision of her standing near the fountain at one o'clock in the morning, radiant in her pink negligée and pearls, rose before his eyes. When she had met him standing guard so gallantly over the sunken sailor, had Lady Amelia been returning from a visit to the Crawsbey rubbish heap?

* * *

"YOU mean to say the fellow's scarpered?" Reggie Arbuthnot demanded in an aggrieved tone. "He cares so little for the presence of the law—in the form of Archie Nettle—that he took off without so much as a by-your-leave?"

"Sitting in the Daimler's hot work of a July morning, rain or no," the constable replied. "Mr. Da Silva said as how he'd be having a pint in The Three Horseshoes, Chief Inspector, and that I was to say you could ask your questions over a draught of bitter as easily as tramping about the back garden."

"He did, did he? Impudent beggar." Arbuthnot stared balefully at the empty spot on the gravel sweep where a cream-coloured touring sedan had once been parked. "Nothing for it, then. I shall have to leg it down to Market Winsome before the day is much older. I must see Her Grace and chat up the other guests, but first I intend to have a look at Admiral Brandon's room. Who've you got stationed there?"

"Begging your pardon, sir?" Nettle looked completely blank.

The Chief Inspector felt his visage purple. No amount of service in the London force had prepared him for the greenness of the country. "Do you mean to tell me," Reggie Arbuthnot demanded, "that you left the Admiral's room completely unguarded—the door unlocked—for a full eight hours after the corpse was discovered?"

"Well—that is—we knew he'd never gone to bed, like—"

"The entire household could have tramped through the place by this time, and you none the wiser, Archie Nettle!"

The unhappy police constable stared at the dusty toes of his work boots. "I was that short-handed," he attempted. "Stood guard myself at the Neptune Fountain most of the night—"

"Bloody hell," Arbuthnot muttered richly. "Come along with me, lad, and learn yourself a proper bit of police work."

He turned on his heel and stumped back through the wide Palladian doorway so lovingly commissioned by the fifteenth duke, then made for the broad staircase that led to the bedrooms on the first floor.

Admiral Brandon had been lodged in a suite of rooms that overlooked the approach to Castle Crawsbey—the driveway that ran for nearly a mile through rolling sheep pasture before dipping down to nod at an excellent trout stream, ending in dramatic style in a circular sweep before the entry. The apartment consisted of a bedroom and sitting room furnished in heavily ornate style, probably dating to Elizabeth's time. A connecting door led from the Admiral's quarters to another bedroom, as Arbuthnot observed when he swung the door open. A crumpled necktie hung over the back of a chair and a straw boater had been discarded carelessly on the counterpane. A black dinner suit lay in a heap on the floor near the foot of the bed.

"Young Mr. Brandon, I'll be bound."

A second door was set into the Admiral's far wall, but when Arbuthnot tried it, he found it locked from the opposite side.

"Find out what's beyond that door, Nettle, when you have a moment."

"But the Admiral didn't die in the house, sir," the Constable said with an air of immense patience.

"Nor he did. Let's have a look at his belongings, then."

A washbasin stood on a sidetable, next to a pitcher filled with water. The Chief Inspector dipped his index finger into the depths. "Tepid," he observed. "Either he never used it last night, or the housemaid has changed the water this morning."

"The face flannel is dry, sir," Nettle told him acutely, "and looks as though it's never been used."

"Same for the bed." The Admiral's shaving kit was a compact affair, such as might serve a man of economy in tight quarters. The contents, however, were jumbled furiously as though someone had misplaced an article and been desperate to find it. A dress uniform, newly cleaned and pressed, hung on the wardrobe door. A faint air of the tropics emanated from the starched fabric.

Arbuthnot raised a speculative eyebrow. "Brandon wore scent? He doesn't seem the type."

"Coconut oil pomade, for his hair," Nettle supplied helpfully. "One of the servants—Lewis, by name—upended the bottle on the Deceased's uniform, and he was forced to wear the late Duke's dinner suit and boiled shirt last evening."

"How very trying for Her Grace." Arbuthnot surveyed the room. "Not a book in sight; he wasn't a reading man. He wrote a letter to someone, however—the stationery in the desk drawer has been disturbed. We must inquire whether Jeavons collected any letters for the post yesterday. That might be significant. What's in the wardrobe?"

"A tweed suit, a pair of plus-fours, and a pair of flannels," Nettle offered. "And a black attaché case."

"Give it over."

The Constable obliged. It was a square black leather case of the sort carried by solicitors or financial men, bound with leather straps. A small gold lock dangled from the clasp. Arbuthnot peered at it narrowly. "Someone has been tampering with this lock—tried to force it with something like a penknife."

He drew from his pocket the small gold key that had

been found among Admiral Brandon's belongings, and fitted it into the lock. With a click, it fell open.

Nettle whistled under his breath. Neat rows of British pound notes filled at least half the available space. "There must be nigh on a thousand pounds in there, sir! Just left lying about!"

"And for what purpose, I wonder?" Arbuthnot gave the uniform bundles of cash a cursory glance, then drew out a pile of papers marked *Minas Gerais Metalworks, Ltd.* He thumbed quickly through them, nodded once, and set them aside. An envelope, poorly secured with a piece of sticking plaster, lay almost at the bottom of the case. He opened the flap and shook the contents onto the bedcover.

A lady's platinum brooch, fashioned in the shape of a phoenix, and set with emeralds and diamonds. A set of photographic negatives. And a sheet of paper, written in a crabbed but flourishing hand.

"It's a list of some sort," Nettle said.

Arbuthnot ran his eyes over the page.

Daisy, Dowager Duchess of Faughstrayne—partial
   payment.
Lady Amelia Crawsbey—paid in full.
Roderick Benfleet—promised.
The Countess Boronskaya—paid in full.
Enrique Da Silva—flat refusal.
Sir Gerard Hawksmoor—

A slight sound from the doorway brought Arbuthnot's head up. He turned and stared at the figure on the threshold.

"Yes, Mr. Benfleet? May I be of assistance?"

The solicitor, Roderick Benfleet, swayed slightly and grasped the doorframe for support. His pallor was dreadful. "I must have—taken a wrong turn. Dashed lot of corridors in Castle Crawsbey, you know. I was looking for—Sir Gerard."

"Indeed? I could have sworn you were looking for something else—something you thought to find among the dead man's effects. Tell me, Mr. Benfleet—what exactly did you promise Admiral Brandon before he died? And did you ever deliver upon that promise?"

Benfleet swallowed painfully, his Adam's apple bobbing. And as he collected his wits in an effort to form a suitable answer, a strain of ancient sea shanty drifted upwards from the gravel sweep.

Put him in the scuppers with a hawse-pipe on him, put him in the scuppers with a hawse-pipe on him, put him in the scuppers with a hawse-pipe on him, ear-lye in the morning—

FOUR

Sea Shanties—and State Secrets

by Walter Satterthwait

"Who the devil is that?" cried Arbuthnot and hastened across the silk Tabriz carpet, a wonderful specimen (if a bit faded and worn in spots) of the Persian weavers' art. He grasped the latch on the casement window with a meaty hand and, grunting slightly at the effort, twisted it up and jerked the window open. He glared down at the circular sweep before the castle.

Except for his faithful old Morris motorcar and two Market Winsome police vehicles, all three autos standing forlornly in the rain that rattled down from a sky so overcast now that it resembled one gigantic complex of bruises, as though the gods had been pummeling the heavens with enormous cricket bats, the drive was empty.

"Sea shanties," he muttered. "I *hate* the bloody things."

Arbuthnot had spent a large part of his unhappy youth listening to—or, rather, doing his very best to avoid listening to—the shanties sung by his father, who at the time was dying a lingering death from paresis and general softening of the brain. Because of her deep distrust of the medical establishment, Arbuthnot's mother had refused to have her husband hospitalized, and had attempted to heal him herself by keeping him chained to a bed in the attic and administering homemade poultices and endless cups of tea. All day and night, except when the old man was drinking his tea, the shanties had droned through the house. Arbuthnot had tried everything to escape them—plunging plugs of cork into his ears, swaddling his head in blankets, howling arias from Puccini— but nothing had worked. The shanties were inescapable.

No one in the family had ever quite understood why Arbuthnot's father had taken such a fancy to shanties, for the old man had never been closer to the sea than Bournemouth, where he'd once spent an afternoon attempting to persuade a shopkeeper to sell him a tea cozy at discount. (Given the celebrated shrewdness of Bournemouth shopkeepers, this was seen in retrospect as an early symptom of his disease.)

But perhaps because of the poultices, or possibly because of the tea, *père* Arbuthnot had in fact lingered for many years, and it was not until Arbuthnot entered the constabulary that he was able to escape their horrid sing-song. To this day he could not hear a shanty without becoming suffused with rage.

Only one other thing in the entire world had the power to disturb him as much. This was Sir Gerard Hawksmoor, who had, blast him, so often interfered with Arbuthnot at the Yard; and who had, through some extraordinary series of accidents, so often been correct in his damnable amateur deductions.

He closed the window. "Scarpered, whoever it was," he grumbled.

When he turned away from the window, he discovered that the singer of shanties was not the only individual who had disappeared. The sole remaining occupant of the room, other than Arbuthnot himself, was Constable Nettle, who stood there with an enquiring look on his handsome face.

"Where the devil did he go?" Arbuthnot demanded.

"Benfleet, you mean, sir?" answered the Constable.

"Who the bloody else would I mean?"

"He left, sir. You were so long looking out the window, sir, that perhaps he felt you'd done with him."

"You let him simply waltz away?"

"He didn't waltz, sir, as much as shuffle. Backwards, like. Shall I go after him?"

Arbuthnot sighed. "No, no, you stay with me. Last thing I need is for you to wander off and get lost. Let's take another look at that evidence, eh?"

HAVING left Daisy, Dowager Duchess of Faughstrayne, in her suite, Sir Gerard Hawksmoor was ambling through the Salon toward the Library. His thoughts, concentrated like a beam of sunlight being strangled by the lens of a magnifying glass, were focused intensely upon a most curious problem. He had just now realised that someone, at some time in the past few hours, had said something that contradicted something said earlier by someone else. Who was it, and what had been said?

His ruminations were suddenly interrupted by the sound of heavy footsteps coming up rapidly behind him.

With his bad leg and injured back, Sir Gerard knew that he was no longer a fit match, at least on the physical plane, for any man whose intention was to do him harm. He cast his glance quickly about the room, looking for a convenient but substantial item he might recruit as a weapon. The antique bracket clock of oak with ebony inlay that adorned on the Charles II cabinet? The Ming Dynasty bowl that decorated the Queen Anne writing desk?

"Sir Gerard! Thank God I found you!"

Sir Gerard turned and saw that it was the solicitor, Roderick Benfleet.

"Ah, Benfleet," he said, relieved—not only because the potential assailant had turned out to be Benfleet, with whom he had in fact wished to speak, but also because he could now, thank goodness, forestall doing damage to the castle's many fine *objets d'art*. He would have damaged any one of them, of course, without hesitation, in order to effect his own survival. Four long years in the trenches had burned into him an involuntary mechanism of defense, one so powerful that even those agonizing months in the hospital had not expunged it.

"As it happens," he told the solicitor, "I've been looking for you. We need to talk, I think, about that letter you received—"

"Damn the letter, man!" expostulated Benfleet. The young solicitor was clearly distressed. He was panting, and his florid face was shiny with perspiration. More significantly, his collar point was askew. "I'm in trouble! We must talk!"

This was not, Sir Gerard decided, the proper moment to upbraid the man for his use of expletives, or for his errant collar point. "Very well," he agreed, with perhaps more grace than the situation, and Benfleet, deserved. "Come along to the Library."

CHIEF Inspector Reggie Arbuthnot returned to the table and glanced down at the items lying there. The platinum brooch, the papers from the Minas Gerais Metalworks company, the photographic negatives.

"Who's this Minas Gerais fellow, sir?" asked Nettle. "Some sort of high muck-a-muck in the metalworks game?"

"It's not a *who,* Nettle. It's a *where.* A state in southeastern Brazil, if I recall correctly." Arbuthnot had no doubt that his recollection was accurate; for years he had been a subscriber to *The National Geographic* magazine. Its frank photographs of aboriginal village life had often been most enlightening, and its detailed maps had occasionally—as now—proved extremely useful.

"The phrase itself," Arbuthnot added, *"Minas Gerais,* means 'mineral mines' in Portuguese. They speak Portuguese in Brazil."

"Why is that, sir?" asked Nettle.

"Why is what?"

"Why do they speak Portuguese in Brazil?"

"Well, everyone has to speak *some* language, don't they, Nettle? In Brazil this just happens to be Portuguese."

"Yes, sir."

That having been dealt with, Arbuthnot turned his attention to the evidence at hand. Carefully, using the tips of his fingers along its edges lest he obscure any fingerprints, he picked up one of the photographic negatives and held it towards the light of the window.

For a moment he couldn't make out what it was he saw. But when, all at once, he understood, his jaw dropped open and his heart skipped a beat.

"Good Lord!" he exclaimed involuntarily.

"What is it, sir?" queried Nettle, reaching for another of the negatives.

"No!" Arbuthnot exclaimed, and held up an imperious hand. Blinking in confusion, Nettle drew back.

Abuthnot's upraised hand was shaking. What he'd seen on the negative had shaken him to the core and he knew that if word of the image contained on that strip of film were ever to get out, it might very well shake the foundations of the British Empire. The images contained on the other negatives—if they bore any resemblance to the first— were of a nature far too explosive for them to be seen by a simple village constable. And especially by a village constable like Nettle, whose simplicity had achieved a level that was very nearly profound.

No, if anyone were to examine the negatives, it must be someone from the Home Office. Someone who would recognize the incalculable threat posed by the images. Someone discreet. Someone who would know the proper steps to take. That chap Finlay, for example. He'd seemed a solid sort, back when the two of them had worked together on the Purloined Letter affair.

Without looking at them—he felt that duty compelled him not to look—and, careful once again not to smudge any possible fingerprints, Arbuthnot gathered together the negatives and returned them to the envelope in which he'd found them. As an afterthought, he slipped in the phoenix-shaped brooch, then folded the envelope and tucked it into the inside pocket of his suit coat.

When he turned back to Constable Nettle, he saw that the man was staring off into space with his head slightly cocked, as though he were thinking, which was unlikely, or as though he were listening to something, which was vaguely possible.

"What is it, Nettle?" Arbuthnot snapped.

"Can't you hear it, sir? It sounds like music."

Arbuthnot glanced furiously around the room. "Not another bloody shanty!"

"No, sir. Some sort of foreign music. Seems to be coming," he turned and pointed to the locked door in the far wall of the bedroom, "from there. . . ."

Arbuthnot listened and, indeed, there was music coming from behind the locked door. He held up a cautioning finger to Nettle, then tiptoed over to the door. He leaned to one side and placed his ear against the wood.

No doubt about it. Music. And as Nettle had said, something foreign. Something with a primitive, savage, decidedly un-British rhythm.

Once again, quietly, he essayed turning the door knob. Locked.

He stood back from the door and looked at Nettle. Softly, he commanded, "Do your stuff, Constable. Break it down."

"WOULD you care for a cigarette?" Sir Gerard asked Roderick Benfleet, once the solicitor and he had taken seats in the book-lined room.

"No, thank you," said Benfleet. He leaned forward. "Sir Gerard, can I rely upon your discretion?"

"Many people have," said Sir Gerard. "And, so far as I know, none have had cause to regret it." He struck a match, lit his cigarette, dropped the match in the crystal ashtray—a Waterford, unless he missed his guess—on the end-table. "What, exactly, is this trouble in which you find yourself?"

Benfleet frowned. "It's rather a long story," he said.

Weren't they all, mused Sir Gerard. "Then I suggest," he said, "that you begin at the beginning."

"Yes. Yes, of course. It has to do with the late Admiral Brandon. Ceebee."

"Ah."

"You know that the Admiral had mining interests in Brazil?"

"Argentina, I thought it was." So Countess Baronskaya had informed him.

"He has interests in Argentina, yes, but his primary concern is a metalworks company in Minas Gerais, in Brazil."

Yes, Hawksmoor remembered now that the Dowager Duchess had mentioned something about Minas Gerais.

A thought flitted so quickly through his mind, like a biplane whizzing through a hangar crammed with aircraft, that he was unable to shoot it down. Something about Daisy.

It would come back to him, he knew. His mind had never let him down. Well, there was, of course, that one absurd moment in Paris . . . but that had been, in the circumstances, forgivable. Absinthe, as everyone knew, was devilish stuff. Thank God his manservant had been at hand.

"Sir Gerard?" enquired Benfleet.

"Yes," said Sir Gerard, turning his head back to Benfleet and his attention back to the present. "You were saying. The metalworks company in Minas Gerais."

"Yes. You know that Dudley, the young Duke of Faughstrayne, has been living in South America?"

"I'd heard so, yes." And had often wondered, along with most of Market Winsome, as well as the surrounding county, why the Dowager Duchess had always been so infernally secretive about the young man's stay there.

"What you may not know," said Benfleet, "—few do—is that the Duke has recently been living in Brazil, in Belo

Horizonte, the capital of Minas Gerais. As you may remember, Dudley resembles his late father in many ways."

Sir Gerard puffed at his cigarette. "I recall the resemblance. Quite extraordinary. Peas in a pod. If one put them side by side, one could scarcely tell them apart."

"It's a resemblance that extends beyond the mere physical. Like his father, Dudley is fascinated by archaeology. Most of his time in South America has been spent wandering through the jungle, seeking out evidence of lost civilizations."

Sir Gerard frowned. Surely there were better ways for a titled young man to occupy his time. But perhaps a pursuit so bizarre would explain the Duchess's reticence. She'd always found her husband's interest in the subject inexplicable.

"As you may realise," continued Benfleet, "wandering through jungles can be an expensive proposition. There are porters to pay for, and victuals, and weapons and ammunition, and insect repellent, and shiny beads with which to ply the natives—"

"Yes, yes," said Sir Gerard. "I comprehend." He stubbed his cigarette out in the ashtray.

"The Duchess has refused to lend her son any further assistance," continued Benfleet. "And so, to fund his most recent expedition, the Duke went to Admiral Brandon. Brandon agreed to provision Dudley, but only on the condition that any discoveries made by Dudley would be shared on an equal basis with the Admiral."

"But what sort of discoveries could the Duke possibly hope to make? As I recall, there are no lost civilizations in Brazil. There are no civilizations of any sort in Brazil. It's all river, as I understand, teeming with unpleasant fauna. Snakes and things. And what isn't river is jungle, clogged with inhospitable vegetation." A shiver of distaste passed over Sir Gerard's frame.

"But that's just *it,* you see," said Benfleet. "The Duke *did* find a Lost Civilization!"

Sir Gerard could hear the capital letters in Benfleet's voice. He smiled. "Come now," he said. "You don't really expect me to believe——"

"But it's the truth! The Duke discovered a Lost Civilization deep in the jungle, perhaps a hundred miles to the southwest of Belo Horizonte. The Kingdom of the Maltecs, an ancient race more powerful and more wealthy than the Incas and the Aztecs. And in their Great Palace, hidden in a crypt beneath a monumental statue of Gorblec, the High Priest, he found treasures that boggle the mind—heaps of gemstones, tons and tons of gold and silver."

"Hang on a moment," said Sir Gerard. "Didn't you tell me last night that no one had heard from the Duke? Didn't you say that you'd received a mysterious letter from some friend in Buenos Aires?"

The solicitor had the grace to blush. Sir Gerard wondered how many of Benfleet's peers would have done the same. "I was testing you," Benfleet said.

"Testing me? For what, pray?"

"I was attempting to learn whether Ceebee—Admiral Brandon—had approached you to become part of the partnership."

"The partnership?"

"The partnership set up by Ceebee. You see, the government of Brazil is terribly touchy about people exporting anything from the country. Particularly archaeological treasures."

"Perhaps because, up until now, there haven't been any."

"Perhaps," said Benfleet. "But if they got wind of this

Maltec cache, they'd swoop down upon it like hawks. Confiscate it. Use it, no doubt, to line their own pockets—you know how treacherous these South Americans are. Ceebee's plan was to move the loot overland to Argentina, very discreetly, and then ship it from there to England."

"And you were attempting to discover whether I'd become a party to all this?"

"Yes. I knew that if Ceebee had, in fact, spoken to you about becoming a member of the partnership, you would've revealed yourself to me."

Sir Gerard shook his head. "I must say, Benfleet, this all sounds terribly dodgy. Whatever the Brazilian government might do, I feel sure that the British government would have something to say about 'tons' of illicit gold and silver flowing into the country."

"Ceebee had photographs."

"Photographs of what?"

"He never told me. But he assured me that with them, he could coerce the highest heads of state into cooperating."

"Surely he gave you some clue as to what was in these photographs?"

Benfleet looked down for a moment, then looked up. "He implied that the photographs had to do, in some way, with the late Queen Victoria."

"*Queen Victoria!* You must be joking!"

Benfleet shook his head. "I can tell you only what Ceebee told me. He seemed utterly confident that with the photographs in his possession, he could proceed unmolested."

Sir Gerard sighed. "All right, look. Let's put all that aside for a moment. Tell me what it is, exactly, that membership in this partnership entailed."

"Each of the partners would provide five hundred pounds.

Ceebee would use the money to arrange transport for the treasure, and to bribe any local South American authorities who might stand in his way."

"Couldn't Admiral Brandon have paid for all that himself? I understood that he was wealthy."

"He was over-extended. His mining operations, both in Brazil and in Argentina, had suffered set-backs. Something to do with the labor unions."

Sir Gerard nodded. "And what would the partners receive in exchange for their five hundred pounds?"

"Each would receive five percent of the proceeds of the treasure, once it was brought to England and sold. The remainder would be divided equally between the Admiral and Dudley."

"And presumably you yourself are a partner?"

"Not a full partner. I paid him what I had at the time, a little over two hundred pounds. The rest I intended to borrow from my great-aunt. She did well in South African real estate."

"And who else has partnered with the Admiral?"

"I know that Lady Amelia has. And I suspect that the Duchess has. I don't know who else."

"And do any of you have any proof, other than Admiral Brandon's word for it, that this treasure actually exists?"

Without a word, Benfleet leaned back and reached into his trouser pocket. When his hand re-emerged, it held a gold figurine, four inches long and about an inch thick. He handed it to Sir Gerard. "Ceebee gave me this."

Sir Gerard examined it. It was roughly cylindrical, with a round head at the top into which primitive facial features had been hammered.

Sir Gerard hefted the piece. It was heavy enough to be gold. He looked up at Benfleet. "Have you had it examined?"

"By a friend at the British Museum. It's genuine gold, all right, but its age is impossible to determine. One can't gauge the age of gold. My friend did say that the piece resembled other Precolumbian gold artifacts he'd seen, and that the gold was similar to the gold used in Incan art."

"Any further proof?"

"A letter from Dudley."

"The Duke."

"Yes. A letter attesting to his discovery of the Lost Civilization, and verifying everything that Ceebee told me."

"You're familiar with the Duke's handwriting."

"Intimately. We corresponded while I was at Cambridge and he was at Oxford."

"Very open-minded of you both. But tell me this, Benfleet. Why have you come to me? You said you were in trouble."

"Yes, well, I'm afraid that Ceebee's death has created some dreadful problems."

"Other than the problem it has created for Ceebee, you mean."

"Yes. Just now, before I found you, I went to Ceebee's room, hoping to find any evidence of the partnership, and conceal it. But I was too late. That Chief Inspector, Arbuthnot, was there, along with Constable Nettle. I suspect that Arbuthnot may already have learned about the partnership."

"You suspect? Didn't he question you?"

"He was about to, but his attention was distracted by a piece of music, some whistling, coming from outside."

"Ah ha! A sea shanty!"

Benfleet frowned. "However did you know?"

"I've heard someone whistling it myself. The Drunken Sailor shanty." He smiled. "It must have driven poor Arbuthnot quite mad. He detests sea shanties."

"Why is that?"

"I—"

Sir Gerard bit off his explanation as the door to the Library opened. Lady Amelia swept into the room, her face clearly marked by lines of concern. Even these, however, could not diminish her splendid good looks.

"Gerry," she said. "Roderick. Have either of you seen the Countess?"

"Katerina?" responded Benfleet. Sir Gerard noted the solicitor's use of the woman's first name. He filed it carefully away among the voluminous but rigorously organised contents of his capacious memory.

"Yes. Have you seen her, Roderick?"

"Not since breakfast." He turned to Hawksmoor.

"Nor have I," said Sir Gerard to Lady Amelia. "You seem worried, Amelia."

"I am. I spoke with her after breakfast, and she appeared despondent."

"Not, surely, as a result of Mr. Da Silva's remarks," said Sir Gerard. "The man is transparently a cad."

"No, it was something else. But I have no idea what it might have been. It was as though something had come over her, some recollection or realisation, something *awful,* and she were suddenly stricken with a dreadful unhappiness."

What an admirable woman, thought Sir Gerard. Even when distressed, she still handled her subjunctives flawlessly.

"You don't think she'll do herself any harm?" Benfleet asked, his voice sounding as troubled as Lady Amelia's handsome face looked.

"I don't know what to think," she said. "First we have this dreadful death on the grounds, and now this."

"As soon as I finish discussing some legal matters with Sir Gerard," said Benfleet, "I should be happy to help you search for her."

"Thank you, Roderick. I do appreciate it." She turned.

All at once, Sir Gerard remembered what it was he'd been attempting to remember ever since he'd first realized that he'd forgotten it. "Amelia, before you go . . ."

"Yes?" she said, turning back to him.

"Didn't you tell me yesterday that Admiral Brandon and his son had arrived only the day before from America?"

"Why, yes. Why do you ask?"

"Just trying to clarify the point. Have either of them ever been in England before?"

"Not to my knowledge."

Sir Gerard nodded. "Thank you." He wondered whether he should question her as to her involvement in the Brandon partnership.

Not now, he decided. She was too concerned about Countess Boronskaya.

Amelia's glance swung to Benfleet. "I'll see you later, I trust, Roderick."

"As soon as we finish," he assured her.

She left the room, pulling the door shut behind her.

Sir Gerard stared at the door.

The Duchess had told him, less than an hour ago, that Whitchell, Admiral Brandon's son, had rowed at Henley this year.

The Henley Royal Regatta, perhaps the most prestigious affair of its kind in the world, took place in early July. At which time, according to Lady Amelia, Whitchell hadn't yet arrived in the country.

Most curious.

"Sir Gerard?" said Benfleet.

"Yes?"

"You were about to explain why Chief Inspector Arbuthnot detested sea shanties."

"No, I wasn't, actually. I was about to explain that I have no idea why he detested them. Most likely it was some event in his childhood that created his loathing, but I cannot speculate as to what that might've been. Perhaps one of his parents went mad and sang shanties all day long. Who knows? When one is deprived of facts, Benfleet, speculation is futile. But to return to your story. Arbuthnot was about to question you when he was distracted by the sea shanty."

"Yes. While he was peering out the window, and taking quite a long time about it, I backed out of the room."

"You do know that running away from a problem has never solved it."

"I know that it has allowed me to discuss the problem with you."

"And why should you wish to discuss it with me?"

"I know of your reputation, Sir Gerard. You are a man to whom, over the years, many people have come with their troubles. I thought that perhaps you might have some suggestion as to what path I should take."

"Had you come to me before you invested in this partnership, I should have suggested that you refrain from doing so."

"Yes, but it's rather late for that, isn't it? The past is past. What do you think I should do *now?*"

Sir Gerard considered. "Very well. This is what I suggest. . . ."

* * *

"KNOCK it down, sir?" whispered Nettle. He glanced about the bedroom, as though it might contain someone who had overheard Arbuthnot's order, and who had disapproved.

"The door is locked, Nettle," Arbuthnot patiently pointed out. "How else will we effect our entry?"

"But the Duchess, sir. Won't she be getting a bit upset, like, if we go banging into one of the locked rooms?"

"This is a police investigation, Nettle. Someone has died in mysterious circumstances. The odds are very good that he was murdered. I believe that the music we're hearing, beyond that door, is being played on a gramophone. The device wasn't playing when we arrived. Someone, therefore, has turned on the machine in the past few minutes. I intend to learn who that person was. Have I made myself sufficiently clear?"

"Very clear, sir."

"Then if you would, please, Nettle. Proceed."

"Yes, sir. If you'll just stand back slightly, sir."

Arbuthnot stood back. Nettle took three steps backward and then hurled himself at the door, shoulder first. With a huge tearing sound, the door swung open. Constable Nettle's momentum was such that he continued through the opening and went plunging into the room.

Chief Inspector Reggie Arbuthnot stepped to the doorway and, for the second time that day, but possibly not the last, involuntarily exclaimed, "Good Lord!"

The room was similar to the room on the far side of Admiral Brandon's chamber, the room in which the Admiral's son had slept. Constable Nettle stood a yard or so into the room. He had been attempting, apparently, to regain his balance when he had become frozen, immobilized by what he saw in the room with him.

The strange, primitive music was much louder now, its savage rhythms pounding at the walls and floor.

And in the center of the room stood a tall, slender woman wearing what appeared to be a brightly colored sheet that hung from her waist, and a shockingly revealing halter constructed of the same multi-hued material. Her hair was long and black, and perched atop it, covering it like a bizarre sort of crown, was a cluster of bananas.

The woman seemed as astonished to see Nettle and Arbuthnot as they were to see her. She had been dancing to the music, so it appeared, but now her hand flung itself between her breasts—a handsome pair of them, Arbuthnot thought in passing, if you went in for that sort of thing.

"*Caramba!*" said the woman. "What a madhouse! One cannot be alone for even a moment!"

"Forgive the intrusion, Madam," said Arbuthnot. "But perhaps you can tell us just who you are?"

FIVE

The Woman in the
Tutti-Frutti Hat

by Margaret Coel

"WHO am I?" the woman shrieked over the dreadful
noises emanating from the gramophone on the marble table
near the door. "You dare to ask who am I?" She took in several gulps of air that sent her bosom rising and falling
within the confines of the skimpy halter, a piece of clothing
that, along with the rest of her ridiculous costume, Chief
Inspector Arbuthnot would expect to find among the inhabitants of primitive villages in South America or some other
land oppressed by an excess of sunshine, certainly not at the
Castle Crawsbey, with Her Grace, the inimitable Dowager
Duchess herself, in residence.

Arbuthnot nodded toward Constable Nettle who, it
appeared had taken his gaze from the woman with some difficulty. As the Constable stepped to the gramophone, the
Chief Inspector made a mental note of the room: four-poster
bed with white canopy and rumpled white bedclothing,
ornately carved wooden tables and Louis Quartorze chairs,

silver tray with the remains of breakfast on the china plate
and a ribbon of smoke rising from the cigarette in the crystal ashtray and curling toward the woman's bare arm.

When, blessedly, the noise ceased, the woman thrust herself forward and began shaking a bejeweled finger under Nettle's nose. "What right have you to burst into my sanctuary? I
demand that you leave my sight immediately."

"Madam," the Chief Inspector began, noting that the
flush of hysteria in her face only accentuated her dark eyes
and increased her exotic beauty. "Please forgive this abrupt
intrusion."

"Get out!"

"Allow me to introduce myself and my colleague."
Arbuthnot motioned towards Nettle cowering under the
woman's wagging finger. "This is Constable Nettle, and I am
Chief Inspector Arbuthnot. We are here to investigate the
unfortunate demise of Admiral Cornelius Brandon, whose
apartment, as you are undoubtedly aware, adjoins your own."

"Demise!" The woman blanched, as if he'd laid a hand to
her cheek. Crossing her arms in a cruciform over her breasts,
she stumbled backward towards the four-poster bed. "Are
you saying that Ceebee is dead? Oh, that cannot be." She
hurried on without waiting for a reply, her eyes flitting
about the room for some safe haven. "Ceebee was well when
I last saw him," she said, positioning herself now at the side
of the bed, as if to conceal the rumpled bedclothing.

"I very much fear, madam, that Admiral Brandon has
met with a most unfortunate . . ." Arbuthnot paused. "A
most unfortunate circumstance," he continued, swallowing
back the word "accident" still half-formed on his tongue.
Surely a man found in a four-foot-deep fish pond, lashed to a
gigantic and, in Arbuthnot's opinion, altogether ghastly

statue of Neptune, by an even more ghastly-hued purple sash, and who, further, had been deceased before he reached the pool, such a man could not be described as having met an unfortunate accident. The Chief Inspector knew a homicide when one floated in front of him, as it were, and the death of Admiral Brandon was decidedly a homicide, most likely brought about by poison, which his medical examiner would undoubtedly confirm on Monday.

"You must tell me everything." The woman slumped onto the edge of the bed, her voice breathless, as if she had exhausted the last of the oxygen in the room.

"Before we begin," Arbuthnot said, struggling not for the first time to lift his gaze from the brown melons protruding from the multi-hued halter, "I must ask you to cover yourself."

The woman allowed her eyes to rest on his a moment before turning around and retrieving from the jumbled bed-clothing a white maracain, which she pulled over her bare shoulders. The sleeves flowed over her arms into a graceful wristfrill. With the motions of a dancer, she lapped the fronts of the gown together and worked the belt into an intricate knot at her waist. Then she reached up and removed the bizarre crown of bananas. After setting it on the bed, she began combing her fingers through her shiny black hair that fell like rain over the shoulders of her gown.

"Thank you, madam," Arbuthnot said, aware of Archie assuming a more relaxed posture beside him. "Shall we begin with your explanation as to who you are and why you are living behind a locked door adjacent to the Admiral's apartment?"

The woman stood up and strolled over to the dressing table beneath the high, leaded casements. She retrieved an item from the table and, with quick, deft movements, swirled her long hair into a tight knot at the back of her head. Then she fastened the knot with a pearl-encrusted comb that gleamed in the gray light filtering through the casements. When she had finished this minor toilette, she turned back slowly, almost regally.

Nettle gasped beside him, and the Chief Inspector had to compress his lips to keep from uttering a similar cry of astonishment at the transformation from hottentot to grand lady, one who might, indeed, grace the finest homes of South America or England.

"You wish to know who I am?" She was smiling, and her smile was both demure and determined. "Very well. You may as well be the first to know the truth. I am the Duchess of Faughstrayne."

Now it was the Chief Inspector's turn to emit an audible gasp, despite his best efforts to remain in control of himself. He had heard the village rumors that the present Duke had shucked all caution, gone native in South America, and married some sloe-eyed beauty, but he had never taken the rumors seriously. And now it appeared he was face to face with the beauty who seemed every whit as regal as the Dowager Duchess herself.

"Come now, madam," the Chief Inspector said, regaining his own balance and better sense, "His Grace remains unmarried and dedicated to a life of scholarship and adventure in the wilds of Brazil, or some such place. What proof have you of such an outrageous claim?"

The woman turned again to the dressing table, opened the center drawer, and withdrew a beige-colored packet wrapped in thin, black ribbon. Turning back, she held out the packet like an offering.

The Chief Inspector crossed the room, conscious of the

soft warp of the carpet beneath his boots, and took the packet. He untied the black bow, lifted the flap, and removed a thin white parchment printed in Spanish by a careful, artistic hand. He was able to make out that on the twentieth day of May, only two months prior, Dudley, Duke of Faughstrayne, and Conseula Imelda Berthold de Cordova had been joined in the holy sacrament of matrimony.

Arbuthnot swallowed hard at the lump arising in his throat at this further complication. His heart ached for the Dowager Duchess, whom he had admired from afar since taking up his post in Rutfordshire. Not only must the poor woman contend with a homicide on the castle grounds, one that involved her guests both as victim and, most likely, perpetrator, but she would now have to give over her rightful place to a South American chameleon. Yes, the woman before him with the satisfied expression and the flashing black eyes was nothing more than a chameleon. An exotic creature one moment, and a duchess the next.

"Perhaps you will be so good as to explain what appears to be your clandestine presence at Castle Crawsbey." Arbuthnot placed the packet in the woman's outstretched hand.

She fixed him with languorous black eyes that, he realized for the first time, were lit with amusement. "*Mi esposo*," she said, "has sent me ahead to Castle Crawsbey to prepare for his return. He intends to assume his rightful position and legacy, and I shall be at his side as his wife and duchess."

"Come now, Your Grace," Arbuthnot said, nearly stumbling over the title. "It is inconceivable that His Grace would send his wife to the ducal seat without notifying the Dowager Duchess. Surely he would want his wife to be appropriately welcomed. Indeed, why wouldn't His Grace have brought you himself?"

"Oh, señor." The woman began shaking her head, a mock look of pity upon the beautiful face. "There is much you do not understand. My husband was delayed by his work in Minas Gerais and, at the last minute, was unable to accompany me. But I assure you, he has already embarked on the voyage home. In his absence, he entrusted me to the capable hands of Admiral Brandon."

At this, the woman slumped against the dressing table, as if the fact of her situation had crashed down on her with the force of carved plaster suddenly loosened from the ceiling. The capable hands to whom she had been entrusted were stilled forever.

Arbuthnot gave the woman a moment, then he said, "I fail to understand why the Admiral chose to . . ." He paused, searching for the exact word. "Conceal you in the castle." He stopped himself from adding, "like some common woman."

"It is very easy to explain, señor." The quiver in the woman's voice, added to the accent that seemed progressively thicker, caused Arbuthnot to incline one ear in her direction. "My husband trusted the Admiral as to when I should be introduced to the Dowager Duchess. The Admiral is . . ." She hesitated, then corrected the verb tense. "Was, how do you say, socially wise? The Dowager Duchess had planned a most elegant event for last evening. It would hardly have done for her to be outshone by the arrival of the new duchess."

As she spoke, the woman turned her head about in the manner, Arbuthnot thought, of a royal person gazing over her subjects. "My husband had planned for such an eventuality," she continued. "He had sent his servant, Lewis, ahead with instructions that Admiral Brandon and Whitchell, that annoying boy, should have the front apartment once occupied by his own father. A convenient arrangement, with an adjoining room inaccessible from the hall. His father's mistress had resided here without causing any disturbance in the household."

Arbuthnot was quiet a moment, weighing her explanation against his own better judgment. Finally he said, "You would have us believe that Admiral Brandon arranged to secret you through the house and into this room without anyone's knowledge?"

"Exactly as it occurred, señor. Have you not heard of a man secreting, as you say, a woman into a house? It is difficult to believe that England is the only country where such situations do not occur." A smile remained on the beautiful face a moment, then, like ice cracking on a frozen pond, the smile broke away. "And now, señor, you say my protector is *demise*? Dead? I cannot believe it is true."

"The Admiral's body was found some hours ago in the fountain below the South Terrace," Arbuthnot said, forbearing to explain the details in the hope that he might ascertain the extent of the woman's knowledge, or even complicity. He hurried on. "When did you last see Admiral Brandon?"

"Oh, sir, forgive me, but I really couldn't say." The woman's dark eyes glanced toward the bed, then lifted upward to him in an appeal of innocence and misunderstanding.

"I'm afraid you must say, Your Grace."

She seemed to consider this a moment. Finally resolve hardened in the dark eyes. "Very well," she said. "I must trust to your discretion as a gentleman. The Admiral came to my chamber sometime after midnight, I believe. I cannot be certain."

"I understand," Arbuthnot said with a flush of confidence that he now understood all. "How long did he remain?"

"Señor!" The slender hands began fluttering like graceful

brown birds flitting across the white gown. "You ask such questions! How can I say? He stayed for some time, and then he left. He said he wanted to walk outside awhile and smoke a cigar. He was fond of the most putrid smelling cigars. I forbid them in my room."

"Very well." Arbuthnot let out a great sigh and stepped toward the door, motioning the constable to follow. Keeping his gaze on the woman still slumped against the table, he said, "I must ask you to remain here until further notice. Also, you are aware that I must inform the Dowager Duchess of your presence."

"No!" The woman jumped forward, as if a spring had released her from the table. "I relied on your discretion, señor. I am a defenseless woman whose protector is now demise diseased. I have no one to advise me except . . ."

"Except, Your Grace?"

"That awful Whitchell, who has only half the wits of his father. There is Lewis, of course, but I haven't seen him since he brought my breakfast tray some time ago. He has yet to retrieve it. How, señor, can I be expected to rely on a servant?"

"If you are the wife of His Grace, as you claim, I can assure you that the Dowager Duchess will accord you every respect. You must understand, I have my duty to inform Her Grace of your residence."

Arbuthnot waved the constable through the doorway and closed the door rather sharply, putting the final snap, as he supposed, on his decision.

"Begging your pardon, sir," Nettle said, a squeak of uncertainty invading his voice. "Won't it be a bit of a shock for Her Grace? I mean, the Admiral getting himself murdered, and now this lady comin' around and saying she's the duchess."

"I have no intention of informing the Dowager Duchess

without the proper intermediary action," Arbuthnot said, concealing the fact that it was exactly what he had planned. He reached for the red velvet butler's pull. "I shall first inform the Lady Amelia. She will prepare her mother."

A muffled cough sounded in the corridor, followed by a soft knock. The door creaked open, revealing the stooped shoulders and birdlike beak of Jeavons, whose sudden appearance caught Arbuthnot by surprise. The thought crossed the inspector's mind that the butler had been lurking nearby, perhaps awaiting the sound of the pull in a nearby room.

"There you are, Jeavons," Arbuthnot said. "Be so good as to take a message to Lady Amelia that I await her company in the Library. It is a matter of some urgency."

"Very good, sir." The butler began backing into the upper hall, closing the door as he went.

"Oh, and Jeavons." Arbuthnot took hold of the brass knob to keep the door open. "Please inform the castle's guests and staff that I shall wish to speak with each one individually in the library. They should remain in their rooms until summoned by you."

"Pardon me, sir," the butler began, "I'm sorry to report that certain guests have already left."

Arbuthnot gave a nod of impatience. "Mr. Da Silva, I believe."

"It would appear, sir, that the Countess Boronskaya has also left. She has not been seen since breakfast, sir."

The inspector exhaled a long sigh. What a bother. Someone else he would have to track down. If that fool Sir Gerard hadn't commandeered the investigation last evening and had instead called him, which was the proper course, no one should have left Castle Crawsbey before he had concluded the official investigation.

"Everyone else present and accounted for?"

"So far as I am aware, sir," Jeavons said, a hint of irony in his tone that confirmed Arbuthnot's suspicions that the butler made it his business to account for everyone at the castle. He wondered if Jeavons had any knowledge of the woman behind the closed door.

"I will, of course, also want to conclude the interviews by speaking privately with you, Jeavons," he said.

"Yes, sir."

The butler bowed his way into the hall, and Arbuthnot closed the door. Then he turned to the Constable, who had not moved from the center of the room. "You will remain here, Nettle," he said. "I do not wish the self-proclaimed Duchess to scarper off until the Dowager Duchess has had a chance to assess the situation."

Confident that he had the matter of the new duchess in hand, Arbuthnot exited the room and started down the spacious hall lined with mellowing oak and a succession of paneled doors that led to apartments on either side. A thick runner covered the center of the floor, leaving the polished wood at the edges gleaming in the dull light. There was the sound of thunder, as if from a great distance, muffled in the ceiling beams. The hall was quite deserted, he realised, and yet, only a matter of seconds prior, Jeavons had taken his departure. The man was like a bird, moving about on little, silent bird feet. Or perhaps the butler had vanished like smoke into the oak walls.

As the Chief Inspector reached the end of the hall, somewhat out of breath, his thoughts now turned to the homicide investigation and the work that lay ahead. The incriminating negatives inside his waistcoat pressed heavily against his chest. There was much still to sort out.

He was about to start down the grand staircase lined with oil portraits of past generations of Faughstraynes when he heard the sound of a door sighing on heavy hinges, followed by a woman's voice: "Monsieur, *s'il vous plait.*"

He swung around. Standing in the small opening of the last door on the right was a tall, full-figured woman, most likely beautiful once, he reflected, but now somewhat past her prime, with streaks of gray shimmering in her dark hair and tight lines of worry creasing her brow. She wore an excellently-cut dress of pink silk, embellished by a large emerald suspended from a gold chain at the front of her thin neck.

Approaching the opened door, the Chief Inspector mentally ticked off the list of Castle Crawsbey guests, which seemed to be diminishing as he wasted valuable time on the matter of the new Duchess, and concluded that this noble-appearing lady could be none other than the missing Countess Katerina Boronskaya.

"OH, Sir Gerard," Benfleet said. "I shall be forever in your debt if you can get me out of this muddle."

"Muddle?" Sir Gerard shook his head in wonderment. "My dear man, you term an illegal plot to ferry contraband onto English shores a muddle? You are a solicitor. Do you not realize the seriousness of your complicity in such a matter?"

Benfleet looked the perfect picture of defeat, which made Sir Gerard want to turn away. The man claimed to have gone up to Cambridge, but neither his diction nor his demeanour suggested this was the case. If he had managed to matriculate at Cambridge, the ivoried traditions of that hallowed institution had failed to take root in the man's character. And

now that Sir Gerard thought about it, hadn't the Dowager
Duchess said that Whitchell Brandon was also up at Cam-
bridge? Odd that Lady Amelia seemed unaware of that fact.
Perhaps it was not the case at all. Certainly, there was no
Cambridge imprint on the brash American.

"I realize all too well," Benfleet was saying. "I implore
you to advise me."

"Very well." Sir Gerard crossed his legs in a futile
attempt to loosen the muscles in his back. He took a long
draw of his cigarette, allowing the smoke to curl between
him and the solicitor, who was now perched on the edge of
his chair. Another inch forward, Sir Gerard observed, and
the man would pitch onto the Tabriz carpet.

"You will return immediately to the Chief Inspector and
inform him of this nefarious plot and confess your part."

"Sir Gerard, that I cannot do." Benfleet gripped the armrests to steady himself. "I must think of my position and of
the Dowager Duchess, who has entrusted me with much of
her affairs."

"You think too late of these matters, Benfleet." Sir Gerard
tapped the ash into the crystal bowl on the side table. "Your
only hope is to throw yourself on the mercy of the good
Chief Inspector," he said, aware of the irony in his tone.
Reggie Arbuthnot was a woolly head of the first order, with
whom Market Winsome was to be burdened until the man's
retirement. It would be no surprise if, in the brief interval
since Arbuthnot had arrived at the castle, he'd managed to
make a complete hash of the investigation.

Sir Gerard took another draw from his cigarette, almost
the only source of pleasure left him. He was resigned to the
unpalatable dish that life had served up, and aware that,

ironically, his incapacity had left him free to do his duty. At the moment, it was apparent that his duty lay in unraveling this unpleasant business of murder because, assuredly, Reggie Arbuthnot would never affect the unraveling.

"I advise you, Benfleet," he said, returning to the matter immediately at hand, "to confess before the Chief Inspector stumbles upon the truth himself." He winced at the unfortunate choice of verb, a momentary lapse that he must strive not to duplicate. It would never do to betray his personal feelings about anyone in an official position, no matter how incompetent the official might be. One never knew when that official might be of some use to one.

Benfleet stood up slowly, his bland face turning the color of strawberries. Altogether, Sir Gerard mused, the man resembled a schoolboy called upon to recite a passage he'd neglected to read. "I'd hoped you'd find another solution," he said, exhibiting a degree of equanimity that took Sir Gerard by surprise. "I'll have to give some thought to it. In the meantime, I'd best lend my assistance to Lady Amelia in her search for the Countess, wouldn't you agree?"

Sir Gerard snuffed out his cigarette in the crystal bowl and stared at the ribbon of smoke that curled over his hand, allowing a moment for the effect of disinterestedness to seep over his companion. What the man did with his future was, after all, of no concern to him. "As you wish, Benfleet," he said finally, an unforced insouciance in his tone. "Give the matter your thought. But remember the words of the bard: 'Be great in act, as you have been in thought.'"

"Thank you, Sir Gerard." Benfleet nodded, his hands clasped at his waist. Then he walked to the door and let himself out.

Sir Gerard could hear the hasty tread of the man's footsteps in the hall as he rose from his chair and crossed to the terrace doors, wincing with the effort. Thunder growled overhead, and the sky had turned the color of dulled steel. He stared out at the pond, with the gray peaks rippling over the surface, and reflected that he didn't care a whit whether Roderick Benfleet took his advice. In the larger scheme, it made no matter. What mattered was the information that the solicitor had imparted, quite inadvertently, Sir Gerard suspected. The fact was that several guests had become embroiled in Admiral Brandon's scheme, and two of them were now missing: Da Silva, off to Market Winsome, and Countess Boronskaya, no doubt hiding from her shame somewhere on the premises. Eventually, Lady Amelia, with no useful help from Benfleet, he was certain, would locate the hiding place, at which time, Sir Gerard resolved, he would have a chat with the Countess.

In the meantime, Da Silva might well decide to hie himself out of the shire altogether before Reggie Arbuthnot realized the man should be detained. Sir Gerard saw his duty as clearly as on the day the Hun had materialized over the top of the trench. He'd taken action then to rout the Hun, and he would take action now to free Amelia, dear Amelia, from this unpleasantness.

Without fetching his oilskin, he opened the door, crossed the terrace and, limping with the arrow of pain in his leg, made his way to the rear of the grounds where he'd left his Bentley. Within thirty minutes, he calculated, he would locate Mr. Da Silva and elicit the foreigner's full involvement in the Admiral's scheme, as well as—it would be no surprise—his involvement in the Admiral's murder.

*   *   *

"PLEASE, monsieur," the woman said, moving backward and motioning for the Chief Inspector to follow. "You must help me."

"Countess Boronskaya, I presume," Arbuthnot said, entering a room suffused in amber light and arranged all around with heavy wooden tables and massive chairs that looked sufficient to support the great King Henry himself.

The Countess closed the door firmly and quietly, then swept past him and folded herself downward into one of the chairs. She flattened her palms together in a praying position and brought the tips of her long, graceful fingers to her lips. The diamonds on her fingers flashed like miniature torches.

"I have been praying all morning, monsieur, that someone of authority would pass through the hall and come to my assistance. You are here in an official capacity, *n'est-ce pas?*"

Arbuthnot sank his ample figure into the overstuffed chair across from the woman. "Chief Inspector Reggie Arbuthnot at your service, Countess. It was reported to me that you had gone missing. I'm pleased to discover that is not the case." He lowered his voice to the courtliest pitch. "Kindly tell me the reason for your distress."

At this the woman visibly relaxed. The graceful fingers fluttered into the silken pink folds of her lap. "I have been in the gravest danger, sir. But now that you are here, I know I will be safe."

"Danger, Countess?"

"Oh, yes. You see, I know who murdered poor Cee . . . Admiral Brandon."

"Perhaps you should start at the beginning."

"The beginning," she said, seeming to gaze at some interior landscape. "There have been so many beginnings for an unfortunate refugee such as you see before you. Ah, well," she swept one hand in front, as if to sweep away the memories. "Let me begin with the shock I experienced when I stepped onto the terrace last evening and saw the man dressed in the dark dinner suit. I thought the Duke himself had returned."

"Returned from South America?"

"No, no." She gave an impatient wave. "Not the boy. His father, Chief Inspector. Ah, there was a duke! Dead now for five years, of course, but for an awful moment I thought his ghost had joined the guests." She laughed and shook her head, her gaze again fastening on some scene available only to her. "It was Ceebee. Admiral Brandon," she corrected herself. "In the late duke's fine suit. Nevertheless, it was quite a shock."

"I don't understand how this may have placed you in danger, Countess." Arbuthnot gently prompted the woman.

"Oh, there was more, Inspector, much more. Never did I expect to encounter such a horrible creature as Enrique Da Silva at Castle Crawsbey, but there he was, strutting about the grounds, like a general reviewing his conquered territory. I tell you, sir, it gave me such a start, and I knew no good would come of Da Silva's presence."

Arbuthnot was quiet a moment, mentally filling in the mortar around the bricks of information that the Countess had set before him. "Am I to understand, Countess, that you were acquainted with all three gentlemen—His Grace, the late duke, Admiral Brandon, and Enrique Da Silva?"

"Gentlemen! Please sir, do not besmirch the memory of the late duke by mentioning him with that creature."

"Forgive me for prying, Countess, but if you were to explain how you were acquainted with His Grace and the others, it may help me to understand your danger."

Countess Boronskaya stood up, walked over to the leaded casements, and laid the slender fingers of one hand along the edge of the brocaded curtains. Reluctantly, Arbuthnot pushed both hands against the armrests and lifted his heavy body into an upright position.

"You must understand, sir," the Countess began, staring past the glass panes into the gray outdoors. "A woman of my birthright . . ." She glanced over one shoulder. "I am the third cousin once removed to Tsar Nicholas II. Naturally I am accustomed to the finest palaces, the most elegant salons. For such a woman to be thrust into the cold with nothing but the clothes on her back, like the crudest peasant woman, was a horror from which I have tried for many years to escape. But, alas, the dreams, the nightmares . . . I am never free. It was only natural that certain men of wealth and power should take pity on such an unfortunate woman and desire her to enjoy material comforts once again."

She turned around and fixed him with a conspiratorial gaze. "I trust that you, as a gentleman, will understand."

"Of course, Countess. But where, exactly, had you made the gentlemen's acquaintances?"

"His Grace? Why, here at Castle Crawsbey." The Countess gave another impatient wave. "Ceebee and Da Silva? In many places. Paris, Madrid, New York, Rio. What does it matter? The point is that I have become entangled in this unfortunate homicide and am now in danger myself."

"Entangled, Countess? How so?"

"I'm trying to tell you, Chief Inspector, that I know the identity of Ceebee's murderer."

Arbuthnot felt himself flush with relief. He had expected a complicated go at it of sorting out matters properly mucked up by that arrogant amateur, Sir Gerard. Instead, it would appear that before him stood a woman with the key to the whole sordid affair.

"The identity, Countess?"

"Da Silva." She spit out the name and tossed her head backward. "I saw him arguing with Ceebee last night."

"At what time?" This was excellent, Arbuthnot was thinking. Possibly nothing less than an eyewitness.

The Countess shook her head. "It's so difficult to be certain about such matters. Time long ago ceased to be of meaning to me. I know only that I was unable to sleep." She paused and inclined her head toward him. "The nightmares, you understand. So I sent my maid to the kitchen for warm milk. But she dallied, as usual, the silly girl, and in my anxiety, I decided to take a turn about the grounds. I saw Ceebee and Da Silva below the terrace."

"You're certain that is who you saw?"

She nodded. "Ceebee, dressed in the late duke's clothing, and Da Silva." She rolled her eyes. "I would know the slouch of his shoulders anywhere. They stood very close, whispering. I couldn't hear them, but they were having a terrible argument, I am certain. I have psychic powers, Inspector, and I could sense the tension between them."

Arbuthnot could sense his own expectations starting to deflate like a collapsing dirigible. It would seem that the good woman had not actually witnessed the murder. "Was there anything else?"

"Only the sound of someone whistling that frightful shanty about the drunken sailor."

"The Admiral? Da Silva?"

"No. No. No." The countess shook her head and closed her eyes a moment. "I have told you, they were whispering angrily. The whistling came from out on the grounds somewhere, near the fountain, I believe. There was no one else about that I could see."

"Did you approach the Admiral and Da Silva?"

"Of course not! I was terrified by their anger. I tried to step back into the shadows, but it was too late. Da Silva had looked around and seen me. The man is like a panther with eyes that pierce the dark! I ran back to the side door through which I'd come and entered the castle. But Da Silva knows that I saw him arguing with Ceebee, and now Ceebee is dead. He will want to make certain that I am also dead!"

"And that is the extent of your entanglement?"

"It is enough, Chief Inspector! You do not know this man. He is evil. He is dangerous."

"Perhaps you could enlighten me, Countess, as to why Mr. Da Silva might have wished Admiral Brandon dead?"

Countess Boronskaya stared at him a moment with astonishment. "You do not know? Ceebee had formed a partnership to bring the treasures His Grace found in Brazil to England. Many people have invested with Ceebee, Mr. Arbuthnot, despite the obvious problems."

Arbuthnot had the sense of a torch suddenly illuminating a darkened corner. This would explain the list he had uncovered in the Admiral's apartment. "By obvious problems," he said, plotting his way carefully so as not to frighten the woman into silence, "I take it you mean legal problems about smuggling another nation's treasure into England?"

"You understand, Chief Inspector, I would never have consented if my own situation had not become desperate. I must throw myself on your mercy. I am, as you can see, no longer young, no longer as desirable to the types of men who had helped me in the past. I must rely on my own resources."

Arbuthnot remained quiet, rubbing his chin, calling on his own powers of deduction that had never failed him in the past, at least not that he liked to remember. Finally he said, almost to himself, "Admiral Brandon's scheme, but Da Silva could have wanted to take control."

"You understand perfectly, Chief Inspector. You are so very clever." The woman was purring now, and giving him such a look that, for a moment, he wondered if she entertained the preposterous notion that he might be of the type of men capable of seeing to her material comforts.

"My dear Countess," he said, "let me assure you that you are no longer in danger. Mr. Da Silva has left the castle. I will have him detained in Market Winsome immediately." Arbuthnot hoped that would be the case. The foreigner even now could be on his way to Dover with the intention of stealing upon the first vessel set to sail across the Atlantic. "For your peace of mind," he continued, "you may wish to remain secluded in this room for the time being. I'll have Constable Nettle fetch a tray of food later, and of course I'll notify you as soon as Mr. Da Silva is in custody."

The Countess slanted her head and gazed at him through lowered eyelids. "Oh, monsieur," she purred. "I knew I could depend upon you."

"Very good, then." Arbuthnot crossed the room and hastily let himself through the door. Once in the hall, he congratulated himself. He'd managed to extricate himself from a most enticing woman and, at the same time, had unlocked the mystery of Admiral Brandon's homicide. Not only had Countess Boronskaya placed Mr. Da Silva with the victim shortly before the murder, the admirable woman had supplied a sound motive.

Arbuthnot gripped the bronze knob at the top of the grand staircase and started down, conscious of the thick odor of polish emanating from the wooden banister, which made his breathing more labored, despite the sense of ease and self-congratulation coursing through him. He intended to speak to the other guests, as planned, but now he expected the interviews to be brief and to support what the Countess had said. He was short-handed at the castle, that was true, what with Constable Nettle stationed in the Admiral's apartment. When he called the station to order that Mr. Da Silva be detained, he would also order more hands to the castle. In any case, the matter of the homicide and the matter of the new Duchess appearing at an inopportune moment should both be sorted out in a matter of hours.

He let himself through the massive double doors into the Library—a grand room filled with leather-bound volumes, worn leather chairs, and carved wood tables that had served generations of Faughstraynes and seemed to embody the very essence of civilization. He made straightaway for the ivory telephone on the table near the doors that opened to the terrace and was about to lift the earpiece when he heard a motor engine backfire and the sound of tires crunching gravel. It struck him that yet another guest was about to depart the castle.

He stepped over, threw open the doors, and hurried onto the terrace just as a black Bentley, with blue smoke pouring from the exhaust pipe, sped along the driveway through the rolling pasture, topped the rise, and disappeared.

"Bloody hell!" the Chief Inspector said out loud. Before he could speak with Sir Gerard, the man had scarpered. Undoubtedly intending to waylay Da Silva himself in Market Winsome. The fool could alert the foreigner that he was under suspicion before his own man might detain him. Da Silva would have the time to compose some sort of story, thus further mucking up the investigation.

Well, there was no hope for it. Arbuthnot started back

inside toward the phone, then stopped. Jeavons stood in the middle of the carpet. Egads! It was as if the man had suddenly dropped from some birdlike perch in the overhead beams.

"Yes, Jeavons?" Arbuthnot said, aware of his own breathlessness brought on by the shock.

"Lady Amelia will be here presently, sir." The butler's head nodded, like a bird pecking at water in a pond. "I regret to inform you, however, that someone else has departed the castle."

"I saw Sir Gerard's auto drive away." Arbuthnot started again for the telephone.

"Sir Gerard?"

Arbuthnot turned back at the surprise in the man's voice. Evidently, there were people other than the new Duchess and the Countess whom Jeavons had not tracked. "Someone else?"

"I'm afraid, sir, that the new servant, Lewis, is nowhere to be found on the premises."

Arbuthnot shook his head at this piece of news, conscious of his investigation entering a downward spiral along with his hopes of concluding matters shortly. "Continue searching for the man," he said and gave the butler a wave of dismissal.

When Jeavons had bowed himself into the hall as quietly as he had appeared, the Chief Inspector lifted the earpiece, connected to the station, and ordered Enrique Da Silva detained at The Three Horseshoes, where he hoped the foreigner was still finishing a pint. He then ordered reinforcements tout de suite to the castle.

He replaced the earpiece, turned around, and took another shock. Standing in the opened doorway as silently as Jeavons had was Lady Amelia herself. She wore a blue serge dress with a starched white collar and sleeve cuffs that rather gave her the look of a governess, not the daughter of one duke and sister of another.

"You asked for me, Chief Inspector," she said, the timber of her voice conveying her ancestry.

"My lady, please be seated." He ushered her toward one of the shiny leather chairs. "I must report some unsettling news."

"If you're going to tell me you've located the murderer, I hardly consider that unsettling." Lady Amelia stepped to the chair and perched on the cushion, a look of serenity in her pale, oval face.

"It would appear," Arbuthnot began, "that your brother, the present Duke of Faughstrayne, has taken a wife."

"Preposterous." Lady Amelia uttered the word calmly, as if he'd notified her that the servants had refused to dust the furniture.

"The woman is here, my lady."

"Here? At Castle Crawsbey? An imposter?"

The Chief Inspector cleared his throat and explained that Consuela Imelda Berthold de Cordova had arrived with Admiral Brandon.

"Ah!" she said, a look of comprehension flooding her face. "So she is hiding in the infamous room."

"You know about the room?"

"Certainly, I know where my father installed his mistresses. Mother pretended not to know, and I suppose she considered Dudley and I too stupid to figure it out, but we always knew. So that explains why that boy, Lewis, insisted that my brother wished the Admiral to occupy Father's apartment. The Admiral was bringing one of his whores to the castle, and my brother, good-hearted as he is, intended to spare him embarrassment. But now that the Admiral is dead, this whore claims to be my brother's wife. Really! This is too much, Chief Inspector. She will leave here immediately."

Lady Amelia rose to her feet and started towards the door.

"One moment, please," Arbuthnot said. "She has a document, my lady."

"Documents can be forged."

"I believe Her Grace will wish to know about the woman. I was hoping you would handle the matter."

"There is no matter to handle, Chief Inspector," Lady Amelia said, whirling about to face him. "I tell you the woman is an impostor."

"Pardon me, my lady, but your brother has been a long time in South America. A man can become lonely."

"My brother has not married, Mr. Arbuthnot. He is homosexual."

Arbuthnot blinked, feeling as if she'd tossed a glass of cold water at him. There were many rumours in the village about the present Duke of Faughstrayne, but never this. . . . After a moment, he realized that it might explain the Duke's long absence in South America and the Dowager Duchess's apparent reluctance to call him home.

Lady Amelia had exited into the hall and was halfway up the Grand Staircase by the time Arbuthnot had recovered himself enough to follow. He labored up the stairs, marveling at the sway of the lady's narrow yet rounded buttocks beneath the unfortunate blue serge and taking every chance to glimpse the white, silken ankles flashing below the hem.

"My lady," he said, gulping for air as he reached the landing and started along the upper hall after her. "I must insist that no one else leave the castle until I've concluded the homicide investigation."

Lady Amelia gripped the knob at the door to the Admiral's

apartment and glanced back, fixing Arbuthnot with a look of icy resolve. "Detain the woman in Market Winsome if you wish, Chief Inspector, but she shall leave the castle."

At this, she opened the door and marched inside, past Constable Nettle, who stumbled onto his feet from one of the side chairs, muttering an astonished, "M'lady!"

"Everything as it were, Constable?" Arbuthnot said.

"Yes, sir." Archie followed the woman's progress to the door. "As it were, sir."

Lady Amelia flung open the door, then whirled about. "What kind of game are you playing, Chief Inspector?" she said.

Arbuthnot walked over and stared beyond her into the tidied room, with bed clothing smoothed over the mattress, the food tray gone, the crystal dish emptied of cigarettes. There was no one there. Only the lingering smell of cigarette smoke hinted to the existence of Consuela Imelda Berthold de Cordova.

SIX

Revelations at The Three Horseshoes

by Carolyn Hart

CHIEF Inspector Arbuthnot surveyed the interior room in disbelief and mounting anger. When it became clear that the apartment contained only himself and Lady Amelia, Arbuthnot turned and glared at his subordinate. "Nettle!"

The Constable's handsome face reflected utter astonishment and growing apprehension. He took one look at his glowering superior and retreated until his back pressed against the wall. Archie Nettle had endured the crash of artillery in No Man's Land, felt the searing slice of white-hot steel against his skin. He'd stood stalwart, met the charging foe though faint with pain. Never in his short life had he yielded to an impulse to flee. Yet had he not at this moment been backed against a wall, he would have turned tail. The Chief Inspector's wrath bubbled like the cauldron in a witches' glen. Not even Constable Nettle's enchantment with Lady Amelia—despite the chasm between their worlds,

even if it could be bridged in the shadows of the night—
would have stayed his feet.

But his back was to the wall.

"Sir!" Nettle's voice quavered.

Arbuthnot drew a deep breath. He felt an ominous
clutch in his chest. His doctor had warned him. "Reggie,
old boy, Market Winsome's just the place for you and that
dicky ticker. Shoot some grouse. Tramp along the lanes.
Nurse a pint with good fellows. But, damn all, man, keep
an even keel." And here he was in a mouldering castle in a
mucked up investigation with witnesses hither and yon and
morphia-deranged Sir Gerard fancying himself a modern
day Vidocq and now, the ultimate blow, a constable with
the sleek handsomeness of a domesticated rabbit and a similar endowment of brains. If it wouldn't have made his chest
ache even more, he would happily have throttled Archibald
Nettle on the spot.

Lady Amelia murmured, "How ever did the door get
broken? It was merely propped upon its hinges. When I
turned the knob, it simply fell away. Curious."

"Nettle," Arbuthnot thundered, "you were charged with
guarding this door." He flung out an accusatory hand. "The
door to the secret apartment where we found Her Grace—"

Lady Amelia swung about from the broken entrance to the
secret apartment. "I beg your pardon, Chief Inspector." Ice
crackling on a winter pond could not have sounded colder.
Lady Amelia's piercing glance made clear her disapproval.

Arbuthnot cleared his throat. "My lady, I can only say
that I was shown a most impressive document, clearly indicating the nuptials of His Grace and Señorita Berthold de
Cordova."

"You recall her name so clearly? Pray then, describe the lady." Lady Amelia fingered the plain white collar of her dress.

There was an instant of silence as he recalled that full-bodied figure. Those breasts . . . the hips that curved so perfectly . . . he cleared his throat. "Quite an imposing lady, my lady. Sleek dark hair upswept with a comb of pearls. Most elegant features."

"Her age?" Lady Amelia stepped into the bedroom with its faint aura of cigarette smoke. She strolled about, flinging open the wardrobe—bare—and pulling out drawers—empty.

"Young." Arbuthnot knew his voice lacked certainty. "In her twenties perhaps." But was that flawless complexion a product of artifice? Whatever her age, the Chief Inspector felt certain, the lady's seductive body was not innocent of experience. He felt his ears redden, the damnable giveaway that had haunted him since his schoolroom days and prompted one master to observe, "Reginald, honesty is your only policy." He cleared his throat. "My lady, Her Gr—" at Lady Amelia's stiletto-sharp glance, he hesitated, "—the subject of our inquiry is clearly a personage of importance."

Lady Amelia's glance skimmed his face. Lingered on his ears? Her tone was wry. "Clearly," she murmured. "But she is not the Duchess of Faughstrayne. I can assure you of that." Lady Amelia languidly surveyed the room. "Whatever she is, whomever she may be, she is not here. That settles the matter so far as I am concerned. Good morning, Chief Inspector." She walked briskly toward the hallway without a glance at either man, though in passing Her Ladyship's slender fingers may have slipped across the back of Constable Nettle's hand.

The Constable looked after her.

A roar. "Nettle."

Nettle jerked to face his inquisitor. He clenched his big hands awkwardly. His blue eyes skidded away from the Chief Inspector's glare.

Arbuthnot folded his arms across his paunch. "I ordered the door to the secret apartment guarded. Why did you leave your post?"

Nettle cracked his knuckles in misery. "The door was locked. I tried it. I did think o' that, sir."

"Oh, that's good. That's very good." The Chief Inspector's voice was almost mellow.

Constable Nettle brightened.

The storm broke, comparing in intensity to the sudden rattle of thunder without, quite on a par with a Shakespearean drama. "You fool. The door was locked on her side. Not yours. Moreover, you previously broke down the door. Do you recall? Clearly, it took only a shifting of the panels for the lady to exit. What good did it do to check the door?"

Archie's blue eyes clouded. "But I thought, sir, that if she'd locked the door she wanted to keep us out and so she'd be staying there. And the door is quite heavy. Solid oak. She must be a very strong woman. However, I was here, at the ready, when I heard the music."

The Chief Inspector's eyes glistened. "That music?" His ears were hot as he recalled the sinuous body undulating to a beat of such savagery that a man might be forgiven the lustful images evoked from a primeval past.

Constable Nettle might be dim, but he understood crimson eartips. "Not *that* music, sir. A sea shanty." His melodious tenor lifted.

Mermaids swim 'round him, fast as the fishes
mermaids swim 'round him, fast as the fishes

mermaids swim 'round him, fast as the fishes,
ear-lye in the morning.

He took a deep breath. "Mermaids swim—"

"Nettle!" Arbuthnot's shout erupted.

"Sir!" Archie stood rigid.

Arbuthnot breathed deeply. Once. Twice. He felt as helpless as a man floundering in a bog and as maddened as a wasp-stung horse thundering toward the cliff and doom. Sea shanties! How could it be that he, Reggie Arbuthnot, should be subjected to sea shanties whilst making an investigation that likely would go down as the most important in the history of Market Winsome?

"This music." He gritted each word through clenched jaws. "Where was it coming from?"

Constable Nettle's blue eyes brightened. "You see, sir, I barely heard it at first. Just a faraway call like a bird's cry. But the minute I could make out the words, why I knew I had to go and see. I knew you'd want me to collar the fellow—"

"Fellow?" The Chief Inspector's tone was sharp.

The Constable nodded, his dark head bobbing. "A man singing, sir. And a fine voice, too. I knew 'twas the other side of the door." He inclined his dark head toward the heavy door to the corridor. "It was just enough ajar that the tune reached me. I moved quiet like a fox creeping up to the hen house. I eased open the door. Out in the hallway, I could hear much better. I ran down the corridor to the balcony. That door was ajar. I poked my head out into the rain. And," he paused, clapped his hands together, "the verse ended. I waited, thinking he'd pick right up, but there was no more. I would have gone out onto the balcony but the rain was coming down in buckets and I didn't think I'd find the fellow."

Arbuthnot's bitter glance took in the comfortable dryness

of the Constable's uniform. "Kept your feathers dry. And then?"

Nettle shrugged his sturdy shoulders. "I waited a moment more." He frowned, his face wrinkled with effort. "Do you know, sir, perhaps it may be important. I was just beginning to shut the door to the balcony when I heard a bang and a rattle and a crump and I knew that Edwin Cooper's taxi was coming up the drive." He looked earnestly at his superior. "Do you think that may be important, sir?"

THE yellow feather quivered upon impact. A muted roar signaled victory by old Sammy Herbert, who claimed he'd lost a leg in the Boer War. Old Sammy had been a fixture at The Three Horseshoes every Saturday since he came home to Market Winsome with one trouser leg pinned to his hip. His prowess was celebrated throughout the county and his mastery unchallenged since the memory of man runneth not to the contrary.

Sir Gerard pulled his gaze away from the quivering yellow feathers of the dart. He couldn't dismiss the bright red feather found at the murder scene. Could his suspicions be correct? Was that vagrant feather a remnant of a blow dart? It would be up to Squiffy Frobisher to determine the cause of the admiral's death. Curare? That would be another link to South America. Sir Gerard stared across the dark oak table at the heavyset man, regarding him with disfavor. The darkness of the table was of a piece with the generally dim interior of The Three Horseshoes: dark paneled walls, dark wooden tables, dark ale, dimly seen faces.

Mr. Da Silva snapped a heavy silver lighter. In the bright flare, Sir Gerard noted every detail of his florid face, a prominent brow, dewlaps beneath bloodshot eyes, a hooked nose, bulging cheeks, and thick, sensuous lips framed by the mustache of a mountebank. The drooping ends lapped down his chin.

Da Silva drew heavily on a thin dark cigar. "Will you have a whiskey?" The mellow scent of expensive Cuban tobacco wreathed about his head.

"I think not." Sir Gerard jerked his head at the barmaid. She nodded. They knew him well at The Three Horseshoes. In a moment she returned with a tall glass of lemonade. "Here you are, Sir Gerard." Her glance was avid. No doubt the locals were already whispering among themselves about the deadly doings at Castle Crawsbey.

Sir Gerard took a sip, wished the sharp tang could speed through his blood, make him young again, restore him to manhood. Before the War . . . He closed his mind against memory, against the days when Lady Amelia might have been his. Enough. His duty was clear.

He leaned his elbows on the table, fixed Da Silva with a penetrating stare. "I know why you came to Castle Crawsbey."

For an instant, the surrounding, comfortable fog of smoke and laughter and movement might not have existed. Sir Gerard and Da Silva might have stood on a windswept moor in utter silence, eyes locked, pistols raised, ready for mortal combat.

"Do you indeed?" The response was sibilant and infinitely hostile.

Sir Gerard's recognition of danger was immediate. He steeled himself for attack as he stared into eyes as cold and hard as any Boche sharpshooter.

"Why did I come?" Da Silva spoke softly. A plump hand dropped beneath the table.

Sir Gerard calculated his chances. His upper body retained muscle and power. He would up-end the table, crush it against Da Silva if he moved. "I know about the arrangements for the removal of the treasure."

Slowly Da Silva's heavy shoulders eased from their posture of readiness. "The treasure," Da Silva repeated the word in a considering tone. His hand lifted from beneath the table. A pudgy thumb and forefinger stroked the drooping ends of his mustache. Abruptly his sensuous mouth curved into a mocking smile. "So you know about treasure. I would," his tone was soft and silky, "be quite interested to understand the extent of your knowledge." He stared at Sir Gerard with unblinking attention.

Sir Gerard knew he was on firm ground here. "I've learned from an unimpeachable source, señor, about the young Duke's success in uncovering a Lost Civilization and the treasure hidden in a crypt beneath the monumental statue of Gorblec. There are mounds of gemstones and tons of silver and gold. I know," Sir Gerard leaned back in the hard wooden chair, his fingers idly turning the glass of lemonade round and round while his eyes scoured the suddenly enigmatic face of Da Silva, "about the plans to smuggle that treasure into England. I know that *you*," Sir Gerard placed great emphasis on the pronoun, "declined to buy into the partnership arranging for that transfer. What I want to know, señor, is why then, given that refusal, did you come to Castle Crawsbey this weekend? Why did you decline to take part? Do you have your own plans for the treasure? Did your plans include disposing of the man sent here by the

Duke to secure funds for the shipment?" Each question was flung at Da Silva with mounting sharpness.

A hearty burst of laughter from Da Silva turned heads their way.

Sir Gerard stiffened. The cheek of the fellow.

Da Silva's face was suddenly agreeable, good humoured. "My dear Sir Gerard, I must confess that I came to the castle this weekend first and foremost because I feel most honored as a mere man of business to be included in such a gathering. The Dowager Duchess has great charm. I needed nothing more than the thought of an evening in her company to make this occasion one of great merit to me. As for the treasure," his plump hand waved in dismissal, "I took it to be nothing more than the young Duke's effort to persuade his *madre* to provide him with yet more money from the ducal estate. Of course I declined, though with courtesy and grace, to donate any of my own funds to such a scheme. I should think you would understand that, Sir Gerard." The ebullient voice was again silky, though this time not freighted with menace. The big head tilted to one side. Dark eyes studied Sir Gerard. "Since you are present at the castle, I assume you are involved in this effort to move the—" a perceptible pause "—treasure?"

Sir Gerard remained impassive. Yet he knew that somehow he had lost control of the moment. It was chafing in the extreme. At one moment Da Silva had looked ready to slit Sir Gerard's throat. And now, damn it all, the man was amused. What accounted for this transformation? Moreover, the banker's question was disquieting in the extreme. Why, indeed, had Sir Gerard been included in this ill-fated house party? It seemed indubitable that everyone except himself was in one manner or another connected to the Admiral's quest for funds. Had the Dowager Duchess invited him as an intimate of the family, there, perhaps, to offer unwitting support? Perhaps the Duchess, despite her baiting of him during their interview, did see him as a possible suitor for Lady Amelia. Perhaps the Duchess preferred a maimed English son-in-law to an American bounder. And no doubt Lady Amelia had kept her dalliance with Archie Nettle a dark secret.

Sir Gerard lifted his glass of lemonade and sipped. "Suffice it, señor, that I am ever and always a willing servitor to the Dowager Duchess. In that capacity, I am endeavoring to discover the truth in this matter of the visiting sailor." Sir Gerard could not quite bring himself to accord Cornelius Brandon the rank of admiral. He felt the Countess Boronskaya's appraisal of the man's antecedents was quite likely on the mark. Indeed, it was possible that the Countess was depending more upon information received than intuition. He tucked back that thought for future exploration. "So, Señor Da Silva," Sir Gerard had spoken quite pleasantly, but now his tone turned to steel, "I must ask how your sash, the purple sash that decorated your chest throughout the evening at the castle, how that sash came to be used to tie Brandon to the statue of Neptune before it came crashing down into the murky water of the fountain?"

JEAVONS flung open the door, but he remained in the hallway, stiff as a starched collar.

Arbuthnot didn't give a damn if the butler turned into another statue on that idiotic fountain, the unlikely site of murder. Poking into servants' quarters clearly seemed declassé to Jeavons. But it was time to find out what was what with this fellow Lewis. Clearly he was a new servant at the castle. The young woman who claimed to be the Duchess of Faughstrayne asserted that the servant Lewis was at the castle at the behest of the young Duke. If that were true, surely the Admiral recognized him. And now Lewis was nowhere to be found. Not a trace of him had turned up. The footmen had returned to the castle after an unsuccessful search of the grounds. The Chief Inspector then dispatched the men to seek the Admiral's son. The young man had remained in his room after being told of his father's demise, but now that room was empty. And no one was in the recently occupied secret apartment. Arbuthnot felt his ears warm. Damn all, now was not the time to wonder who the late Duke had installed in that secret room. Certainly it had no relevance to the matter at hand. What mattered was its most recent occupant. Where had the exotic beauty gone? Where had everyone gone, departing like pigeons startled by gunfire? Where was the new, unproven Duchess? And the banker Da Silva? And Sir Gerard, who'd raced away in his black Bentley? And the Admiral's son Whitchell? And, most importantly perhaps, the dark-haired servant Lewis?

Arbuthnot strode into the room that had been allotted to Lewis. It was as bare as a dungeon, though possibly more cheerful. Watery sunlight spilled down from a high casement window. The furnishings were Spartan in the extreme: an aged, narrow wooden bed with a plain white coverlet, a modest chest, a warped table with a worn chair.

There was a faint scent of coconut oil pomade. Arbuthnot wrinkled his nose. Ah yes, Lewis was the clumsy fellow who had splashed the Admiral's uniform, necessitating his appearance in a dinner suit of the late Duke. The Chief Inspector felt a quicksilver dart of excitement. No uniform . . . dinner suit . . . all cats are black at night . . . A motor raced outside in the drive, effectively vanquishing the evanescent thought.

Arbuthnot noted that the bed was not well made, the coverlet drawn up crookedly, the pillow askew. Was the fellow simply all thumbs? At least nothing had been spilled upon it.

That smell . . . he rounded the end of the narrow bed, and in a step reached the chest. He pulled open the top drawer. Two bottles rocked and fell. He reached out, then stopped himself. Both appeared well stoppered. Perhaps he'd better take care over fingerprints. He was beginning to have grave doubts about Lewis.

Arbuthnot pulled a handkerchief from his pocket. He carefully eased over the nearer bottle, peered at the label. Ah yes, here was the famous coconut oil pomade. Curious that it should be here rather than in the Admiral's room. As Arbuthnot understood it, Lewis spilled the pomade while unpacking the Admiral's kit. The clear inference was that the pomade belonged to the Admiral. So why was the bottle now in the servant's chest? Hmm. Curious. Arbuthnot eased his handkerchief-shielded fingers around the second bottle. He stared at the label for a long moment: *Miss Pinkerton's Rectifying Beauty Preparation.* Now this was deuced odd, a compound for a lady's skin lotion. Using the cloth, Arbuthnot carefully lifted the bottle and unscrewed the cap, all the while protecting possible fingerprints. He poured a spoonful into his palm. Lotion oozed onto his skin, thick and brown as molasses. Why if anyone smeared this muck about, they'd look dark as a native. Arbuthnot restored the cap, replaced the bottle in the drawer, thinking furiously. He swung about. "Jeavons."

The butler stood in the doorway. "Sir."

The Chief Inspector glowered. "Describe Lewis."

Jeavons' nose wrinkled in disdain. "A motley-looking fellow. I'd been planning on telling the Dowager Duchess that he should be dismissed. Her Grace has a kind heart, sir, and as I understand it, she'd taken on the fellow to please an old friend. He'd just arrived the very day that the guests came. But we have no use for such clumsiness here at Castle Crawsbey. He tried to ape the manner of a better servant, but he was not well trained. And it was shocking how that foreigner—the one that got himself killed—took umbrage with Her Grace over the accident with the hair dressing."

The Chief Inspector looked sharply at the butler, but Jeavons's manner indicated nothing more than honest anger over rudeness to the Dowager Duchess. But if the man Lewis was sent by the young Duke, how then could the Admiral feel free to criticize Her Grace's staff? Arbuthnot felt there was more here than met the eye. Damn all, he had to find Lewis.

"What did Lewis look like?" Arbuthnot snapped.

"Dark-skinned as a native. Coarse hair black as pitch and a sight too much of it. But," the butler's usually expressionless face crinkled into a puzzled frown, "he had light eyes, blue as a piece of Wedgwood."

"How did he speak?" The chief inspector pulled open a second drawer. His gaze was arrested and he scarcely heard the butler's reply.

Jeavons's tone was sharp. "He scarcely spoke a word. A grunt here, a nod there. Sometimes I wondered if he was all right in the head."

The Chief Inspector once again used his handkerchief. This time he picked up a mop of curly black hair. He held the wig up to the light. By God, here was a bit of a shock.

Skin lotion and a hairpiece. Who was to know how Lewis appeared now? There could be no doubt, the fellow had shed his identity and scarpered from the castle.

ARBUTHNOT strode into the Library.

Roderick Benfleet swung around from the window. "Chief Inspector, may I have a word with you? I've looked for you everywhere." Benfleet's tone was anxious. His thin sandy hair drooped down his wrinkled forehead. His ill-fitting suit definitely was off the peg. As was the Chief Inspector's. But what was fitting for a policeman was surprising for a man who appeared to be an ultimate of the Dowager Duchess.

Arbuthnot hesitated. He was eager to sound the alarm for the pick-up of Lewis. There was no time to waste. The fellow might be en route to the coast and a ship to South America. Or perhaps he was on his way to London, never to be seen again. Or certainly not to be seen as a servant named Lewis. Dash it all, who was the man and what had been his business at Castle Crawsbey? He'd arrived the same day as the members of the house party. Hmm. Perhaps it would be best to inquire of the Dowager Duchess if her son had sent the man. And perhaps the Admiral's son might know more about the incident of the spilled pomade.

Arbuthnot frowned. Whitchell Brandon had yet to be interviewed. Unfortunately, he was not the only important witness unseen. This investigation was as muddled as Constable Nettle's mind. Arbuthnot held up his hand. "In a moment, Benfleet." Arbuthnot waited for the Constable to appear. He'd been right behind him, actually trod on his heels at one point, and now that he needed Nettle, where . . .

Nettle burst into the Library, his face flushed.

"Constable," Arbuthnot heard the clip of a woman's shoes. Hmm, no doubt Lady Amelia has just passed this way. Village gossip had swirled about her and the Constable in recent weeks. But Nettle had better hew to the course while the investigation proceeded. "Look sharp. I want the Admiral's son and I want Sir Gerard. Post haste." Sir Gerard seemed eager to involve himself in the investigation. Well, he might as well make himself useful. The Chief Inspector was hardly eager to make inquiries of the Dowager Duchess. Sir Gerard would be an excellent intermediary.

"Yes, sir." The Constable backed out of the Library.

The Chief Inspector strode to the desk. First, he'd send out an alarm about Lewis . . . He reached for the telephone.

"Chief Inspector." Benfleet was plaintive. "There is no time to waste. I implore you to grant me a moment. There is a thief at Castle Crawsbey."

Arbuthnot's hand fell. His eyes narrowed. "A thief?"

Benfleet swept a hand across his thin hair. "I regret that there is much you do not know. I must start from the beginning. The Duke has discovered a Lost Civilization in a remote area of Brazil . . ." Benfleet sketched the history of the hidden gold and silver, the plans to smuggle the lot into England, and the Admiral's search for funds to support the effort.

Arbuthnot reached into his inner jacket pocket for the envelope that contained the Admiral's enigmatic list. He drew it out, once again aware to the very ends of his toes as well as the tips of his reddening ears, that the shocking negatives were also contained in that envelope. He knew he must deal with the negatives soon or the very foundations of England might rock. What the devil was he to do? He was careful not to reveal the negatives as he drew out the sheet of paper with the names written in that cramped handwriting. The inspector re-taped the envelope, thrust it back into his inner pocket, sensitive to the telltale crackle of the negatives. For the moment, he must concentrate upon this new information. He interrupted Benfleet's narrative, "You say the dead man came here to the castle seeking funds." That explained the money in the black attaché case. Arbuthnot reread the list, this time in its entirety:

> *Daisy, Dowager Duchess of Faughstrayne—partial*
>   *payment.*
> *Lady Amelia Crawsbey—paid in full.*
> *Roderick Benfleet—promised.*
> *The Countess Boronskaya—paid in full.*
> *Enrique Da Silva—flat refusal.*
> *Sir Gerard Hawksmoor—the phoenix.*
> *Dr. Squiffy Frobisher—appointment made.*

Arbuthnot nodded in satisfaction. Clearly the case was taking shape. Now that the purpose of the house party was plain—though Frobisher was not among the guests and that remained to be explained—the truth of the murder could not be far behind. There was nothing like gold and silver to result in murder. Someone—possibly one of those on the list—might have decided to keep the Admiral from sharing in the booty. "Very well, Benfleet. I see there is a conspiracy afoot. But what is this about a thief?"

"The Duke sent me a gold piece to verify the treasure. I had shown it to Sir Gerard—"

Arbuthnot frowned. "That was most irregular. I am in charge of this investigation."

Benfleet tugged at his collar. "Chief Inspector, that was precisely what Sir Gerard said. He urged me to report this matter to you. I know that was quite good advice, but I hesitated to take such a step without the approval of the Dowager Duchess. I spoke to her and to Lady Amelia and to the Countess and everyone agreed the matter should be laid before you immediately. However, in the interim, I had returned the gold statue to my room. A few minutes ago, I went to my room and opened the chest. Chief Inspector, the gold is gone."

ARBUTHNOT drove fast, his old Morris clacking like horse hooves on cobbles. The damp air swirled around him. He smiled. For once Nettle had served him well. The Constable was still a bit breathless from his bicycle ride into Market Winsome when he called with the startling information that Whitchell Brandon was pacing up and down on the platform at the train station. Moreover, and Nettle deserved a commendation here, Sir Gerard Hawksmoor had just departed The Three Horseshoes after a long conversation with Mr. Da Silva and appeared to be en route back to the castle. In fact, halfway to Market Winsome, the Chief Inspector swung almost to the verge to avoid a crash with the black Bentley.

Arbuthnot's usual flare of irritation with Sir Gerard subsided as he recalled that Sir Gerard had dutifully encouraged Benfleet to reveal the plans to smuggle treasure into the country. Perhaps Sir Gerard was realizing that this matter was far too serious for the intrusion of an amateur. Arbuthnot's nose wrinkled. Sir Gerard had horned in and spoken with Da Silva and must be instructed to refrain from interfering with other witnesses. Arbuthnot would see to it as soon as he returned to the castle, but first things first. The train to London departed in twenty minutes. The Admiral's son must not scarper. Arbuthnot frowned. How had that young man thought he could simply leave the castle without permission? But, hang it all, there didn't seem to be a soul at the castle.

Arbuthnot parked. He studied the dripping sky as he clattered up the stone steps. Surely it was too wet for Squiffy Frobisher to be tramping about the golf course. Arbuthnot wanted information about the cause of death, but more importantly, he wanted to know if Frobisher had ever spoken with the Admiral. Did Squiffy know about the treasure? If so, he should have informed the Chief Inspector. In any event, if Lewis could be rounded up and if Whitchell was privy to information about his father's search for funds, the Chief Inspector was confident he'd be near a solution in time for tea.

At the top of the steps, Arbuthnot paused, breathing heavily from exertion. Ah, there the young man was, his red hair beneath his straw boater almost as garish as his striped blazer. Odd how these Americans dressed. No sense of proper attire. Whitchell Brandon munched on a chocolate bar.

The Chief Inspector marched toward him. "Mr. Brandon."

The redheaded youth slowly turned to face him.

"Mr. Brandon, I'm Chief Inspector Arbuthnot. In charge of the investigation into your father's death." He held out a brawny hand. His fingers were momentarily crushed in a ferocious grip.

The young man looked at him enthusiastically. "Gee, I never thought I'd ever meet a real Chief Inspector. What a weekend. Hey, Pop, you're a real treat."

Arbuthnot blinked. Pop? And where was the sorrow that could be expected after the demise of a parent? He cleared his throat. "I know you've suffered a blow, young man. I regret exceedingly that your father met his end at Castle Crawsbey. I am hoping that you can be helpful to me in seeking the murderer."

A freckled hand shoved the straw hat to the back of his head. "Pop, I'd help you if I could. But Ceebee wasn't my old man. He rented me for the weekend." At the Chief Inspector's blank look, the young American spread out his hands ruefully. "You know how it is, you meet someone in a bar and it's old home week. I mean, one Yank talks to another. The old boy had seen me row in a regatta and he won a packet on me. We got to talking and he said he had some business at a mouldy castle this weekend and wanted to appear to be a family man and how would I like to come along as his son and he said there was a beautiful daughter of the house and so I said I'd be glad to help out. And there was a little matter of a hundred pounds." He rubbed his sunburned nose. "I'm Twitchell Turley. My old man's big in copper. Two-Tone Turley, they call him. Anyway, Pop, I'll have to say, this was a weekend to remember."

SIR Gerard eased his pain-wracked body from the Bentley. He surveyed the front of Castle Crawsbey. The parapets appeared to be wreathed in steam, quite likely an interesting result of the recent rainstorm and the uncommonly hot weather.

"Gerry." The soft call came from the South Terrace.

Sir Gerard followed the graveled path to the opening in the marble balustrade.

Lady Amelia stood near the steps leading down to the fountain. She half turned towards him. The classic perfection of her features was marred by a slight frown. Her slim figure was regal. Her lips parted, then closed. She said nothing as he approached, the sound of his steps sharp, almost menacing, in the heavy quiet.

"Amelia." Sir Gerard wished he could draw back her name. He had revealed too much in his tone. His longing. And his fear.

Lady Amelia's wary gaze softened. She reached out, took his hands. "Gerry, why don't you go home?"

He managed a wry smile. "Has the legendary hospitality of Castle Crawsbey degraded to nothing?"

Her grasp tightened.

Sir Gerard welcomed the soft feel of her skin, the warmth. The life.

"Oh, Gerry."

Abruptly, he drew her close, slipped his arms around her, felt the silk of her soft hair against his face, smelled her faint, unforgettable scent. But he had to know. "Amelia." Now his voice was abrupt. "Da Silva told me. After dinner in the garden you asked for that damned purple sash. He gave it to you. What happened then?"

SEVEN

The Other C. B.

by Carolyn Wheat

HE was going mad. That was all there was to it. Those everlasting sea shanties were driving him round the proverbial bend. He would soon be a case for the trick cyclists.

Reggie Arbuthnot couldn't possibly have heard what he thought he'd heard.

Then he heard it again.

"There's a C. B. Brandon to see you, Chief Inspector," young Pomfrett announced.

"Admiral Brandon is dead," Arbuthnot replied through clenched teeth. "That's what we're investigating, Pomfrett. His death. So kindly do not tell me he's waiting outside for me, there's a good lad."

"It isn't a him, Chief Inspector," the imperturbable constable said. "It's a her, and she says she wants to see the body if you don't mind."

"Wants to see the—If I don't mind—What's all this, then?" Faced with the impossible, Reggie Arbuthnot reverted to the jargon of his own bluebottle days. He fairly flew out of his office to greet the cheeky newcomer, who stood in the doorway of the village police station with an awed expression on her young face.

She was perhaps five-and-twenty, with blonde hair tucked up under a cloche hat. A black cloche hat that matched her black coat, black skirt, and black shoes. Very stylish, cut in the latest short-skirted fashion, but unmistakably a mourning costume.

"Madam, I am Chief Inspector Arbuthnot," he said in an austere tone. "And you are——?"

"C. B. Brandon," the young woman replied in an unmistakably American accent as she thrust out a small hand gloved in black kid. She gazed up at him with limpid blue eyes. "I suppose you want me to identify my father."

"I——er, that is, yes, if you feel up to it, Miss Brandon." Arbuthnot pulled a handkerchief from his pocket and mopped his suddenly damp brow. "But surely you have a Christian name."

A wan smile greeted these words. "It's Cecily," she said. "Cecily Barbara, but I went by C. B. ever since I was in school. Just like my Daddy. I was always," she went on with a slight sniffle, "Daddy's little girl." She dabbed at her nose with a linen handkerchief edged in black. Harrods, the Chief Inspector noted with patriotic pride, had everything.

Arbuthnot led Miss Brandon down the cold stone corridors that went to the dead house, which had been a creamery in a former life. The Admiral, lying under a white shroud on a stone pallet, was the sole occupant. As he raised the sheet from the dead face, Arbuthnot turned toward his companion just in time to see her swoon and drop to the floor, too late for him to catch her.

For a horrible moment, Arbuthnot wondered whether Dr. Frobisher had been careless again and forgotten to re-attach the man's scalp to his skull. Even the no-doubt awful sight of a murdered parent didn't usually send a healthy girl diving towards the cobblestones.

But once he'd picked up Miss Cecily Brandon and carried her to a chair, once he'd called in a W.P.C. to administer smelling salts, and once the young lady had come round, he learned the reason for her fainting spell.

"It isn't him," she said in a wondering tone. "It isn't Daddy after all."

"THE sash?" Lady Amelia stepped back, her eyebrows raised and her chin lifted in a way that reminded Sir Gerard forcibly of the Dowager Duchess addressing a pert parlormaid. "You think I had something to do with the murder of that dreadful man?"

"Of course not, Amelia," he lied. "But when Mr. Da Silva told me you asked him for his sash—whatever possessed you to do such a thing?"

"Well, how was I to know it would end up on a corpse, Gerry? Honestly, if I'd known that, I wouldn't have asked for it, would I?"

"But why did you want it in the first place?"

"What difference does it make?" Lady Amelia's eyes were blazing now. "You think I'm a murderess."

"I do not." Sir Gerard's pain was evident, he was sure, in his voice. "That is," he continued, misery and honesty mingled in his tone, "I don't want to."

Her soft hand reached out and stroked his cheek. "Then don't."

"What about the blowpipe your brother sent from Bolivia?"

"Oh, that silly thing." A genuine smile warmed her pale face. "I've had the most awful fun with it. You've no idea how thrilling it is to prick some pompous ass with a dart and watch him turn round and round looking for a wasp."

"Amelia, doesn't it occur to you that the Admiral was probably poisoned?"

"What if he was? I didn't cook dinner, did I?"

"Poisoned by means of a dart. I found a feather near the body—a feather that came from an arrow—or a dart."

"Dudley said the Brazilian natives use poison on their darts," Lady Amelia mused. She turned away, staring into the distance as if seeking enlightenment in the raised flowerbeds of the Italian garden. "Perhaps one of the darts still had poison clinging to it and I never knew."

Gerry's heart sank. Was he hearing a confession?

"Did you shoot the Admiral, Amelia?"

"He would have deserved it, wouldn't he?" Lady Amelia faced him with the forthrightness he admired so much. "What amazing cheek the man had! And that impossible son! Do you know he tried to grope me in the upstairs hallway?"

"I can't say I'm surprised. The boy was a bounder. I wish you'd told me. I'd have—" Gerry broke off and hung his head. Whatever he might have done in such a case before the war was immaterial; the way he was now, he could have done nothing even if he'd been on the spot.

"Where is the blowpipe now?" He steeled himself for the answer. Would she lie or tell the truth? Would there be a telltale blush of guilt on her damask cheek?

"In my room, I suppose. At least," she said with a toss of her head, "that's where I saw it last."

"Let's go look for it," Sir Gerard suggested. He wasn't certain whether he intended to turn it over to Arbuthnot, confiscate it, or throw it in the nearest fire. "On the way," he added, taking Lady Amelia's arm, "you can tell me all about Mr. Da Silva's purple sash."

"I hoped you'd forgotten about that, Gerry," she murmured.

"NOT your father, Miss Brandon?" Arbuthnot tried to keep the eagerness out of his tone, but this was a development of the first magnitude. Ever since he'd found those scurrilous negatives in the "Admiral's" room, he'd doubted that the man held the rank to which he'd pretended. Even in the States, a man of Brandon's black stripe couldn't rise to the top rank of the navy, could he?

The discovery of the bogus Whitchell Brandon on the platform at the train station added more evidence to his growing conviction that the deceased admiral was no more an admiral than he was.

But where there was one fake offspring, could there not be two? Was this young lady who she claimed to be?

He resolved to check every single aspect of her story, taking nothing on faith.

The woman who called herself Cecily Brandon shook her head. "No. I was—oh, dear, it was so upsetting to read in the *Times*—the *London Times,* of course—" Arbuthnot inwardly cursed the flapping tongue of Ned Chapman the milk carter. "—that Daddy had been murdered at Castle Crawsbey. Upsetting and strange, too, because whatever would Daddy be doing in a castle, anyway? He hates castles, and country houses, and museums, and—really, Chief Inspector, the only thing Daddy likes about England is the boats. He dragged me to Greenwich and Plymouth—we have a Plymouth, too, in America, you know, the one with the rock?—and I said I couldn't stand to see one more ship, so he let me go to London for some shopping while he went on to Southampton for a look at the *Olympic*—that's the *Titanic's* sister ship. Daddy always said if he'd been the captain on the *Titanic,* more people would have been saved, so it seemed a good place for him to visit while I caught up on all the things he hates in London. And that's where I read that he was dead."

"Only he isn't," Arbuthnot said, realizing with dread that he was actually following this tangled narrative. "Dead, that is."

"Well, it doesn't look like it, does it?" The words were tart, but not the tone. She was still, Arbuthnot realized, adjusting to the fact that her beloved parent was probably still in Southampton boring the pants off the poor souls at the White Star Line. She really was a taking little thing, he reflected as she turned the full force of her cornflower eyes on him.

"I did telephone, of course," Cecily Brandon went on, "but the Southampton hotel said Daddy checked out and went to Brighton, and none of the Brighton hotels I called knew anything about him, so I thought I'd better come here."

"Quite right," the Chief Inspector replied, patting her hand in a fatherly way. "Let me order you some tea while you tell me more about your family. Your brother, for instance—is he in England too?"

"Whitchell? In England?" The girl's light laugh brightened the stone cell. Arbuthnot rose and offered her an arm. They walked together towards the warmth of his office and the promise of a nice cup of tea. "He's at Annapolis, following in Daddy's footsteps. Why do you ask?"

"Because someone, Miss Brandon, took his place at Castle Crawsbey. The Dowager Duchess entertained two men: one who called himself Admiral Brandon, and the other of whom passed himself off as your brother."

"But why would anyone want to—" The black-clad hand flew to her rosebud mouth as if to stop the words from tumbling out. When she removed her little hand, the lip-rouged mouth was set in a thin grim line.

She knows. She knows, but she isn't going to say, Arbuthnot thought to himself.

And so it was; Arbuthnot offered tea, the admiral's daughter accepted, and he questioned her for another twenty minutes, learning absolutely nothing.

EDWIN Cooper hadn't had such a profitable day driving people to and from the castle since Lady Amelia's scavenger hunt. First the red-haired American and then the pale-faced man with the spots of brown color near his hairline wanted rides to the train station. Then the foreign-looking cove with the oily black hair rode to the pub. Now this blonde American girl ordered him to take him to the Castle and asked the name of every house, every road, and every tree between Market Winsome and the family seat of the Crawsbeys.

"I've heard so much about this place," she said eagerly, bouncing in her seat like a child. "I can't wait to see it!"

The taxi driver shook his head. "I told you, miss, the public tours are on Thursday. All you'll be able to do today is look at the outside of the house. No picnics allowed, either."

Her reply was a superior little smile. "Oh, I think they'll let me in when they find out who I am," she replied.

IT was the Dowager Duchess who found the missing Consuela Imelda Berthold de Cordova—in Her Grace's bedchamber, on her knees measuring the drapes.

"We shall put lace from Barcelona in here," the young woman said in her charmingly accented English when her erstwhile mother-in-law stepped into the room. "I have the perfect silk for the chairs, a rose color. One should always use rose in the boudoir, it makes everything so sexy, don't you think?"

Her Grace's basilisk eye should have turned the dark-haired girl to stone. Instead, the would-be young Duchess walked—did she walk, or did she sidle like a snake? Recounting the incident in later years, the Dowager Duchess tended towards sidling—towards the massive bedstead in which her son had been conceived. (She had thought of England.)

The young woman ran her hands along the carved cherry posts and purred, "This bed will do. It is strong and sturdy enough to stand up to many nights of passion." As if her words weren't outrageous enough, the baggage was dressed as if for a costume party, in a multicolored skirt tiered with ruffles and a lacy blouse that showed a great deal of shoulder and offered teasing hints of what lay beneath the sheer cotton.

"Who are you and what are you doing in my bedroom?" If anyone could ever have been said to "thunder" a sentence, this one was thundered. The Red Queen couldn't have ordered the girl's head cut off with more menace than the Duchess packed into those words.

"Oh, *Dios mio*! I am forgetting—you do not know who

I am!" The woman opened her dusky arms, plastered a toothy smile on her face, and strode towards the Dowager Duchess with a happy cry of "Mamacita! I am your dear Dudley's *esposa*."

Without realizing it, the Dowager Duchess emulated Cecily Barbara Brandon. She collapsed on the fortunately well-carpeted floor in a dead faint.

JEAVONS opened the door and was in the process of informing the young person that Her Grace was not receiving today when the slight blonde American cut in with a cry of "Oh, aren't you just the cat's pajamas! A real English butler!" Before he knew it, the child was inside the hall, loudly admiring the Chinese vase that held umbrellas and walking sticks.

"Miss, I told you—" Heedless, the girl continued into the Reception Room, pointed at the painting of Her Grace that hung on the landing of the carved staircase, and exclaimed, "Oh, is that Lady Amelia? She's so pretty. But then I knew she would be, because—"

Family pride overcame Jeavons' intense desire to see the door shut on this extraordinary apparition. "No, miss, that is the Dowager Duchess when she first married the Duke."

"Oh, when she was Daisy Digby the chorus girl," the young lady said with a nod of understanding.

"Her Grace was not," Jeavons corrected in freezing tones, "a chorus girl. She was a—" He broke off and stepped in front of her, blocking her way. "Madam, you cannot stay here. I have no authority to admit you, and no one here will receive you."

"You are just so precious," the girl replied with a delighted clap of her gloved hands. "You couldn't be more perfect if they got you from Central Casting." She made her way toward the Grand Staircase, evidently intent upon examining the family portraits that lined the walls.

"What is Central Casting, and what are you doing here, and, miss, you can't go up there, really you can't." He scampered up the staircase but was not fast enough to block the young woman's light steps.

"Mr. Jeavons," a frantic female voice called from the top of the stairs, "come quick. There's a strange lady up here what made Her Grace faint."

The butler drew himself up to his full height, slowed his pace, and made his dignified way towards the landing, muttering, "There's a strange lady down here too."

"SO it was curare?" Chief Inspector Reggie Arbuthnot drew on his pipe and settled into his chair. "I thought as much." Puffs of satisfied smoke gathered round his head, and he smiled benevolently at Dr. Frobisher. Things were, he felt, finally falling into place. He knew now that the dead "Admiral" was a fake and a blackmailer and he knew how the man had become a corpse.

"Nasty stuff, curare," the doctor opined with a lugubrious shake of his head. "Saw natives bring down a jaguar with the stuff when I was in Brazil."

"You were in Brazil?" Arbuthnot's complacency melted like snow in May; he sat up in his chair and gazed at the doctor with consternation. One of the drawbacks of not being a local man, he thought ruefully, is that people didn't bother telling you things because they assumed you already knew them.

"I was a ship's doctor for twenty years," Frobisher replied, resting his plump hands on his ample waistcoat. "Happiest days of my life. The bounding main, the adventures, the wide ocean." He lowered his voice and gave a wink. "The handsome *señoritas* in port—I expect it was my stories of South America that inspired young Dudley. He certainly seemed intrigued by them when he came down from Cambridge for the weekends."

Arbuthnot had neither the time nor the inclination for smoking-room stories of Frobisher's conquests in exotic climes. "Curare kills instantly, does it not?"

"No, more's the pity." The doctor's round, humourous face took on a serious cast. "It paralyzes the body, rather like anesthesia. The victim slowly asphyxiates, thanks to increasing paralysis of the lungs, but he's conscious the whole time. Conscious and unable to cry out, unable to move. It must be rather a horrible way to die."

"It comes from a South American plant, I believe," Arbuthnot said, looking up from the notes he'd made.

"Yes," replied the doctor, "from a plant found in the Amazon basin. The Brazilians call it *pareira brava* but I find the French name more descriptive: *vigne sauvage.* Savage vine."

"Savage indeed," the Chief Inspector agreed. "But how would someone in England get hold of it?"

"Excellent question," Frobisher said. "The natives boil the bark of the vine and make a dark, viscid paste. They dip the tips of their darts into the paste and shoot the darts through blowpipes. I can only assume—although, strictly speaking, this isn't my brief as a pathologist, you know—that someone brought the stuff from South America. It isn't," he added, "the sort of thing you pick up at the village chemist's."

* * *

"HONESTLY, doesn't anyone in this house know the first thing about South America?" Cecily Brandon surveyed the assembled occupants of the Dowager Duchess's bedroom and placed her hands on her hips. "This woman isn't Brazilian. She speaks Spanish, not Portuguese. So she can't be the daughter of Tomás Berthold de Cordova. She's a liar—and she's certainly not the Duchess of Faughstrayne."

The most interesting fact about the young lady's declaration was that she pronounced the name correctly.

"Even if she's lying about her family connections," Sir Gerard pointed out in his most reasonable tone, "she could still be married to the Duke."

The Dowager Duchess, who had been revived by a judicious application of cold water and smelling salts, uttered a low groan.

"No, she couldn't," the blonde woman replied with a withering glance at the smoldering South American. "Because I am."

The Dowager Duchess's head fell heavily onto the breast of her distraught maid. Lady Amelia jumped from her chair and cried, "Impossible!"

"You lie!" The dark-haired woman who called herself Consuela stepped towards the slight blonde with a menacing look in her black eyes. "*I* am the rightful Duchess! I have papers to prove that Dudley married *me* two months ago!"

Cecily Brandon gazed at the fiery Consuela with cold blue eyes. "And *I* have a perfectly valid marriage certificate that says my father the Admiral married Dudley and me *three* months ago. So put that in your pipe and smoke it!"

"Your father!" The Latina snapped her fingers. "You think anyone will believe that! You take up the pipe and you smoke it! My marriage was performed by a priest in a church."

"A priest?" The wan little voice belonged to the once-formidable Dowager Duchess, who was being vigorously fanned by her attendant. "Not a *Catholic* priest?"

"Gerry, do something," Lady Amelia begged. "This is intolerable!"

But there was nothing to be done. The two claimants to the title squared off like bare-knuckle boxers, circling one another like tigers. One blonde, one dark—it was, Sir Gerard thought, like a scene from a morality play. Only which was Virtue and which Vice?

"As if a hot-blooded lover like *mi querido Duddito* would be content with *una pescada fría* like you!" The self-proclaimed Consuela Imelda Berthold de Cordova tossed her dusky curls and stamped her foot. The Cuban heel made a less than satisfying thump on the carpeted floor. "*Sí,* I call you a cold fish, you American *puta.*"

"Well, if I'm a cold fish, I'd hardly choose prostitution as a profession, would I?" Cecily's high, girlish voice was ice. "But then you'd know all about that, wouldn't you, señorita? You who danced the tango in cheap bars for all of Argentina to see, you who spread your legs for every sailor at liberty in Buenos Aires? My Duddy," she said with simple dignity, "is a gentleman. He wouldn't wipe his hands on a woman like you."

"Oh, he did more than wipe his hands. Let me tell you what *mi caro esposo* does when we are in—"

"Don't you dare! The thought of my precious Duddy having anything to do with you makes me sick as mud. My Duddykins is an explorer, a man of honor, a—" Here she paused and lay her hand on her breast, gazing towards heaven—"a Peer of the Realm."

The outraged Argentine launched into a torrent of rapid Spanish, stamping her feet and whipping her skirt with her hands, punctuating her words with a rhythm that would have been instantly recognised in her native Buenos Aires as belonging to a particularly passionate tango. To Sir Gerard's surprise, the blonde American replied in kind, her own Spanish apparently matching Consuela's for speed and breadth of invective.

When the dark-haired beauty had been driven from the field, sobbing and shouting imprecations, Cecily turned to her audience and said with a satisfied smile, "I didn't spend my childhood at a convent school in Santiago without picking up a bit of the language."

"I doubt she learned many of those words in a convent school," Sir Gerard muttered.

"Well, of course, Daddy's interests in silver mines did bring me into contact with some of the rougher sorts of men," the blonde admitted with charming self-deprecation.

Perhaps it was her sense of duty as the chatelaine of Castle Crawsbey, or perhaps the mention of silver mines, but the Dowager Duchess rose from her chair, turned towards Jeavons, and said, "Please show Miss Brandon around the house and grounds."

AFTER the butler led the black-clad American from the bedchamber, Lady Amelia returned to her chair, her mouth settling into a very pretty pout.

"For a man of my brother's proclivities to marry one woman is nothing short of astonishing. But for him to marry two is outside the bounds of credulity!"

Sir Gerard knew not what to say. To hear a gently-reared girl like Lady Amelia talk so frankly of "proclivities" shocked him profoundly.

Her ladyship's mother, who had settled herself in the chintz-covered armchair, showed no signs of his inner turmoil. "Don't be silly, Amelia. Marriage, as your late father's example should have demonstrated, has little or nothing to do with 'proclivities.' It is a matter of alliances, not physical gratification. For that," and now the Dowager Duchess raked Sir Gerard with a look that could only be described as scornful, "men have other outlets."

"But why," Lady Amelia cried, raising her eyes toward heaven, "should Dudley wish to ally himself with either a hootchy-koochy dancer or a flapper?"

The Dowager Duchess's voice was plummy with indulgence. "*Cherchez l'argent,* my pet," she replied. "The *genuine* Admiral Brandon possesses silver mines, and the *genuine* Señor de Cordova owns one-fifth of Brazil, which I'm told is rather a large country." She lifted a scented handkerchief to her nose and added, "On the whole, your brother seems to have done better than I expected. This South American folly of his has turned out rather well after all. Whichever unsuitable bride turns out to be who she says she is as well as his lawful wife will bring a pretty penny into the exchequer."

"Mother, please." Lady Amelia's blush cut Sir Gerard to the quick. He empathized fully with her feelings but dared not speak.

"We might get the roof fixed," the Dowager Duchess said in a dreamy voice, "and perhaps hire an undergardener or two. Do you think the budget would extend to restoring Neptune to his rightful place at the fountain, and providing him with another prong to his trident?"

"Bident," Sir Gerard corrected under his breath, and was rewarded with a smile from Lady Amelia. His heart sang; no one else, he was quite sure, had the power to make Amelia smile like that. She might lust after a strapping country lad like Archie Nettle, but wit would not be hers so long as she dallied with someone so far below her in intellect.

Intellect—that was the ticket! He could win her, he knew he could, if only he could solve this mystery, clear her name, restore her honor, reveal to the world the true killer of the late, unlamented non-Admiral. Perhaps, he thought, letting his fancies take flight, he could even figure out which of the two ladies was the real wife of Dudley, Duke of Faughstrayne.

"CHIEF Inspector Arbuthnot wishes to see you, Your Grace," Jeavons announced with a slight bow that seemed to convey his complete appreciation of the fact that a Duchess shouldn't be bothered with such trifles as a murder on her premises, or with such low persons as the police, but that ever since the Great War standards had fallen and old ways discarded, and this fact lay heavily on his heart but could not be altered. Since this was precisely Her Grace's view of the matter, Jeavons' manner went down well, and the Dowager Duchess rose to her feet, prepared to receive the Chief Inspector with all the civility of a lady of the manor dispensing charity to a particularly feckless tenant.

Arbuthnot sat in the late Duke's Library and ran his eyes over the titles that crammed the shelves. Most, he was quite sure, still boasted uncut pages, the late lord of the manor having been a man not noted for his intellect. His eye was drawn to a shelf containing a number of volumes in English, Spanish, and Portuguese dealing, apparently, with details of South American explorations. He opened one and flipped through the pages until he came to a photograph of a Brazilian blowpipe being used by a scantily clad native. The pipe was long, about the size of a javelin, and according to the accompanying text, it was made of bamboo. It was also, the writer assured him, a very easy weapon to master. It was light and could be aimed quite accurately with little practice.

All the Chief Inspector needed now was to find a blowpipe on the premises and his suspicions would be confirmed.

"WE must find that blowpipe!"

"Why are you whispering, Gerry? There's no one here but us." Lady Amelia led Sir Gerard along the upstairs corridor towards her bedroom as if the two of them were in flight.

"Can we be certain of that? Either one of those so-called sisters-in-law of yours might be snooping around."

"Please don't joke about that!" To his dismay, she stopped walking and turned towards him. "Honestly, Gerry, I've spent years living in fear that my mother would find out the truth about Dudley—why he was sent down from Cambridge, why Father had to endow that chair at Eton, why that young footman burst into tears when he left for Brazil. I wouldn't have turned a hair if a handsome boy turned up and said he was Dudley's 'special friend,' but this—" She broke off with a frantic wave of her hands. "It defies everything I know about my brother."

"The blowpipe," Sir Gerard repeated through clenched teeth. "And the sash. Tell me why you wanted Da Silva's sash, for heaven's sake."

"Because it was purple. Because it was the Order of the Apothecary, if you can imagine such a silly thing. Because

I'd had too much champagne and the night smelled of jasmine and I lost my head. I felt like teasing the odious man because I couldn't do anything about those awful Brandons and I had to take my feelings out on someone and Mr. Da Silva was at the fountain smoking a perfectly poisonous cigar. I started flirting with him and asked if I could wear his sash for a bit and he very gallantly said yes and then someone came up to speak to him and I went away, still wearing the stupid sash."

"Who wanted to speak to him?"

"The egregious Admiral, of course. Wearing my father's dress suit, if you please. Of course, now we know why, don't we?"

"Do we?"

"His luckless servant didn't spill coconut oil on his uniform, Gerry. He didn't have a uniform because he wasn't a real admiral. He made that petty scene so we'd think he had one that he couldn't wear."

They had reached Lady Amelia's bedroom. "What did you do with the sash?"

"Oh, Gerry. I feel so stupid now." She stopped and turned her face to him again, and he was swept by another rush of love for her. Did she know how she affected him? Was she using her charms deliberately to keep him from insisting upon the truth? "But how could I have known?"

"Amelia. Just tell me." He stepped back, resisting with all his might the urge to plant a kiss on her delectable lips.

"I walked about the garden for a bit. You can't see the colors at night, of course, but the scent is intoxicating. Then I looked down at myself and realized I was wearing the sash. I felt silly, so I slipped it off and left it on a hedge. A box hedge, I think." She blushed prettily. "It wasn't kind to

Mr. Da Silva to leave it there, but I'd had too much to drink and wasn't thinking straight. All I wanted to do was go upstairs to bed and I thought it would be better to leave it where he'd find it instead of taking it up to my room. I know that makes no sense, but that's what happened."

"That means anyone could have found the sash on the hedge and used it to tie up the 'Admiral,'" he said. "That is," he continued, honesty overcoming hope, "if the Chief Inspector believes your story."

The male voice made them both jump like startled rabbits. "If the Chief Inspector believes what story?"

Arbuthnot stood in the doorway of Lady Amelia's bedchamber, suspicion etched on his face.

CECILY Brandon knew a great deal about her alleged husband's native land, and she'd learned all of it from murder mysteries. Upon being shown the ha-ha, Cecily remarked, "Oh, yes, Sir Roderick Basingstoke broke his neck jumping over one of those in *Tragedy at Tantalus Abbey*." She lowered her voice confidentially, "Of course, the groom, who was really the long-lost heir to the estate but ran off to Australia when he was a young man, had cut the cinch on the horse's saddle."

"B-But I never, miss," the groom attending her said with a pale face and trembling voice. "Why, Her Grace came in and fed sugar to Bellerophon just before His Grace set off on that fatal hunt. She tested the cinch herself, she did, and told me it was right as rain." The wiry little man, who smelled rather strongly of equine, shook his head sadly. "It was a dark day when His Grace took that tumble. A dark day indeed."

When she learned that Sir Gerard was an amateur

detective bent on solving the murder of the man who'd posed as her father, the American said brightly, "Just like Lord Peter Wimsey! Only a Duke like my Dudley out-ranks a mere knight, doesn't he? And I must say the Dowager Duchess isn't at all like Lord Peter's mother, but I'll bet this house is as nice as Duke's Denver."

Jeavons rolled his eyes. He was as fond of Dorothy L. Sayers as the next man, but it had never occurred to him to regard her fantasies of English nobility as anything at all like reality.

The butler's pantry was greeted with delight. "It's the bee's knees," Cecily Brandon proclaimed.

"As you say, miss," the beleaguered butler replied, "the bee's, er, knees."

THE blowpipe stood at the back of Lady Amelia's wardrobe, between a pair of dancing slippers and stout walking shoes. It was about three feet long and was made of split bamboo lashed together with strands of tree bark wrapped along its length. The mouthpiece was made of bone and a handsome woven basket sat next to it, red-feathered darts protruding from its mouth. The red feathers were an exact match to the feather Sir Gerard had picked up at the murder scene. Tied to the side of the basket was a gourd with a small hole on top.

"That's for the curare," Lady Amelia said in a flat voice. It seemed to Sir Gerard that she'd given up, that she was surren-dering herself into Arbuthnot's custody, refusing to defend herself or explain anything. As he'd feared, her story about the purple sash sounded thin and unbelievable.

"If Dr. Frobisher tests these items," Arbuthnot asked, his

eyes narrowed, "will he find traces of curare in the blow-pipe?"

"He might," she replied, trying for a nonchalant toss of her head and succeeding only in looking guilty. "Dudley said it was authentic, not made for tourist traffic."

"Look, Arbuthnot," Sir Gerard began, uneasily aware that he sounded condescending but unable to modulate his tone, "anyone could have sneaked in here and taken the thing out. I daresay most of Lady Amelia's acquaintance knows she owns it—I imagine she's shown it off to nearly everyone who's visited Castle Crawsbey by now."

A shrewd gaze from the Chief Inspector greeted his remark. "Did you know about it, Sir Gerard?"

"Yes, of course I did," he bluffed. He didn't dare look at Lady Amelia, knowing full well that her honest features would reveal the truth.

"No, of course you didn't," she cut in with some asperity. "Kindly refrain from making this worse, Gerry. I appreciate your gallantry, but it can only lead to more trouble in the long run."

"So the presence of this blowpipe was not generally known?"

"No, Chief Inspector, it was not. Only a few select friends knew I had it—and my mother, of course."

"Surely you can't believe the Dowager Duchess—"

"I believe nothing. I disbelieve nothing. I am merely collecting evidence," the Chief Inspector replied. He turned back to Lady Amelia. "Who among the visitors who were here when the 'Admiral' died knew about the blowpipe?"

"Let me think. Roderick Benfleet, because he knew Dudley and I wanted to show him Dud's latest present to me. Mr. Da Silva because he's from Argentina and I thought he'd be interested. Doctor Squiffy, of course, he said it was quite fine and I should give it to a museum someday. Archie, because—" She broke off with a blush and a giggle. "Just because."

A slow flush spread up from Arbuthnot's neck to the top of his head. Sir Gerard realized that the Constable had seen the red feather from the dart and had said nothing to his superior about Lady Amelia's blowpipe.

Dr. Squiffy Frobisher stepped into the room brandishing a bamboo cane. "Thought you might like to take a gander at this," he said, waving the cane like a baton. "Haven't seen one of these since I was in Rio last," he went on cheerfully. "Rather regretted not buying one myself. Found it in the umbrella stand in the front entrance hall."

"Why would you think that?" The Chief Inspector's tone was not encouraging.

The plump doctor pulled off the handle and pointed the cane at the Chief Inspector. "Look through the bottom," he ordered.

"I haven't time for this now, Doctor," Arbuthnot replied. "I'm in the middle of interrogating witnesses."

"You're in the middle of trying to prove that Lady Amelia's blowpipe is the murder weapon," corrected the pathologist with a glance at the offending artifact. "Well, you'd better know that it's not the only candidate for that honor. This cane is hollow. Take the handle off and you've got a mouthpiece. I think this had better be tested for curare as well."

Just what he needed, thought Arbuthnot resentfully. Find one murder weapon and it turns out there's another. Worse, the cane, unlike the blowpipe, had been found in a place accessible to everyone in the house. With his damnable luck they'd both test positive for curare.

Or worse, they'd both test negative.

Jeavons stepped into the doorway and said in a lugubrious tone that somehow managed to convey the impression that this was the policeman's fault, "Chief Inspector, I regret to inform you that there is a corpse in the fountain. Again."

Two murder weapons. And now, two bodies.

EIGHT

What the Butler Saw

by Dorothy Cannell

"*H*AD a bad day, love?"

Arbuthnot sat in a dimly lit corner of The Three Horse-shoes pulling on his pipe that he had failed to light. The locals hovered round the bar as shadows from a bygone age. Their voices seeped his way and then retreated like the murmur of the sea at ebbtide. Smugglers . . . sea shanties . . . horse-shoes. Horseshoes for luck. And blast it all, luck was what he needed as never before! He had come—been sent—to Market Winsome like an old donkey put out to pasture. At first he had inwardly railed against those in command who had seen him as used up—done for—and even possibly as a liability. But then he had been lulled by the beauty of the countryside. By the daffodils peeking up in the garden at Mortmain Cottage, by so simple a thing as the milk bottles on his doorstep—on those days when they didn't stand too long in the sun—into thinking that what he had was a fresh start. He would make a success of things down here. And if he didn't go out with the flags flying it would at least be with his head up. Now there was this damnable case with all its inconsistencies and the accusation at the ready that he was allowing the bodies to pile up. Consuela. Beautiful Consuela. Sultry, sinuous and, until today, so vividly alive.

"You poor lamb. Must have been a really bad day. Want me to fetch you another pint of bitter?"

The voice came at him like a sledgehammer. But for all her false blondness and coy bosom the woman standing over him had a motherliness to her that swept Arbuthnot back to childhood days in the nursery where Nanny was always close at hand with words of comfort and the inevitable beaker of warm milk.

"Thank you. But I think I'll finish what's left in my glass and call it a night." He produced a strained but genuinely appreciative smile for the barmaid. Alice was her name. A downright good sort with the knack for being able to soothe any ruffled feathers among the locals before matters got out of hand.

"Not much good for business, you aren't." She placed her hands on her ample hips and scowled with just sufficient fierceness to let him know she was joking in an attempt to cheer him up. "Might as well close this place up if we get any more the likes of you. We've already got Sir Gerard as comes here when he's in these parts, and never touches a drop of what's good for you. Always lemonade for him." Her face softened, putting Arbuthnot further in mind of dear, long-departed Nanny. "Shouldn't be making jokes about him, I shouldn't. A proper gentleman if ever there was one. No surprise to me when I heard he was a war hero. Got it from Fred Lumpkin," Alice turned her blonde head and thumbed towards the bar, "him that's your Constable Nettle's uncle. Fred said Sir Gerard don't drink on account of seeing some of his officer pals go down the road to ruin, trying to drown out the pain of the injuries they was left with. Along with the memories of what they heard and saw when they was in the trenches. Doesn't bear thinking about, does it?" Alice bent to wipe off the table that didn't need wiping with a cloth pulled from her apron pocket. "A wonder more of the poor devils didn't end up in mental homes." Her voice receded. The words "Now you stay sitting comfortable, Chief Inspector" were sucked into the waves lapping against some distant shore. To be drowned completely by the sea shanties bellowing in hoarse delirium inside his head.

Arbuthnot's hands shook as he picked up his unlit pipe and stuck it back in his mouth. He had thought he had mastered the tremors along with being able to empty his mind at will of his father's hideous renditions of songs made the more vile by the fact that normal people clapped and danced to them in exuberant jollification. What would Alice—kindhearted, salt-of-the-earth Alice—think if she knew the truth about himself and the noble Sir Gerard? That they had met and come to know more about each other than either cared to remember in a ward at St. Benedict's. An institution euphemistically termed a convalescent home, where the windows were narrow strips of glass high against the ceiling, and the doors were kept locked because, as that angel-faced nurse with the worried eyes had always been careful to point out, "It wouldn't do for them to create a draught and cause any of the patients to catch a chill. Such a shame that would be, now wouldn't it, Reggie?"

Strange to think, Arbuthnot mused as he gazed around the dark polished coziness of The Three Horseshoes, that one of the worst things about that hellish three months at St. Benedict's had been being called Reggie by everyone from the ward maid on up to the head man. Dr. Edward Lestrada with his steepled fingers and his pinstriped suits, that infuriatingly gentle smile . . . and those dark hooded eyes that seemed to suck some damning revelation out of every second of silence. The Phoenix. Why did he think of The Phoenix when he remembered those sessions with Dr. Lestrada?

Arbuthnot put down his pipe and picked up his glass with its inch or two of remaining bitter. His hands were steady now. But that was only because he felt that old numbness creeping back. He had to fight against it. He had to focus . . . focus . . . tell himself that his mind was still his own. He would not allow it to be drowned out by the sea shanties. He had told Gerard Hawksmoor about them. Was that the reason he now so disliked the fellow? Would he have tolerated the man's amateur sleuthing with no more than a perfunctory contempt but for the memory of that night when they had been returned to the ward late at night confused and befuddled as to where they had been and what had transpired? They had sat crouched in the space between their beds, trying to put the pieces together. A long narrow room . . . instruments . . . voices. Dr. Lestrada's face—no— just his eyes. The rest was all mask. With him had been another man whose presence had added a measure of comfort to Arbuthnot. Here was a friend, a colleague of long standing, someone to be trusted. Sir Gerard had vehemently disagreed. A wolf in sheep's clothing . . . a subservient snake . . . a sewer rat, had been his rambling denouncement. Who? Who? The answer was as elusive now as it had been then.

"Chief Inspector?"

Arbuthnot roused himself to look up into Archie Nettle's good-looking, if not intellectual, visage. "Sit down, lad, for God's sake. You won't grow taller standing up."

"Well, I can't say as I mind taking a load off." The Constable eased himself into the seat on the other side of the table. "It's been a long and difficult day, you might say, and I could do with a pint if it's allowed, sir."

"Don't go 'sirring' me," Arbuthnot growled back at him. The Chief Inspector was mentally back where he belonged, on the job with his nose to the ground. It happened that way. One moment he was trapped in that other place where only patches of sharply delineated memory penetrated the fog that blew and swirled around him. Then all was sharp and clear once more. Or as clear as anything could be in life. "Have a beer, lad. Have two if it suits you."

"Thanks, Gov. Him that was here before you took over was always one to go on about—not during working hours. Easy for him to say; he was a teetotaler."

"Very creditable. But he's gone and I'm inclined to do things my way." Arbuthnot patted his jacket pocket and produced his tobacco pouch and a box of matches. Alice appeared with a foaming tankard and set it down at Constable Nettle's elbow.

"That's what I like," he said, "a woman as knows what I want without having to be told." There was something in his voice that caused Arbuthnot to look up sharply and survey him over the match flame before blowing it out.

"Think yourself quite a charmer with the ladies, eh, Nettle?"

"Oh, I wouldn't say that, sir."

"Wouldn't you, now? Why, that does sound modest

coming from the lad who is rumoured to have found favor, if only on the now and then, with the lovely Lady Amelia." Arbuthnot's eyes narrowed as he tamped more tobacco into the bowl of his pipe. The handsome, dark-haired constable was undoubtedly smirking.

"I've known her since she and me was children. If we wasn't from different stations in life she'd have married me like a shot. Oh, I'm not bitter about it, like. And," Constable Nettle's mouth thinned out, "I'm not going to apologise to you, sir, for what I've got going on away from the job with the woman as I loves."

"I asked you to stop 'sirring' me." Arbuthnot's voice was mild, but as he clamped the stem of his pipe between his teeth his thoughts were angry. This young jackanapes didn't know the meaning of love. All he knew was physical passion—the stirring of the senses in response to an attractive woman. Arbuthnot remembered his own reactions to the sight of Lady Amelia's rounded rump under the blue serge skirt as she had mounted the staircase at Castle Crawsbey and the even more powerful sensations evoked by the now deceased Consuela. He did not condemn himself for those responses. He was a man. A man who had been without a woman for several years now. But he did not confuse those feelings with love. The sort of love a husband feels for the wife who has lived with him, slept with him, shared all the best and worst of herself with him and uplifted him with her courage when illness confined her first to a bath chair and then to bed. Sophie! Beloved Sophie! When she could no longer talk she had spoken to him with her eyes. She had been dead only a few weeks when he had begun his investigation of what came to be known as the Dockside Murders. If Sophie had lived he would have talked the case over with her night after night until he had it straight in his head—such had always been their custom. And he might not afterwards have had to live with the terrible unease that he was responsible for sending an innocent man to the gallows. Arbuthnot took out his pipe and cleared his throat.

"What's that you say, Gov?" Archie was lolling back in his seat, his beer tankard positioned on an upraised knee. The very picture of nonchalance. Or was it insolence? Arbuthnot became convinced at that moment that he had seriously underestimated his subordinate. He could only hope that it would not prove to be a mistake anything near as costly as the one that had seen Froggie Nelson-Whyte hang.

"I didn't say anything. I was clearing my throat. But if you're eager for a word or two, harken to these. Do not allow your relationship with Lady Amelia to muck up this investigation any more than may already have occurred. Do I make myself indelibly clear? And for God's sake stop slouching."

"Sorry. I was trying to avoid catching my uncle's eye. He's over by the bar."

"So Alice mentioned before you came in."

"Jaws on and on, he does. All about nothing except when he's interfering, as is most of the time. And we don't want that, do we, sir? Not with already having too many fingers in the pie, like. That Major Hawskmoor trooping around the place acting like he's Sherlock Holmes come back to life."

"Twice might be considered improbable."

"Don't take your meaning, sir."

"Holmes already came back to life." Arbuthnot tapped out pipe ash in a brass bowl that served the purpose. "Surprised

you didn't know that, Nettle. I was picturing you and Lady
Amelia in the Library at Castle Crawsbey, chummily boning
up on Sir Arthur Conan Doyle."

"Them leather-bound books aren't for reading, they're
like for show. Not a penny dreadful among them, so Ammie
says." Constable Nettle displayed his impeccable teeth in
another of his superior smirks. "But I expect you're wanting
me to give you my report, Chief Inspector. Don't want to be
accused of dragging my heels. Wouldn't want to set your
nerves on edge when you're already under stress, what with
this second murder to think on."

He knows, Arbuthnot thought grimly. He knows about
St. Benedict's. That's what's different about him. That's why
he's taken off his dim-witted yokel smock and is letting me
glimpse the real Archie Nettle. He didn't know yesterday,
or earlier today. So who's talked to him? Forget about that for
the moment. What's important is not to let the bugger know
he's got under my skin. "Let's have it then, Constable—the
report. Did you follow my instructions?"

"The ones you gave me as you was leaving Castle
Crawsbey after Dr. Frobisher had finished examining the
body and arrangements was being made for its removal?"
Nettle was back to sounding dim-witted. "That I did, sir.
Followed them to the letter. There'll be two men watching
the house and grounds around the clock. Called in reinforcements from Winsome-Under-Ware, Winsome St. John,
and Winsome-le-Hatch, I did. Just like you wanted. Told
the Dowager Duchess you'd be back to talk with everyone
again in the morning if you didn't come back tonight. I
explained it had been a busy of days for you and can't go
overdoing things given you're at an age where your health
could be a problem."

Arbuthnot's vision blurred. A pulse was beating in his neck. It took every ounce of strength he had not to uncurl his fingers and fasten his hands around Nettle's despicable neck. God help Lady Amelia if she thought the man was dancing to the strings she pulled. And God help England if The Phoenix rose from the ashes. Where had that thought come from? The answer, if there was one, was drowned out by the ever-increasing eruption of sea shanties inside his head.

"YOU knocked, madam?" Jeavons spoke with commendable aplomb given the fact that he was not in the habit of receiving nocturnal visits from young ladies, attractive or otherwise, when he was about to remove his dressing gown and climb into bed. It was a handsome dressing gown presented to him by the late Duke, shortly before that regrettable hunting accident. Regrettable because it had not been seen at the time—or since—for what it was. Murder most foul.

"Oh, how cute you look." C. B. Brandon, otherwise known as Cecily Barbara when she wasn't introducing herself as the newlywed Duchess of Faughstrayne, closed the door behind her and tiptoed towards the abashed butler.

"Cute is not a word that frequents my vocabulary, madam." Jeavons looked longingly towards his socks that he had placed on top of the used linen basket, because he had been in two minds as to whether it would be acceptable for a man of his position in the Castle Crawsbey household to wear them one more day. He would have felt more adequately dressed had he been wearing his socks. Bare feet had always been, in Jeavons' view, a vulgarity that one was forced to accept along with original sin.

"Madam?" Cecily kept coming towards him until he had

no choice but to hop onto the bed to avoid physical contact. "Shouldn't you say 'Your Grace'?"

"I would not betray my loyalty to the Faughstrayne family by addressing a wicked," Jeavons' voice spiraled upward, "truly wicked imposter by that noble address."

"What else could I do but come up with a lie that would give me an excuse to stay on here at the castle?" The outrageous American girl perched herself on the edge of the bed and crossed her legs, displaying more thigh than Jeavons had yet witnessed in a lifetime of service to his betters. And that given the fact that the late Duke had offered a particular hospitality upon occasion to females who were not ladies—titled or otherwise.

"I must ask you to leave this apartment on the instant, or I shall find it necessary to pull the bell rope above that bed post," Jeavons pointed a trembling finger, "and summon the footman on duty to come to my assistance."

"Oh, why do you have to be such an old crosspatch!" Cecily nibbled at a pearly pink fingernail. "You're the only one I can turn to, the only one who might possibly understand why I did it. You do recognise me, don't you?"

"You have me completely at a loss, miss."

This was bad. She had been demoted even from "madam". But he had yet to reach for the bell rope. "You mean you really haven't guessed? I was so sure that my eyes would give me away. There was no way to change them from blue to brown. Everything else was easy. The black wig! The skin-darkening lotion! When I looked in the mirror I hardly recognized myself. Of course, being an actress helped. Even so, my voice might have given me away. But playing a foreigner simplified things. The English consider those from other countries to be automatically inferior. I think it's rather sweet, really. Anyway, it wasn't hard to convey by a few grunts that I understood the language but didn't speak it."

"You . . . you," Jeavons' voice quavered. "You were Lewis."

Cecily nodded. "Until it seemed sensible not to be him anymore. And I can't really say I was sorry. That stuff I put on my skin itched and I began to wonder if certain parts of my upper body would ever recover from being bound up for hours on end. Oh, I can see I am shocking you, Mr. Jeavons, but when I explain everything I know you will be fully in sympathy with my acting such a low-brow part. And given your own responsibility in the matter."

"My what?" Jeavons recoiled deeper inside his dressing gown while his cheeks paled and his hair stood up on end.

"Well, it was you that kept in regular touch with Duke Dudley, so he properly had the wind put up him that nasty doings were afoot at Castle Crawsbey. But we'll get to Duds in a minute, because it strikes me I should start at the beginning. And that's with Mother, who was married to Daddy B., as he likes me to call him. He's not really my father, the poor precious. But he wishes he were. And of course he was devoted to darling Mother. She was the most beautiful creature you ever saw. Your Lady Amelia pales to an insignificant drab in comparison." Cecily emphasized this point with a most unladylike sniff. "Poor Daddy B., he believed right until the end that he was married—properly married to Mother."

"And he wasn't?" Jeavons consoled himself that he was having a nightmare—the result of partaking cheese before bedtime.

"How could he be when she was already married? The Duke was still alive, you see, when Mother lay on her death-bed. We are talking about seven years ago, you understand.

And there had been no divorce. That's the part Daddy B. took so hard when Mother confessed all to him within hours of her passing. He just couldn't take it in when she told him that she had always hoped that her noble Duke would come for her and his children."

"His what?" Jeavons could not handle these revelations, true or false, with any semblance of equanimity without a stiff drink. He slid as gracefully as a man of his years could do off the bed and set a saucepan on the wood stove in the corner of the room. A cup of very thick hot chocolate was surely what Dr. Frobisher, so dutiful in his visits to Castle Crawsbey, would advise.

"His offspring. Perhaps that is a better way of putting it." Cecily watched him stir the contents of the saucepan. "For even at that time my brother and I were no longer children. But I can see, Mr. Jeavons, that you are still very much confused. What happened is that Mother and the Duke met when they were young enough to be wildly romantic, poor sweets. His family was against their marrying because hers was in trade or some such nonsense. So what could they do but elope to Gretna Green? It was all quite legal, and Mother had the marriage certificate to prove it. They planned to break the news to his parents upon their return. But fate was against them. The old Duke—my grandfather I suppose I have to call him—had suffered a heart attack, and it was feared that the least upset would produce another. Mother agreed to keep the marriage secret. Time passed and Grandfather refused either to die or get well. It must have been a terribly trying time for everyone. But worse was to come. And I'm sure," Cecily sat on the bed grinding her pearly teeth, "that you know what I'm talking about, Mr. Jeavons."

"A marriage was arranged between the now Dowager

Duchess, formerly Daisy Digby, and . . ." The butler stared austerely into his saucepan.

"My mother's husband. Can you imagine anything more outrageous? Well, I can. It's that he somehow managed to convince Mother that he'd had no choice because Daisy was—preggers, I think you call it—with Duds, as it turned out, and she'd have seen him dead if he hadn't shown up at the church with a ring in his pocket. Mother went to America for a while, but she couldn't stay away from her one true love. She put pride aside and came for visits to Castle Crawsbey. Visits," Cecily took the cup of hot chocolate Jeavons handed her and set it on the trunk at the foot of the bed, "that resulted in me and, a few years later, my brother."

"Your mother's name?"

"Elizabeth—Lizzie. Maiden name—Muire."

"Ah, yes." Jeavons inclined his head. "I recall her well. She was, as you described, a great beauty. And if it is any comfort to you, I always considered her to be the late Duke's favourite mistress. Always roses in her room upon her arrival and boxes of French chocolates that were particularly to her taste."

"But do you believe me that they were really married?"

"Did you bring the marriage certificate with you?"

"It is in a safe place. Ready to be produced when the time is right."

"Then for the moment I neither believe or disbelieve."

"I suppose I had better tell you what came next. After Mother's death, that is. Daddy B. was all broken up. There were times when my brother and I wondered if he'd gone and lost his mind.

"But Whitchell and I couldn't help being curious as two cats about our real father and the old ancestral hole back in jolly old England. We'd been brought up in America almost from day one, never thinking of ourselves as aristocrats. And I can see you're busy taking that in, Mr. Jeavons, while you pretend to drink your cocoa. It can't be easy to accept the fact that Whitchell—not Duds—is the current Duke. Not being a completely unfeelinged pair, we realized that our appearance on the scene could be a mighty big blow for all concerned, so I persuaded Whitchell to let me take charge. I hired us a private detective, truth be told I hired us several because, although there was no difficulty in providing us with information about Dowager Daisy and daughter Amelia, there was no word to be had about Dudley other than he was believed to be off in foreign parts. And for some reason—call it blood being thicker than water, Whitchell and I weren't comfortable taking Castle Crawsbey by storm until we had made contact with our half-brother who, through no fault of his own, believed himself to be the Duke. Just when we had about given up hope a few months back—the detective we had hired a few days previously got in touch to say that he'd found the man we were looking for in Brazil—near Minas Gerais. Whitchell couldn't abandon his studies to go with me, which was tough, because we've always supported each other in everything. But meeting Dudley . . . dear Duds wasn't anything near as harrowing as I'd expected. It took a while for me to explain the situation to him . . ."

"So I would imagine," intoned Jeavons.

"But when he had everything clear in his dear head, he expressed relief that he wasn't after all to be saddled with the title and the old ancestral pile. What mostly occupied his mind were those letters you so faithfully sent him. What worried him most of all were the rumours that his friend Sir Gerard Hawksmoor had become addicted to morphine.

Duds assured me that it couldn't be true, that Gerry, as he called him, just wasn't the type. Someone had to be intent on smearing his good character. But to what purpose?"

"To destroy his credibility would be my suggestion." Jeavons had forgotten his embarrassing bare feet. "Sir Gerard is a gentleman of exceedingly high intellect, if I may be permitted the assertion. He was also regarded, until these recent slanders, to be above reproach in his habits and character. I have known him since he was a boy. And it has grieved me to suspect that he is at the mercy of some dangerous enemy—or enemies—determined to bring about his downfall. I believed it to be my duty to state my suspicions in my letters to the Duke, as I will still call him for the time being. You may think me guilty of disloyalty when I say that he was always somewhat lacking in bottom, as it was called in my youth, and it did not surprise me that my missives did not result in his return to England. His friendship for Sir Gerard is sincere. I doubt not that he feels for him greatly in this matter while continuing to spend his time playing at unearthing Lost Civilizations and accepting as his due the attentions of every passably attractive female who happens his way."

"Lady Amelia—I really can't think of her as my half-sister," Cecily curled her lip, "said in her mother's presence as well as mine that Duds is a homosexual. You don't think she would have said the same sort of thing to that Chief Inspector?" Her face paled and her periwinkle-blue eyes widened. "That could mean he could be arrested if he returns to England. Homosexuality is a criminal offense, isn't it?"

"Tut! Tut!" Jeavons shuddered and tightened the belt of his dressing gown. "Let's not talk about it, other than to say that I believe myself in a position to assure you that Lady

Amelia is of a devious disposition, and the Duke has never displayed a partiality for a certain kind of interaction with men in any walk of life. A certain footman left Castle Crawsbey having taken umbrage not at any advances made to him, but for the lack thereof."

"Oh, I'm so glad!" Cecily dimpled at him. "That you don't like Lady Amelia any more than I do, for I am quite persuaded that she is absolutely wrong for Sir Gerard. Well, to bring things up to date. After I left Duds I told the detective to start fishing around to see if there really was something that didn't seem right going on. With a connection to Sir Gerard Hawksmoor, who was a frequent visitor to Market Winsome and, in particular, Castle Crawsbey. And he came back to me with the strangest piece of information. It seemed there was this man, an American that went under all sorts of assumed names, who was planning to show up here pretending to be Daddy B. with a fake Whitchell in tow. Can you imagine how that put my head in a spin? Could it be that someone was out to ruin my family's reputation in conjunction with Sir Gerard? Let me tell you, my blood was up. I came with the detective to England and, upon discovering that a new servant was due to arrive shortly before the supposed Admiral Ceebee Brandon put in his appearance, we arranged a surprise meeting with the boy and, just like I already told you, I entered Castle Crawsbey as Lewis. I'd made up my mind not to draw any unnecessary attention to myself, but when "the Admiral" was about to put on that uniform it seemed to me like sacrilege, Mr. Jeavons, and I pretended to accidentally pour that coconut oil pomade over it so he couldn't wear it. Afterwards I took the bottle to my room, hoping it would provide some clue as to its owner. But in my rush to get away I left it behind."

"And was spilling the Cumberland sauce down Lady Amelia's white gown also an accident?"

"Believe me or not, Mr. Jeavons, it was. If you remember, Sir Gerard was seated directly across from her and, when I realized who he was and looked at him, the jug just slipped in my hand." Cecily Barbara Brandon rose from the bed and walked towards the window, to stand looking out at the night with eyes misted with tears. "It was like I'd read about in books, but never thought happened to real people. Love at first sight. That's how it seemed to me at that moment. But perhaps I'd loved him all along from listening to Duds talk about him. Whatever way it was, I won't let Lady Amelia sink her fangs into him. I swear I'll die if need be to save him from her and another dozen enemies." She stepped suddenly back from the window to clutch at Jeavons's arm. "There's someone out in the garden; whoever it was just disappeared behind that beech tree."

WITH a feeling of inexpressible relief, Arbuthnot had bidden Constable Nettle good-night outside The Three Horseshoes. His intention had been to make his way directly to Mortmain Cottage, but his feet walked him towards Castle Crawsbey. He had to talk with Sir Gerard, however late the hour. He had to explain that the memory of sending his friend Froggie Nelson-Whyte to the gallows had resulted in his not having the stomach to press Squiffy Frobisher for an explanation as to why he had been on the "Admiral's" list of "partners." And whether the appointment noted thereon had in fact taken place. If this case were ever to be solved, Arbuthnot knew he had to call a truce with Sir Gerard or it would destroy them both. The stars spangled the sky like diamonds scattered from a broken necklace. The air was softly warm and fresh from the storm. But tonight he had no thoughts for the wonders of nature. Deep in thought, he was walking up the drive to Castle Crawsbey when he caught a whiff of tobacco. Not from a pipe or a cigarette. More like a cheap cigar favored by the sort of man who wore flashy suits and fake diamond cuff links. Someone stepped out from behind the dark shape of a beech tree to take hold of his arm and murmur in silken tones in his ear, "What a happy surprise, meeting you again, Chief Inspector. Shall we take a gentle stroll in the direction of the pool, in order to admire the fountain and the statues?"

NINE

Blackmail!

by Deborah Crombie

"DA Silva!" Chief Inspector Reginald Arbuthnot whirled around, his heart thumping dangerously in his chest. "What the deuce are you doing here, creeping about in the garden like some Transylvanian native?"

"There is no law against walking in the garden in the moonlight, Chief Inspector," Da Silva said smoothly. "And I must admit I was restless. Could it be that I am not alone in my need of a calming influence?"

"I've no idea what you're talking about." Arbuthnot's irritation, which had been simmering since his chat with Nettle in The Three Horseshoes, threatened to boil over into outright rage.

"You jumped like a startled colt, Mr. Arbuthnot. But then, perhaps one's nerves are not what they were before the war."

It seemed to Arbuthnot that Da Silva's glance was as sly and knowing as Archie Nettle's—surely the man couldn't have learned the truth about St. Benedict's, as well? And if so, who had told him? "Mmmph," he answered, determined to ignore the inference. "Who wouldn't be nervous, Mr. Da Silva, with bodies turning up as common as kippers for breakfast? And where were you, for the matter, when the foreign lady turned up her toes in the fountain this afternoon? I had my constable search the house and the grounds for you."

"I had to run up to London to attend to some . . . business, Chief Inspector. Nothing to do with matters here at Castle Crawsbey, I assure you." Da Silva puffed out a great cloud of smoke from his cigar, and Arbuthnot coughed. "Unfortunately, my tobacconist had sold his entire stock of Cuban cigars to a woman with a Russian accent, but that is beside the point. I was as distressed as you when I arrived this evening to learn that the lovely Consuela was dead."

The progress of their stroll across the grounds had taken them to the fountain itself. Arbuthnot saw again the body of the Latin beauty, lashed upside-down to the one-eyed Nelson in a parody of an embrace by a woman's white evening gown, the carp nibbling happily at the floating mass of her dark hair.

"A fine woman," Da Silva continued, gazing into the now-empty depths of the fountain. "With a figure like that, one could almost forgive her affinity for blackmail."

"Blackmail? Consuela? Surely you're mistaken, man. If she were a blackmailer, why would she pretend to be married to the Duke?"

"All a ruse to cover her real activities. She was in league with the man who called himself Ceebee—in fact, she may have even been his wife. They were both blackmailers of the first order."

"But the treasure—"

"Don't tell me that a man of your experience and stature was taken in by the Lost Civilization tale, Inspector. A child's ploy, invented in haste to distract your attention from the secrets of Ceebee's victims."

Why, indeed, thought Arbuthnot, should he have believed the solicitor, Benfleet, with his nervous air and ill-fitting suits? Anyone could see that the man was besotted with Lady Amelia—could Benfleet have invented the story to protect her? And what proof was there, other than Benfleet's word? The golden statue supposedly sent from South America by Dudley as proof had vanished without a trace.

"How do you know so much about it, then, Mr. Da Silva? In their confidence, were you?" Arbuthnot regarded the other man's sleek hair with suspicion. No dependable person would use so much pomade. And what was that awful, sweet smell? You'd think the man had been rolling in cheap perfume. Arbuthnot felt himself flushing as he followed that thought to its logical conclusion. Perhaps *that* was what Da Silva had been doing in London.

"I heard them here in the garden that night, Chief Inspector. They were arguing about how best to persuade the Dowager Duchess that they meant business."

"You're saying they were blackmailing the Duchess? Whatever for? Why, Daisy Digby is as fine a woman as you could meet. Struggling to keep up this crumbling pile" —he gestured at the dark bulk of the castle, looming behind them— "with no help from that wastrel of a son." Arbuthnot couldn't help but think of the Dowager Duchess's handsome features and regal bearing. He liked to think that if his Sophie had been born to wealth and position—and if she hadn't been confined to a wheelchair, of course—she would have matured as gracefully as the former Daisy Digby.

"She may be a fine woman, Chief Inspector, but she's not a duchess," Da Silva told him with an air of satisfaction. "Somehow Ceebee found out that the Duke's marriage was never legal. He and Consuela meant to reveal all unless the Duchess paid up. Overhearing that little tidbit saved me from making a costly mistake, I can tell you."

"What are you talking about, man?" Arbuthnot's eyes watered as the soft, evening breeze cloaked him momentarily in a haze of cigar smoke and perfume.

"The Dowager Duchess invited me here this weekend to woo me, Chief Inspector, and I was inclined to let her succeed. She wanted my money; I wanted her title. An equitable arrangement, don't you think?" Da Silva's smile was sly. "Except that she has no title. So the deal's off, as they say in America."

"Not married to the Duke? But that's impossible!"

"Not if the Duke had a prior marriage, unacknowledged."

"But the Dowager Duchess would be ruined. And the children, Dudley and Amelia—" Arbuthnot stopped, chilled to his very marrow by a sudden thought. If this dreadful thing were true, Dudley and Amelia would be illegitimate, without an inheritance. On the list he'd found in the late "Admiral's" possession, the Dowager Duchess had been shown as making a partial payment, but Lady Amelia had paid in full. Did that mean she'd known about the blackmail as well? And if so, what else would she have done to save her name and her position in the world?

While Lady Amelia might be quite happy to make a fool of Constable Nettle, Arbuthnot couldn't imagine her settling down in Nettle's cottage in Market Winsome as a constable's wife.

And what about Dudley? Did he know, too? It was Dudley, after all, who had sent Amelia the Peruvian blowpipe—might it have been accompanied by instructions to kill anyone who threatened their security?

His head reeling from the implications, Arbuthnot grasped Da Silva by the shoulder. "Tell me exactly what you overheard!"

Smoothly, Da Silva shrugged away Arbuthnot's clutching hand and brushed at the shoulder of his evening jacket. "Please, Chief Inspector. There is no need for violence." He relit his cigar and puffed a few clouds of blue smoke into the air, while Arbuthnot ground his teeth in impatience.

"It was after dinner yesterday evening. I had been having a little tête-a-tête with Lady Amelia behind the yew hedge, and I must admit I was asking myself if the daughter would be a better investment than the mother."

Arbuthnot felt himself flushing. The sheer effrontery of the man, speaking of the Dowager Duchess and Lady Amelia as if they were prize cattle! He forced himself to hold his tongue, however.

"When Lady Amelia pleaded a headache and retired to the house—still wearing my sash draped jauntily across her shoulders—I decided on another turn around the garden. As I was coming back along the hedge, I heard voices coming from the direction of the fountain. At first I thought it was Lady Amelia, talking to another man. But then, as I came nearer, I realized the man and woman were arguing, and that the woman's voice was accented. I stopped and peered through a gap in the yews." Da Silva paused and pointed at a darker gap in the hedge.

"I could tell by the uniform that it was the 'Admiral'. The woman in the white evening dress, however, was someone I had never seen before, a dark and fiery beauty. She was furious! 'You will ruin everything,' she spat at him, 'with your drinking and your foolishness. No one will believe you are really Brandon!' She went on to say that they must go cautiously with the Duchess, that Her Grace had powerful friends who would help her keep the Duke's bigamy a secret. But Brandon just laughed at her. 'Daisy Digby won't do a thing as long as I have the brooch,' he told her. 'If the truth came out about that, the Duchess would have more to worry about than losing her title.'

Arbuthnot remembered the diamond and emerald brooch in the shape of a phoenix he'd found among Ceebee's possessions. "Why should the Dowager Duchess have been frightened of a brooch?"

"I didn't hear any more, I'm afraid," Da Silva answered. "The woman—Consuela—seemed to hear something. She was off towards the house like a startled hare. I followed her—I must admit I was curious—but once inside the house, there was no sign of her."

"She must have disappeared into the secret room," Arbuthnot mused. "But look here." He fixed Da Silva with a suspicious glare. "If you knew all this about Consuela, why didn't you say something when she came forward claiming to be the Duke's wife?"

"It was amusing to see everyone running around like your proverbial chickens, Chief Inspector. Especially the Duchess, as she had tried to cheat me. How was I to know anyone would be harmed by it?"

"There was already one dead body! You've willfully impeded a police investigation, Mr. Da Silva, and in so doing, you may very well have been responsible for Consuela's death." Arbuthnot's fury rose another notch. "And another

thing. If this Lost Civilization story is bollocks, then Brandon tried to blackmail you, too. Your name was on his list."
Enrique Da Silva—flat refusal, the list had stated.

Da Silva's eyes flashed. "So he did! And I told him to go to hell, Chief Inspector, even before I heard the truth about the Duchess. He threatened to reveal my . . . history . . . with the Countess. Now," Da Silva added speculatively, relighting his foul cigar, "there you have someone with a great deal to lose."

"The Countess?"

"Katerina Boronskaya, she calls herself." Da Silva gave a snort of derision. "That woman is no more descended from royalty than I am. Her family were Russian peasants, potato farmers. She's made her living these many years by trading on a myth—a myth built on a few second-hand evening gowns, some bits of paste jewelry, and a strategically placed tattoo picked up in a back street in St. Petersburg. I was taken in myself, for a time."

"And then what happened?" asked Arbuthnot, fascinated in spite of himself.

"I was flattered by her attentions, at first. My interests in the silver mine had just come in, and I had not yet time to develop a proper cynicism about such things. But little things began to raise my suspicions: the rifling of my wallet, my jewelry case, her disappearances at odd times of day and night. Then, one day I followed her, saw her handing over my cufflinks to some sailors at the wharf, then screeching at them like a fishwife when they didn't pay her what she'd expected."

"Sailors? The Countess—I mean Madam Boronskaya— had a connection with sailors?" Arbuthnot shook his head like a horse trying to dislodge a blowfly, but the faint, whistled melody persisted.

"An intimate connection, I would say." Da Silva gave him an evil smile, his teeth still clamped tightly on his cigar. "Now, if you will excuse me, Chief Inspector, I believe I've inhaled enough fresh air for one evening." Saluting Arbuthnot with his cigar, Da Silva made off towards the house.

Arbuthnot stared after him. The jaunty strains of a sea shanty seemed to come from all round him now. He grasped his head between his hands, trying to shut out the damned whistling. By God, he must be going mad. Utterly mad. And there was only one person who would understand.

SIR Gerard Hawksmoor settled himself more firmly in the leather armchair positioned just under the lamp in the library alcove. The night was stifling; only the occasional breath of air moved the heavy draperies at the sides of the open windows. He had his book open in his lap, a fresh cup of tea resting on the side table, but he found himself unable to concentrate on the mysteries of Stonehenge. This damnable case was driving him to distraction.

It had been he who had discovered Consuela's body in the fountain. He'd thought himself inured to the face of death, after the many horrors he had seen in the trenches of France, but the sight of such a beautiful woman, bound upside down, her hair floating like seaweed, her skin bleached to the pallid hue of some undersea creatures—well, it didn't bear thinking of. And, even worse, she had been exposed, her colorful Spanish skirt falling down over her upper body in a sodden mass.

It had taken all his self-control to leave her as she was while he went back to the house to ring the police. Lady

Amelia had found him in the hall and had immediately known, something was wrong.

"Oh. Gerry," she'd gasped, her hand going to her throat in the gesture that made his heart ache, "what is it? Not another—"

"I'm afraid so, my dear." He took her hand, gently. "It's Consuela. In the fountain. I've rung for Chief Inspector Arbuthnot, and sent Jeavons to guard the body until the police get here."

Lady Amelia gave a little moan and slumped against him, but just for an instant he thought he'd glimpsed something unexpected in her eyes—a certain hardness—or had it even been . . . satisfaction? Thinking back on it, he doubted his own perceptions, and it was that that bothered him more than anything.

Had he let his long-standing feelings for Amelia cloud his judgment? There was the matter of the blowpipe in her possession, after all. He supposed he could understand Amelia killing Consuela, with the woman's claim to be Dudley's wife, but why would Amelia have killed Ceebee? On the other hand, if Amelia had murdered Consuela, why lash her body to the fountain with her own dress? For Amelia had identified the white evening gown as her own, the one she'd worn the night of the Admiral's death. When Hawksmoor had questioned her as to its whereabouts in the interim, she gazed at him blankly.

"Why, I'd assumed the maid took it be cleaned," she'd told him demurely, and he couldn't very well admit he hadn't found it when he'd been snooping among her soiled linen. "Why would anyone use my dress? My dress . . ." she'd murmured in horror, and he'd felt even more a cad.

He'd left the harassed Chief Inspector Arbuthnot to deal

with the body and had undertaken to question the household maids himself. None of them admitted having removed the white evening dress stained with Cumberland sauce from Lady Amelia's bedroom. So either Amelia was lying, or someone else had taken the garment. His tea cooled beside him as that thought led him to recall Lewis, the singularly inept servant.

The drapes framing the French windows suddenly billowed out, and into the Library stumbled Chief Inspector Reginald Arbuthnot. He was perspiring heavily, and he ran a hand distractedly through his thinning hair. "Hawksmoor! Thank God you're here."

"What is it?" Hawksmoor pulled himself half out of the chair. "Not another—"

"No. But that fellow Da Silva's been telling me the most remarkable tale." Arbuthnot collapsed into a nearby chair, looking round as if missing something. "You wouldn't happen to have—"

"Sorry." Hawksmoor raised his cup in apology. "Nothing stronger than cold tea, I'm afraid."

"Never mind." Arbuthnot settled back with a sigh. "Would you believe that the Duchess isn't a duchess? And the Countess isn't a countess?" He proceeded to relate the details of his interview with Da Silva to Hawksmoor.

"Ah," Hawksmoor mused when he'd finished. "I never did set too much store by stories of lost treasure. If Da Silva can be believed, that explains a few things, and it ties in with what I've learned." He held up a hand to forestall Arbuthnot. "No, I haven't deliberately been withholding information from you. Jeavons only came to see me this evening. It seems that recent events have been a bit much for the poor old chap, with having to stand guard over the lovely Consuela's body proving the last straw. He was afraid that the demise of one claimant to title of Duchess would cast suspicion on the other—"

"Little Cecily Brandon?" Arbuthnot frowned. "The girl has no alibi for her activities this morning."

"Nor does anyone else, except for Da Silva, who was seen by one of the servants to leave the house just after breakfast this morning." Hawksmoor studied the Chief Inspector for a moment, then came to a decision. "It seems that Cecily Brandon was less than honest with you. She's not the wife of the current Duke, who is actually illegitimate. She is, in fact, Dudley's half-sister, and she and her brother are heirs to this estate." As Arbuthnot goggled at him, Hawksmoor told the girl's story as Jeavons had told it to him, discreetly omitting the part about Cecily and Jeavons seeking to salvage his, Hawksmoor's, reputation. Even now he felt touched at the girl's defense of him.

"Well, I'll be buggered," Arbuthnot said coarsely, rubbing at his face in consternation. "The little minx. I'll have her into the station first thing in the morning for obstructing my investigation, and God knows what else. If she could lie about one thing—"

"Begging your pardon, Reggie," Hawksmoor interrupted diplomatically, "but it might be better to handle Cecily Brandon with solicitous encouragement. There are several questions left unanswered by her statement, and I had hoped that if I gained her confidence, she might reveal the truth to me.

"First, if she was masquerading as Lewis, why did she leave the castle? She told you she didn't know the false Admiral was dead until she saw the notice in the newspaper, but that was part of her pose as the young Duke's wife."

"And why did the girl faint when she saw the body?" Arbuthnot mused. "She said 'That's not my father,' but according to what she told Jeavons, she already knew that the Admiral was an imposter."

"That brings us to a matter of utmost importance, and one in which Miss Brandon may not be of any assistance. Who was this man who pretended to be Admiral Brandon?"

"Consuela could have told us—"

"But Consuela is conveniently no longer with us. She—" Hawksmoor stopped, listening. His keen ears had caught the faintest line of melody, borne into the stuffy confines of the Library on the sultry July breeze. "Did you hear that?" he asked his companion, but Arbuthnot had gone white as parchment, then a shocking shade of puce.

"Sea shanties," he whispered hoarsely. "Someone's trying to drive me mad." He grasped Hawksmoor's arm. "But who would know? For God's sake, man! You didn't tell anyone?"

Hawksmoor gently removed his arm from the Chief Inspector's beefy hand. "Of course not, Reggie. What happened in those dark nights at St. Benedict's remains between us alone."

"Someone knows," Arbuthnot insisted. "And someone's told Archie Nettle, just today. He was mocking me tonight in the pub, the two-faced snake."

"Constable Nettle!" Hawksmoor saw again Nettle's dark head bent over Lady Amelia's as he whispered in her ear, and he felt an uncharacteristic irrational rush of fury. For a moment he focused on the meditation technique he had learned on his sojourn to India, then he spoke more calmly. "Nettle was a good soldier. But for all that, I have to admit that there were times when I saw a certain . . . slyness . . . in his behavior . . . times when I doubted the altruism of his motives. I believe Nettle would use any untoward information that came his way to his advantage, but who could have told him about your . . . um . . . difficulties . . . with sea shanties?"

"There's some link between what's happened here at Crawsbey Castle and our time in hospital, Sir Gerry." Arbuthnot leaned forward, hands on his knees, his blunt face intent. "And that connection is buried somewhere in my brain, if only I could remember what it was . . ."

THE storm rolled through in the early hours of the morning. Mortmain Cottage shook as with the blows of celestial hammers, and flashes of lightning lit the leaded casements with blue fire.

In Reggie Arbuthnot's sweat-soaked, restless dreams, the intermittent blaze of light became the fierce glare of a spotlight, trained on his hospital bed. There was pain, then the cessation of pain, and a soothing voice. He knew he would do anything the voice told him, because the voice had the power to halt his torment. Still, some part of his mind remained unscathed, and he knew he must make out the face behind the voice. But the light blinded him, and if he sometimes caught the shape of a nose, the outline of a chin, the pieces refused to fit together in a coherent whole.

He woke at dawn, unrefreshed, haunted by the images of his dreams. Nothing that a good cup of tea wouldn't fix, he told himself resolutely as he washed and dressed, but when he opened the door of the cottage to the rainwashed morn, he discovered that the storm had smashed his milk bottles.

* * *

ARBUTHNOT arrived at the dank halls of the mortuary in a foul temper. If the truth be told, he found Squiffy Frobisher's incessant jolliness hard to take in the best of circumstances, but without his morning cuppa, it was well-nigh unbearable.

"What ho, Chief Inspector?" Frobisher said cheerfully as he threw back the sheet covering the body of the late Consuela.

Blanching, Arbuthnot breathed hard through his nose. "For heaven's sake, Squiffy, how can you be in such a good humor when this poor woman is lying on a slab?"

"She's not a woman to me any longer," Frobisher explained. "She's a challenge. And I have to tell you, Chief Inspector, that this one threw me for a bit."

"Curare again?"

"So I assumed. It seems the logical choice, does it not? She was killed in an exposed place where someone could have come along at any moment—"

"Because the blowpipe can be used from a distance?" Arbuthnot nodded. "But someone still had to tie her to the fountain."

"They choked her, first." Frobisher handed the Chief Inspector a ceramic dish in which several bright blue beads rolled like balls in a pinball game. "I found these strung on a bit of thread, lodged quite firmly in her throat."

"Turquoise . . ." Arbuthnot said softly, nudging the beads with a fingertip. "Like the beads we found near the 'Admiral's' body. How very odd . . ."

HER secret should be safe for a little longer, thought Cecily Barbara Brandon as she opened her bedroom door and peered out into the hall. She had agreed that Jeavons could tell Sir Gerard, if he felt he must, and she would have to trust to Sir Gerard's discretion. He'd been mum at breakfast that morning; but then hardly anyone had uttered a peep, what with being upset over yesterday's events.

Cecily shuddered. Not that she had *liked* that awful trollop, Consuela, but she hadn't wished her dead. And certainly not dead like that, her lower limbs bared for all the world to see, her face beneath the rank green water. And all in broad daylight! Such daring argued for a callous and fearless killer—were any of them safe?

A rumbling, gurgling sound made her start. She held her hand to her throat, her heart hammering, but after a moment she realized it was only the repercussions from one of the toilets flushing. Even by British standards, the plumbing at Castle Crawsbey left much to be desired.

Cecily took a deep breath to steady herself and continued down the corridor. She wasn't going to let fear of a stalking killer stop her from doing what she could to solve this mystery, and the next thing on her agenda was to see what she could learn about that slimy solicitor, Benfleet. He was in cahoots with the Dowager Duchess and Lady Amelia, of that she was sure, but just what were they all hiding?

Earlier that morning, she'd gone to the Dowager Duchess's suite, hoping to do a bit of snooping around. Getting no answer to her knock, she'd opened the door quietly and stepped inside. There was no one in the sitting room, but as she peeped into the bedroom, she saw the Duchess rummaging frantically through a chest of drawers.

Her back was to Cecily, but some sound must have alerted her for she turned with a start, the color draining from her face. "You! What are you doing here?"

To Cecily it seemed that the older woman's outrage was

tinged with relief. Had she been expecting someone else? "Oh, I'm so sorry, Your Grace. I was looking for your maid. It's just that I had a little problem with my bath." Putting on her brightest smile, she inched forward to get a better look at the chest of drawers. "Is there something I could help you with?"

"Oh, no," the Duchess had said, hastily closing the drawers. "It's nothing. Just a scarf I've misplaced." She gave Cecily an equally bright and equally false smile, but at least that was an improvement over her previously frosty demeanor. Cecily knew that the Dowager Duchess, like most of the snooty Brits, thought her stupid because of her accent. Well, if they didn't know the value of a Bryn Mawr education, she wasn't going to enlighten them. Being thought dimwitted just might play to her advantage.

The Dowager Duchess had then proceeded to ring for tea in her sitting room, and had politely and mercilessly pumped Cecily for information about Dudley. Cecily had obligingly mooned and swooned over "dear Duddy" without revealing anything of importance, and all the while her sympathy for the poor boy grew more pronounced.

Who could blame him for staying as far away from this mausoleum as he could? God knew she didn't want anything to do with the place, now that she'd seen it, and she didn't think Whitchell would, either.

Once the tea and small talk had been exhausted, the Dowager Duchess had still seemed reluctant for Cecily to leave. Cecily came to the conclusion that not only was the woman desperately worried about something she'd lost or misplaced, but that she was quite simply afraid of being alone.

Cecily, however, had worries other than the Duchess's

nerves. Although the tale she'd told Chief Inspector Arbuthnot about her father having gone missing from his Southampton hotel had been entirely fabricated, her father was, in fact, missing.

After the false Admiral's murder, she'd made a transatlantic telephone call to Annapolis, only to be informed by the houseboy that her father had not returned home for several days. Nor did any of the Admiral's friends and colleagues know where he might be. He had not packed a bag or left word with anyone, as far as Cecily had been able to ascertain.

Next, she'd sent a panicked telegram to Whitchell at the Naval Academy. Her brother—always a dependable sort, thank goodness—had wired back, "HAVE TAKEN TEMPORARY LEAVE. WILL FIND DAD." But Cecily wasn't satisfied that she'd undertaken every means of tracing her elusive stepparent. Could her stepfather's disappearance be somehow connected with the murder of the false Admiral? And if so, how?

There was only one thing to do, Cecily decided. Benfleet would just have to wait. She was going to confide in Sir Gerard.

HAWKSMOOR was on his knees beside the fountain, searching through the fine grass with his fingers, when a shadow fell across him.

"Whatever are you looking for?" said a female voice.

Recognizing Cecily Brandon's flat American accent, he got up and brushed off the knees of his flannels with rather more force than necessary. Not only did he dislike being interrupted when he was concentrating, he was irritated with himself for failing to detect her presence.

"Clues," he said shortly to Cecily. "I don't trust Constable Nettle not to have missed something. What are you doing here?" Now that he could see her, his bad temper lessened. She wore a navy and white dress with the wide collar of a sailor's uniform, and with her sleek, bobbed hair and fair, faintly freckled skin, she looked quite fetching.

"I wanted to see you—to ask your help, Sir Gerard." So winning was her expression that the last of his aggravation melted away.

"Why don't we sit over there, in the shade." He guided her to a bench near the hedge. "And you can tell me all about it."

She clasped her hands in her lap and turned a trusting face to him. "It's my stepfather, the real Admiral. He's disappeared." She went on to explain the situation.

"How very odd," Hawksmoor mused when she had finished. "As far as you know, your stepfather has no connection with anyone here at Castle Crawsbey?"

"Well, Jeavons will have told you about my mother." She colored and looked away. "But that was before she married my father—I mean my stepfather, the Admiral. I don't think he's ever even been to England."

"And your stepfather's job—" Sir Gerard tried to think of a discreet way to pose his question."—is he much involved with government?"

Cecily drew her brows together in a most appealing frown. "He has friends in the White House, and he's always being called to meetings and conferences and things, if that's what you mean. But what has that to do with this?"

What, indeed, thought Hawksmoor. For a moment, he was tempted to tell her the truth, about himself, and about what he was doing here at Castle Crawsbey. For he was, in fact, not as crippled by his war injuries as he led people to believe. It was a useful deception, one that kept people from taking him too seriously, and in his trade, deception was a necessary evil.

It was during his time in hospital that he had been recruited by the Home Office, and he had been working for His Majesty's government ever since. Sir Gerard Hawksmoor was, not to put too fine a point upon it, a spy.

His superiors had bade him wangle a weekend invitation to Castle Crawsbey because they'd received information indicating that someone associated with the Castle posed a grave threat to national security. So far, Hawksmoor had come to believe that the false Admiral was somehow involved, but he had got no further.

And of course, he thought with a sigh of regret, he could tell no one, not even poor Reggie Arbuthnot, who was being driven quite mad by fragments of memory from their time in hospital together. Arbuthnot had seen things he shouldn't have seen, heard things he shouldn't have heard, and had had his mind tampered with to ensure his silence. Now someone seemed to be making use of the knowledge of what had been done to Reggie—but to what end? Could it even be Hawksmoor's own superiors? The thought made his blood run cold.

He turned back to Cecily Brandon, summoning a smile. "I'll tell you what, Miss Brandon. I'll make you a deal." Seeing her eyebrows rise in surprise, he added, "Isn't that what you Americans say?"

"Yes, but what do you mean?" she asked, her voice trembling.

"Just this. I'll help you find your stepfather, if you'll tell me why you left the castle the morning after the 'Admiral' was killed. What happened to drive you away?"

She stared at him, and he noticed that her eyes were the blue of morning glories. "I should have known I couldn't keep anything from you, Sir Gerard. You're too clever by half. It happened like this." Taking a breath to compose herself, Cecily looked out over the fountain and began to speak.

"Like I told Jeavons, seeing *that man* in a naval uniform, impersonating my stepdad, really brought it home to me. I was so furious I spilled the hair pomade right down his front—it was all I could think of to do. I couldn't reveal that he was an imposter without coming forward myself, and I wasn't quite ready for that."

"And the Cumberland sauce on Lady Amelia's dress?" Hawksmoor asked curiously.

Cecily gave him a shy glance. "That was entirely an accident. As I was saying, later that night, I decided I had to confront the 'Admiral,' tell him who I was, and that I knew who he wasn't. So I changed out of my servant's clothes, washed my face, and went down to the garden. I saw Da Silva talking to the 'Admiral' by the fountain, and from a distance it looked like they were arguing. But then Da Silva started up towards the house. I hid in the shrubbery as he passed, not wanting to have to explain myself, then I crossed the lawn to the fountain. I told the 'Admiral' the game was up. At first he didn't believe me—he even tried to flirt with me, the horrible man. But when I told him what I knew about the Dowager Duchess, and why I was here, his face began to change. His eyes grew colder and colder, then suddenly his hands went round my neck and he started to throttle me. 'You're not going to spoil this,' he hissed at me," Cecily gave a little shiver at the memory. "I thought I was a goner, I can tell you."

"But you got away?" prompted Sir Gerard, moved by the girl's bravery.

"Not exactly." Cecily Brandon glanced at him, then looked away, as if unsure of his reaction. "I pulled an urn off the balustrade and smashed it over his head. The last I saw of the so-called Admiral Brandon, he was lying unconscious in the grass."

TEN

Journey Into Fear

by Alexandra Ripley

THE night train moved with an irregular, lurching motion, as if it were as fatigued as the passengers aboard. But—fatigue notwithstanding—one by one their drooping heads lifted when the mysterious woman walked through the coach. She was as beautiful as a dream come to life. Her movements were graceful and controlled, like a dancer's—or an athlete's. The pale green skirt of her linen frock swirled when she turned into the W.C. at the end of the car. The dream had vanished.

Inside the restroom the woman cursed sotto voce as she stared at the poorly lit mirror while she removed her clothes. She was a Special Agent for the Home Office, known as a master—no, mistress—of disguise, but it was far from easy to become a new person when one couldn't see what one was doing. She rummaged through the intricately woven straw satchel that she had carried as a handbag.

When the train stopped at the High Winsome station,

a thin, stoop-shouldered old woman stepped off. Disorderly tendrils of gray showed at the edges of the crumpled black turbanish scarf that covered her head, and the faded gray skirts of her shapeless garment hung unevenly over the tops of her high-faced, once-black ankle boots.

Sir Gerard Hawksmoor hurried acoss the platform to meet her. His imitation limping wasn't necessary because there was no one around to see him. "Thank you for coming," he said fervently. "I truly need your help, Miss—"

"Mrs. Ledbed," the woman interrupted. "And don't you forget it, and stop acting so pleased to see me. Someone on the train might be watching. Go to your car. I'll follow, but at my own pace."

"I'll carry your bag—"

"Imbecile! Go!"

FLICKERING light shone dimly through the thin summer curtains of the Dowager Duchess's sitting room windows. The storm had passed long since, but Castle Crawsbey's electric wiring had not yet recovered, and there was an oil lamp on the table in front of the gilded loveseat where the Duchess was seated close to her daughter.

"Amelia, we must devise a way out of the quagmire in which we find ourselves."

Lady Amelia groaned. "If I could only retrieve my five hundred pounds. Why did I ever let you talk me into that horrible 'Admiral's' scheme? What kind of mother would do such a thing to her own daughter?"

"A desperate one." The Dowager Duchess's words snapped like a whip. "What's done is done, and whining won't change it. You must set yourself to wrap that Chief Inspector person around your little finger, next to poor Gerry. We know the man took the money from Brandon's room; he must have taken those dangerous photo negatives, too."

"WHAT in God's name are you talking about?" Sir Gerard demanded of Mrs. Ledbed. "What negatives?"

His Bentley was parked under a thick canopy of tree branches on a narrow dirt road away from any possible traffic. It was so dark inside that he couldn't see the grimace of rage on her face, but its vibrations reached him like tongues of flame through the night's thick heat.

"You really know nothing, Hawksmoor! Arbuthnot managed a hasty phone call to our chief, Finlay, after he found them. He said he would bring them to the Home Office at once, but two days went by with no Chief Inspector, no message, no anything. So Finlay sent me here to make some sense of what is—or is not—happening. A good thing, too. Don't ask me questions, but tell me what you know, or think you know, before the Chief Inspector's London charwoman shows up at his door at dawn."

LIGHT from many candles illuminated the bedroom of the Countess Boronskaya, but it could not possibly be seen from outside because thick draperies were closed on top of the summer voiles. The room's contained heat was oppressive, yet it did not bother the naked bodies side by side on the rumpled bedclothes. On a table beside the bed a decorative Limoges porcelain basket held the remains of half-smoked cigarettes.

"Say you forgive me for the insults I made, my beloved, it was vital to make these fools believe that we were not together in this scheme." Da Silva kissed Katerina's breast, holding it in a caressing hand.

Her throat gurgled with laughter and pleasure. "I would hardly have opened my door and my body to you, Enrique, had you not been forgiven. . . . Be cautious about those kisses, my love, regardless of how they delight me. You mustn't remove my tattoo or people might suspect that those lies you told about me are all true. If Ceebee had not been murdered in such a timely manner, he might have begun to suspect the jewel I gave him for payment was really paste, as you told the world."

"And the lies you told about me?" Da Silva's teeth nibbled Katerina's earlobe.

"Mmmmm, that's lovely. So were my tales. Only a man of high standing and great wealth would be permitted inside the doors of the Monte Carlo casino to lose that much money."

Da Silva pulled her close. "When all this is over, we will have such a fortune that the casino will lay a red carpet for our entrance," he murmured before he kissed her.

". . . I think that's everything," said Sir Gerard. He longed for a drink of water after what seemed a full hour of recounting the complexities of the situation to Mrs. Ledbed.

Her laugh was a half-snort. Hawksmoor winced. He still longed for a drink, but something stronger than water now.

"It's no wonder that you are so pitifully confused," said his interrogator. "There are so many females involved, and your training as an English gentleman renders you incapable of even beginning to comprehend that a 'lady' is fully as capable as a man of all kinds of deception. Plus, generally more skillful. She has to learn it in the nursery in order to live in this world of ours where Man is King. It's a good thing Finlay sent me. I'll see right through your Duchess's grandeur and the Countess's pitiful deposed aristocracy. As for the absurdities that American girl is telling, our embassy in Washington has excellent investigators. I will telephone the code room at the Home Office and dictate a message to send at once."

She took a deep breath. "Now, Hawksmoor—about this Amelia person . . ."

"*Lady* Amelia." Sir Gerard's protest verged on a shout.

"I earnestly beg your pardon, Your Gentlemanship. It is clear that you are besotted with the girl, so I will generously help you find relief in one insignificant aspect. The feather you found at the murder scene was red, you told me. But, even though your heart's burden admits to merrily shooting her blowpipe at guests below her window, the darts in her closet have yellow feathers. And anyone at all might have gotten the bamboo weapon from the umbrella stand in the entrance hall."

"Of course!" Sir Gerard was so happy, he didn't mind feeling like a fool.

"I said 'insignificant,' remember? For now, the women must be shelved until I have the opportunity to see them for myself. Tell me more about the change you think has become apparent in Constable Nettle."

"I'm not really the one who saw it; it was the Chief Inspector, and he told me about it. Unfortunately, I can't be sure it's true. Reggie Arbuthnot is in a bad way. He hears sea shanties all around, is afraid he's losing his mind."

Mrs. Ledbed grabbed Sir Gerard's arm. Her tone was urgent. "You're managing those drugs for him, aren't you?

That's the most important thing of all, to keep him from remembering what he saw at hospital." Her fingers were digging painfully into his flesh.

He made his own voice low and calm. "A closer look at Nettle is what we need first. He's the one who is doctoring Arbuthnot's morning milk delivery so that he'll get the medication with breakfast tea."

"Idiot!" she screeched. "Take me to the Chief Inspector's home immediately. Let me out some distance away so he won't see your car when his faithful servant's pounding fists awake him to open the door."

MORTMAIN Cottage had a picturesque thatched roof. Reggie Arbuthnot had been secretly charmed by it even when he was most angry about being moved from London to a new post in a tuppence-level country village.

But as the mantel clock struck midnight, the sound seemed to activate a faint scurrying rustle overhead. Did he have some kind of animal companions, or was it more evidence that he was going mad? He sunk lower in his chair, bent his heavy head, covered his ears with his hands.

If only he could remember—whatever it was that escaped him again and again just when he felt that success and sanity were only centimeters away.

"Lon-don," he groaned aloud. The rustling answered him. "City," he whispered. He'd give anything to be back there, in his old home, his old life. Where he could sleep at night instead of sitting up, afraid of unknown dreams that might come. That might bring that music, that relentlessly jolly sea shanty.

His large hands formed fists at his ears. When daylight

came he was going to take the horrifying negatives to the
city, to Finlay at the Home Office. No matter if a hundred
new dead bodies showed up in that accursed fountain. He'd
been delayed too much already. Nothing, he promised himself, nothing is going to stop me this time. He raised his
chin, lowering his arms.

The barely audible chuckle came from an open window
behind him. Then the whistling, the nightmare tune. The
heavy chair crashed backwards when the Chief Inspector
lurched to his feet. Overhead, the scurrying became frenzied.

It took only an instant for him to reach the window.

There, he groaned again. There was nothing to see and
no longer any sound.

SIR Gerard Hawksmoor was driving too fast for safety. He
knew it, and he didn't care; he wanted freedom from the
silent but tangible disapproval beside him.

"Stop the car," said Mrs. Ledbed. He ignored her. "It's
urgent, Hawksmoor. I need to complete my disguise. Now,
stop!"

The abrupt braking nearly overturned them. Sir Gerard
felt her body jolt into his arm, heard the impact of her form
against the dashboard. My God, what had he done? She was
a woman, after all, and part of the Battle to Preserve the
Mother Country. "Are you all right, Mrs. Ledbed? I'm sorry,
so very sorry. Can I do anything to help you?" He couldn't
see a thing inside the automobile.

Her voice was unsteady when she answered, but it was
strong. "I've survived much worse. Do you have a torch?"

"Yes, of course. Right here in the tool box." Gerard

fumbled at the lid beside his left foot, then inside among the things tumbled by the sudden halt.

"Where is the auto's mirror? Beside your door?" She was climbing down to the road through the door she had opened. "Hand the torch to me and turn off the headlamps."

SIR Gerard stared. It was rude, he knew, but he couldn't help it; he was fascinated by the scene so close, on his right. She was holding the lit torch in her left hand, out ahead of her, the beam bright on her face, which was duplicated in the large mirror on the side of the car. The fingers of her right hand looked almost transparent when she moved them across her forehead and cheeks, pushing aside the tendrils of false elderly hair that were attached to the headpiece she wore.

Then, quickly and efficiently, she hauled up a handful of skirt and scrubbed her skin clean, using the perspiration thick on it for washwater. The hand dropped down to an unseen pocket and returned, holding a dark glass jar. The torch found a resting spot in her armpit while she opened it and scooped up some of its contents. Then her face was starkly lit again.

Why, she's really beautiful, Sir Gerard marvelled silently.

She spread some dark butter-like substance over her face and throat, then arranged the hair tendrils carefully. Her big, dark eyes look sad and worried, he thought. Was there something he should say to her? He searched his mind for he knew not what—some words of comfort, or at least of comradeship.

But Mrs. Ledbed spoke before he found them. "I know you are staring, Hawk. Brace yourself. Any minute now you will want to scream in horror. Don't, please."

I won't either, thought Louisa Ferncliff—'Mrs. Ledbed's' real name—I want to every time I do this, but I always hold it in. Along with the terror that the other jar might not work, might not bring me back to myself again.

Silently, the two of them stared at the mirror and the transformation it displayed. One after another, her cheeks and eyelids and throat seemed to puff outward, then subside slowly—oh, so slowly—into lines, then sagging, uneven wrinkles made from splotched and darkened skin. She dabbed the tears from her eyes as they welled, before they could roll down onto the horror taking place. Gerard felt his own eyes fill, too, in—sympathy? Fear? Revulsion?

"Done," she said at last. "I can do hands and arms as we drive on." Gerard was grateful for the dark when she climbed back inside. He turned on the car's headlamps and drove carefully, slowly, to the lane where Arbuthnot lived.

"I will leave my travel case with you," she said as she rubbed her hands and wrists. "When we reach our destination, extinguish the headlamps, put it in the boot, lock it, and give me the key."

"But if I do as you said and stop some distance away, how will you see to get to the cottage? The sky is full of dark clouds."

"I'll use your excellent torch. It is in one of my capacious pockets. Thank heaven, so is a goodly supply of the Chief Inspector's sanity medicine."

AS Mrs. Ledbed marched along the muddy lane, she allowed herself the luxury of a few stifled sobs. It was difficult being businesslike all the time. Why had she been so extra-harsh with Hawksmoor? Was it because he was so masculine, or because he was so very good-looking, and considerate, in spite of it? What was wrong with her? Had he noticed when she slipped up and called him "Hawk," the name he should have?

She should be concentrating on Arbuthnot. He needed her help. She was so afraid for him. How he must be suffering! It was insane to be half in love with a fat, creaky creature at least twice her age. But she had missed him dreadfully in the three months since he left London, missed being needed, missed the five-days-a-week shared tea in the mornings, when she slipped him his medicine and was some little help in his loneliness. And some large help in her own?

Good, there was the cottage. With a light in the window, he must be awake. Excellent. She would make tea right away, the drugs would soothe him and put him to sleep, poor old angel. Then she could find the negatives. Time now to concentrate on her mission.

"Love . . ." whispered her heart.

"I'll think about that tomorrow," she whispered back.

Then she raised both fists to beat a noisy demand for welcome on the door of the charming thatched cottage.

ELEVEN

The Lady Investigates

by Eileen Dreyer

SHE sat in the shadows, perfectly still. Watching. It was what she did best these days, all that was really left to her after all the work she'd done to get here. Her legendary beauty had faded like the light at the edge of day, her elan eroded like a carpet too long tread upon. And her children . . . well, that wasn't a subject worth pursuing when one sat alone in the dark at the end of night.

So she watched. She watched the South Terrace that stretched out below her window with its crumbling balustrades. She watched the gardens that had once been sculpted into designs as precise as her plans. She watched the lawns, rolling gently into a vague distance, indistinct enough in the predawn gloom to imagine perfection.

And she watched the fountain.

That ugly bloody fountain she had loathed from the first day she'd set foot in Castle Crawsbey. The blasted, useless, gap-toothed fountain that was causing so much trouble.

As if a fountain dedicated to sea battle made any sense when set on a lawn far from the nearest English shore. As if any foot in Rutfordshire had so much as dipped in the ocean, except for the odd holiday.

As if the fifteenth Duke of Faughstrayne had for any reason whatsoever. The fountain-building Duke had never been any closer to Trafalgar than the admiralty building in London, where he had been responsible for the ordering of naval salt pork. Where he had, in actuality, built up the once legendary Faughstrayne fortunes by short-changing the admiralty over their pork. For that, generations of perfectly comfortable, bucolic peerage had been punished with a positive orgy of ugly marble right outside their bedroom windows.

It wasn't to be borne.

Still, it shouldn't be treated *quite* this badly.

Although if they were unfortunate enough to see another tragedy enacted over tea, she wouldn't absolutely mind seeing that ridiculous Benfleet fellow go next.

She would have been perfectly happy spending the sunrise ticking off every insult the Faughstraynes had ever visited on this piece of land. She would have been happy watching. But she knew it was time to act. She knew she had to do something to oust these people from her home, and to do it, she had to offer herself up to the very gossipmongers she'd risen above so many years ago.

They would believe, after all, that the blackmail was about the surprise real first wife. That pasty bitch who had taken her home over, even though she'd never seen her. They would believe that it was enough for her, the woman who had made her name as the Dowager Duchess of Faughstrayne, to give in to the kind of blackmail that might well end up in murder in her own fish pond.

They would believe her.

They had to.

Because the alternative, the real secrets she hid, would not bear the light of day.

It was time, then. She had business to attend to.

So she did what any duchess would do in that situation. She rang for the butler.

THEY crept on their knees through the grass.

"Are you quite sure this will do any good?" Jeavons asked, his woeful countenance focused upon the grass stains on the knees of his good trousers.

"We don't want anyone knowing we're out here looking for that hidden door," Cecily Brandon whispered, her attention on the nearest window that led into the little-used Library.

"And you say that His Grace informed you of this egress into the house?" the butler asked behind her.

"Nope. He told me there was a door. Under the ivy next to the Breakfast Room. It was how his father got my mother up the stairs so her nibs didn't see 'em visit in the secret room. It was the room they found the fake Duchess in."

"The *other* fake Duchess, you mean?

Cecily gave him a bright grin over her shoulder. And her very shapely bum. "Don't be a spoilsport, Mr. Jeavons. I've explained myself."

"Yes, my lady. But why could we not simply test the entrance from the more . . . civilized end?"

Jeavons was glad the young lady didn't turn around to see his blush at his unfortunate turn of phrase. Especially since he couldn't seem to take his eyes from said end.

"They have cops covering the door to the suite," she was

saying as she crawled past the Library toward the Breakfast Room. "Just think, Mr. Jeavons, maybe we'll find something nobody else did."

"That, my lady," the butler said in egregious tones, "is what I fear."

"Well, we have to do *something*," she insisted, stopping a moment to face him. "Both the Chief Inspector and that wonderful Sir Gerard are gone, and my stepfather's missing, and now I hear that he was supposed to be here, too."

"Your stepfather, my lady?" the butler asked, forgetting to feel ridiculous there in the dawn grass on his hands and knees in his butling uniform.

"The other one," she said, resting back on her haunches. "The real admiral. I heard from my brother. Actually, I heard from the State Department. My father was supposed to be here for this weekend. Isn't that odd? At the behest of the U.S. Government. I wish he'd told me. We could have saved so much time and bother."

"But what would the U.S. Government want with a country party in England?"

She shrugged and pointed forward again to begin crawling past mullioned windows that were just beginning to reflect gray from the lightening sky. "Something to do with Brazil and a person named Phoenix." Heaving a sigh, she shook her head. "This is getting to be a very complicated weekend, Mr. Jeavons."

"Indeed, my lady."

"So I thought if I could help in any way to set things in quicker motion, I might find out where my stepfather really is. And why the Chief Inspector hates sea shanties and what all those bodies are doing in the fountain. Do you know someone named Phoenix, Mr. Jeavons?"

"I'm afraid not, my lady. The only phoenix I know of is the mythical one." For a moment, Jeavons failed to maintain forward momentum. He'd remembered something, which brought him to a considered halt. "There is the brooch, of course."

Cecily stopped moving as well. "The brooch?"

"The Romanov phoenix brooch. Commissioned by the Dowager Empress when all that bother in Russia began." He shook his head, troubled to the soles of his plebeian shoes by the threat that country now posed to a well-regulated, comfortable world. "Unfortunate, that."

He didn't notice how wry a smile Cecily passed back to him. "You've seen the brooch?"

"Why yes, my lady. Quite often, as it has been passed among the various royals of Europe. This is Castle Crawsbey, after all. Even a Dowager Empress needs funds on occasion. I do wonder if there aren't a few copies, however. I have seen it more than I ought, I have to admit."

"Well," Cecily decided. "We'll see about that, too. Now, we need to find that door and see what it hides."

Find it they did. Under the ivy. A cleverly hidden door with a handle that had been oiled in the not-too-distant past.

"I just can't imagine that Duddie would have told the fake admiral about this," Cecily mused as she pulled open the door to discover darkness, dankness, and not a few disturbed cobwebs. "Not Duddie. No matter what anybody says, he loves this place. Now that he knows Whitchell and I will take charge, he's even thinking of coming back."

"Splendid."

Cecily looked back at the butler, not sure whether his delight was sincere. The butler was busy brushing off his knees.

"Okay," Cecily whispered, her fingers to her lips, as if Jeavons couldn't hear her admonition. "We have to be very quiet. We go right by Lady Amelia's bedroom to get there."

Neither Cecily nor Jeavons allowed a reaction to the sounds they heard coming from Lady Amelia's bedroom. They were too busy staring at what they found in the stairwell.

NO one paid any attention to the sudden rumble and bang that echoed throughout the castle that morning. After spending three days with the castle plumbing, they did no more than turn over and, as their want, go back to sleep, or whatever else claimed their attention.

Only the new upstairs maid reacted. Maisie, who had been hired to help staff the house party, remained firmly convinced in her half-Irish soul that the mouldering, half-decayed grandeur of the castle was haunted.

Maisie had just scratched on Lady Amelia's door to announce the imminent arrival of morning tea and toast. She was in the process of easing the door open with her elbow so as to not overbalance the silver tray that weighed almost as much as she did when the noises startled her. Down went the tray. Down went the tea and the toast, all over the Aubusson rug that had once been such a beauty.

Maisie didn't shriek at the noise. She knew better than to insult ghosts. She did shriek at what she saw in Lady Amelia's room. It was why she was summarily dismissed. It was also why she didn't mind.

HE stood in the roadway next to his Bentley. The light was growing apace from pearly gray to shell pink, and all Sir

Gerard could think of was that the dew wasn't doing his bloody leg any good at all. He'd given up pushing that harridan from the Home Office to move more quickly. He'd given up on getting more help from Reggie Arbuthnot. The Chief Inspector was going to be out of commission.

He should have been back at the castle, rummaging through the rest of the rooms. He waited, though, because he had something to say.

"You're still here," she said without preamble, her face still shattered into old age by the makeup, her body lithe and supple in spite of it.

"We have a few things to clear up," Sir Gerard said, straightening from where he'd leaned against the bonnet. He'd be damned if she saw him wince with the effort. "I won't stand by any longer and watch you lot tinker with that man's brain. Let him come back to himself."

"Or else?"

"Or else I go to the *Times* with the whole story. How the powers that be keep a man in a mental twilight rather than admit their own muckups."

"You think you can dictate to us?"

"In this case, yes. I'm the one with the VC from the Somme, Mrs. Ledbed. I'm the one who will be listened to."

"Unless word of your own mental instability leaks out."

"From whom, a pathologist who can't scratch his own nose without a golf club? I'm tired of this, Mrs. Ledbed. I've worked for the Home Office for three years without complaint. I will do so no longer if something isn't changed."

He actually thought he saw that arrogant face sag a little. Caught a brief spark of emotion. He discounted it. She was one of their best agents, after all.

"If we didn't need you so much right now, I would shoot

you on the spot," she said, sounding more tired than threatening. "But someone managed to get to the Chief Inspector before I did. The only negatives I found were of a child bicycling in Hyde Park. Certainly not the ones Arbuthnot found. We simply must get those negatives back."

Sir Gerard sighed. "Brilliant. Do you tell me now what the Phoenix has to do with the Minas Gerais mines in Brazil and an English house party?"

She looked off into the east, where the birch that lined the Ware rose in silhouette before the lightening sky. "The Duke," she said.

"Which one?"

"The present one. He works for us."

Sir Gerard stared. "Good Christ," he snapped. "Does everyone work for you without knowing who else does?"

She actually cracked a wry smile. "Possibly. The Duke has been helping with a certain mining issue."

"Mining?"

Another small smile. "National security does not rest merely on cannon and horse, Major. There are minerals being discovered in that jungle that have certain long-reaching consequences. His Majesty's government and the United States are working together to make sure they don't fall into—shall we say, unreliable hands."

"The kind of hands who might well control the Phoenix," he said.

"Exactly."

For a moment, Sir Gerard simply stood where he was. "Well," he said. "I imagine, then, that I have some investigating to do."

"There is one question I do have," Mrs. Ledbed said, pulling a paper from her apron pocket.

Sir Gerard waited, keys in hand.

"Would you like to tell me what this means?"

She handed him a piece of paper, on which a list of names were marked with mention of payment. Except for his. Against his was written "The Phoenix."

"Good Lord," he muttered.

"Exactly," Mrs. Ledbed answered.

SIR Gerard walked into the breakfast room at the castle exactly thirty minutes later. Early enough to see that Cecily Barbara Brandon was attacking a positive mountain of eggs and kippers, and that Enrique Da Silva stared abjectly into a cup of coffee. Jeavons, for some reason, was trying to hide his knees with a platter as he slipped from the room.

"Why, there you are," Cecily greeted Sir Gerard with a bright smile and a leap to her feet, breakfast evidently forgotten. "I need to talk to you."

"The Duchess," Jeavons said stiffly from the edge of the green baize door, "wishes to speak to you, sir. At your convenience."

"The Duchess is here," that eminent lady intoned from the doorway.

"But you need to know about the third blowpipe," Cecily insisted.

Sir Gerard turned back from where he was just about to greet the Dowager Duchess. "A *third* blowpipe? Good God, are we hiding a tribe of amazon natives in the vicinity?"

"We could," Cecily muttered to herself.

Even at that moment, Sir Gerard noticed how endearing she was, with her little upturned nose and the smattering of freckles across her fair skin. Straightforward and true, he thought. No wonder these Americans were appealing.

"But I need to talk to you, too, Gerry," Lady Amelia said, stepping up in between him and her mother.

He could smell her scent, the scent that had always drawn him. He could also, this time, smell something else. Something that made him frown.

Lady Amelia didn't notice the hot blush that stained Cecily's cheek, or the one that darkened Jeavons's neck at her entrance. Sir Gerard did.

"In a few moments, if you all don't mind," he said. "I need to speak with Squiffy Frobisher first. There are some questions that need to be asked."

"There sure are," Cecily agreed with a militant look in her eye.

For the first time since he'd seen that first fallen statue, Sir Gerard felt like smiling. He wasn't used to anyone leaping to his defense. So he smiled back at the cheeky American chit. And he ignored the fact that Lady Amelia immediately scowled.

"Now, then," he said, addressing the room. "I was told that Dr. Frobisher had been called here for some reason. Anyone know where he is so I may talk to him?"

"I'm afraid I do," came a voice from the hallway behind them. "Not that it will do you any good."

It was Constable Nettle, out of uniform and a little disheveled. And looking over his shoulder as if seeing something unpleasant.

"Oh, no," Sir Gerard protested.

"Not the fountain again!" Lady Amelia cried, flinging a dramatic white hand to her sleek bosom.

Nettle walked up to stand just beyond her. "The fountain."

"Good Lord," the Dowager Duchess sighed, then brightened just a bit. "I don't suppose it was Benfleet this time."

"Uh, no, Your Grace," Nettle apologised. "Frobisher."

"Just as well," she said and sat down.

The rest of the party turned for the hallway towards the Library, from which they could access the South Terrace. Sir Gerard was just pulling open the French doors when at the back of the crowd he heard someone mutter, "Take 'im and shake 'im and try an' wake him. . . ."

Arbuthnot.

Arbuthnot, who was repeating the line from a verse of the Drunken Sailor shanty.

Brilliant. Just brilliant. Sir Gerard wondered as he stepped out into the new sun whether Mrs. Ledbed had some of that brain freezer she'd been feeding to the Chief Inspector for him. He thought he was going to need it.

TWELVE

The Phoenix Rises

by Jan Burke

"CHIEF Inspector?" Constable Nettle said, an expression of uncertainty on his face. "Cooper said I was to tell you and Sir Gerard that he's here to pick you up."

Arbuthnot could not recall ordering a cab, in fact he was sure he'd driven over in the Morris, but as he stood dazed he heard Sir Gerard Hawksmoor say, "Quite right. Just in time for our appointment." Sir Gerard turned to the others and added, "If you'll excuse us? We'll return as soon as possible."

Arbuthnot was vaguely aware of the Dowager Duchess's protests, and various and sundry exclamations from the others, but Sir Gerard placed a surprisingly firm grip on his elbow and steered him—with Jeavons's aid—into the sultry July air, and Edwin Cooper's cab.

"That's right, gentlemen," the elderly but muscular cabbie said, helping Sir Gerard in next. "Just you sit back and enjoy the lovely scenery. We'll have you all right and tight in two shakes of a lamb's tail."

"Where are we going?" Arbuthnot asked.

"To see the Phoenix," Sir Gerard said, turning to wave to someone on the front steps.

Arbuthnot looked through the rear window and saw both Lady Amelia and Cecily Brandon smile and wave back, then scowl at each other.

Arbuthnot sat in silence for a moment, then said, "You've spoken to him already, then?"

"Briefly. He was dressed as an old woman. A dashed ugly one, to tell the truth, but he will have his disguises. I forced myself to think of him as a female the entire time we spoke, but it was close run thing."

"I quite understand. If he thinks you've betrayed him by so much as a gesture—"

"Precisely."

"I've known him many a day, gentlemen," said Cooper. "You'd be wise not to question his ways."

Sir Gerard and Arbuthnot exchanged a look. Best not to start Cooper reminiscing. As far back as the days of his impoverished London boyhood, Cooper had known the Phoenix.

Arbuthnot, still a bit queasy, rested his head against the window and tried, without success, to rid his mind of sea shanties and to bring the Phoenix's face to mind.

At an unmarked crossroads, not far beyond High Winsome, Cooper made a left turn.

"Winsome-Under-Ware?" Arbuthnot guessed woozily.

"Yes," Sir Gerard said.

"Always wanted to see Winsome-Under-Ware."

"You mean you've never gone any farther than High Winsome?"

"All the way south to Winsome-le-Hatch, once," Arbuthnot said with a dreamy smile, "but didn't trouble myself to stop at Winsome-Under-Ware."

Winsome-Under-Ware, Arbuthnot thought to himself. Even in his muddled state of mind he found it revealing. The Phoenix hadn't, after all, banished him. Something wrong in even thinking such a thing. All this while, the Phoenix had been close at hand.

They passed through the small village, with all its frilly little shops, and continued into a nearby woods. The ride grew a bit bumpy. They passed what appeared to be a small pond. Cooper turned sharply toward it, and Arbuthnot held his breath, thinking they were about to plunge into the pond's depths. But the cab rode as if it were a boat, and he discovered that just below the surface of the water, and disguised by it, was a well-tended lane.

They passed through curtains of vines and entered a tunnel. Arbuthnot, in his disordered mental state, was unable to suppress a gasp of fear. In the darkness next to him, he heard Sir Gerard say, "Steady on, Reggie. All shall be well. Keep the window closed."

"You, the most claustrophobic man I know, want me to keep the window closed?"

"You'll see why."

As they emerged from the tunnel, he did indeed see why. They had driven straight into a swarm of bees. Cooper seemed unperturbed, although he slowed the car. They came clear of the swarm, and eventually only a few bees could be seen clinging to the cab's windows—although Arbuthnot thought there were still a damned sight too many of the creatures buzzing near the cab when the vehicle rolled to a gentle stop before a small stone cottage.

Cooper, oblivious to the menacing insects, helped his passengers alight, if one could use such a term to describe Arbuthnot's clumsy exit from the cab. Arbuthnot felt a new wave of dizziness as he stood; the droning of the bees seeming to match a buzzing inside his head. Above this humming came another sound: someone inside the cottage was playing a violin, a dark and melancholy melody that immediately cleared Arbuthnot's mind of sea shanties.

He stumbled along between Cooper and Sir Gerard, feeling a little stronger now, lured by the violin. Cooper opened the door without knocking. Arbuthnot caught the scent of a pipe tobacco—exactly his own mixture, he thought, which troubled him, but he wasn't quite sure why. There was another scent here as well, of something sweet and familiar.

The violinist turned towards them, but did not cease playing. He was a gaunt old man—older even than Cooper. His pale skin lay thin and papery over his sharp features. His fierce stare riveted them where they stood.

I know him. Arbuthnot thought. I know him. But who—?

"Cooper!" the violinist said in a commanding tone. "Give him the mixture on the table—and be quick about it!"

Cooper moved at once to pick up one of two steaming cups of tea. He brought it to the Chief Inspector's lips and said, "Drink up—now, there's a good lad."

Arbuthnot found he could not resist. The tea tasted odd, though not unpleasant—not his usual milk and sugar. He looked toward the table and saw—of course, of course—honey! A glass jar of the lovely amber sweetener bore a neatly printed label: Phoenix Honey, Special #863.

The tea was delicious. He took the cup from Cooper and downed it greedily. Cooper was saying, "And this one for you, Sir Gerard," when Arbuthnot heard the violinist exclaim, "Catch him!"

But by the time Cooper reached for him, Reggie Arbuthnot had fallen senseless to the floor.

HE awoke to find himself on a narrow cot. He heard a soft sound and turned his head to see the violinist's gaze on him. The old man sat in a chair, filling a pipe.

Feeling amazingly clear-headed, and yet somewhat alarmed, the Chief Inspector glanced towards a hat rack near the door.

"Yes, Reggie, a deerstalker. You expected me, perhaps, to take up wearing straw boaters?"

"No, sir." He sat up, and straightened his clothing. "Only—it's been so long, I thought—"

A faint smile curved the old man's lips. "You gave up on me, Reggie?"

"No, but—truth be told, I thought you'd given up on me, sir."

The smile faded. "I shall never know exactly why I haven't, given the present state of affairs. Hullo—I believe Sir Gerard rejoins us as well."

"Yes, sir," said Sir Gerard, rubbing a hand over his face. "Although I'm not quite sure why—"

"Why it was necessary to give you a cup of the same elixir? My dear Hawksmoor, what could be more logical? You've both received the antidote because you've both received the poison."

"Poison! Not curare?"

"Not at all," the old man said, a bit impatiently. "A rather different chemical reaction altogether. A drug that paralyses the mind, not the body. I do hope it won't be necessary to administer another dose of number eight-sixty-three to you, Sir Gerard. That antidote is difficult to come by."

"A drug that paralyses the mind," Arbuthnot said, looking up as the old man stood. "Then that would explain—"

"Why you've made nearly no progress in matters at the castle? Precisely. Why you've become preoccupied in a rather morbid way with sea shanties? Absolutely. Why Sir Gerard has spent the weekend stealing sniffs of ladies' undergarments and believing his own cover story? Yes, indeed. In fact, gentlemen, nothing else on earth could explain what a wretched mess you've made of your assignment. You've ingested a rather nasty brain poison."

"But how was it administered?" Arbuthnot asked. "I've not eaten a single meal at the castle."

"Reggie. Think. I've more hope for you at the moment."

"But sir!" Sir Gerard protested.

The man they knew by the code name Phoenix turned an icy stare towards him. "Shall I tug on that bit of silk masquerading as your handkerchief, Sir Gerard? Lady Amelia has that scent prepared especially for her by a Parisian perfumery. She applies it only to certain regions of her person for a reason—you will find it leaves a peculiar stain on the lining of your pocket, if not elsewhere. Your valet, you will recall, is in my employ."

Hawksmoor blushed and fell silent.

"Go on, Reggie," the Phoenix said. "Eliminate the impossible."

"Not food—not drink—but something we've both made use of."

Arbuthnot frowned in concentration, then suddenly said, "Tobacco!"

"Excellent!" the Phoenix said. "We make progress. The dosage you received, I'm afraid, was higher, because your pipe tobacco was more easily tainted than Sir Gerard's cigarettes—the poisoner had to wait until Sir Gerard opened a packet, and then had to individually taint the cigarettes in a way that would not reveal the tampering. In your case, he or she simply applied the poison to the contents of your pouch or jar of tobacco. Although Sir Gerard was not unaffected—I could tell when I spoke to him recently that he couldn't correctly recall much of anything I'd said."

Arbuthnot said, "When I came into your cottage, I noticed that the scent of your tobacco seemed somehow different than my own."

"Although we use the same mixture. On some level, Reggie, that useful brain of yours still tried to function. Tell me, have your memories of our mission started to return?"

"Yes, sir," he said with some relief. "The Home Office—where your very existence is a secret known only on the highest levels—contacted you and asked you to do a particular service for your country."

"I am, alas, a soft-touch for such appeals."

"You used your networks of old friends and called in markers, and recruited Sir Gerard and me to aid you. The Home Office was unsure. We seemed an unlikely pair of recruits—I am getting on in years—"

The Phoenix gave a bark of amusement. Arbuthnot blushed, but continued.

"And Sir Gerard's war injuries—although he has learned to manage quite well—engendered some prejudices against him by the Home Office. You ignored their objections. I was chosen for my investigative skills, Sir Gerard for his abilities in espionage work."

"And my access to social circles closed to you," Sir Gerard added.

"Yes, that's so, Gerry."

"Go on," the Phoenix said to Arbuthnot.

"Knowing that most people want the mentally ill to be utterly hidden from view, you chose an asylum— St. Benedict's Hospital—as our briefing ground, which would allow you to maintain the highest level of secrecy.

"Sir Gerard and I were to appear to be constantly at odds with each other—I would appear to be hot-headed and insecure. Sir Gerard would seem to be an insufferable, meddlesome lunatic who nevertheless succeeded, at times, to solve my cases."

"The moonlit nudity episode," the Phoenix said, "was in unforgivably poor taste."

"Yet convincing?" Sir Gerard ventured.

"Too convincing," the Phoenix said with a shudder. "I understand the locksmith in Winsome St. John is doing a brisk business."

"I was only doing my part for my country," Sir Gerard said. "You told us of the disappearance of one of our British operatives in South America, the patriotic Duke of Faughstrayne, an expert in the mining of certain strategically important ores, and a man empowered to make certain arrangements with the various countries where these ores were to be found. He vanished at a critical juncture in these delicate negotiations. His opposite number among the Americans managed to get a message through to his government before he, too, disappeared. The message indicated that His Grace might have been brought back to England against his will, perhaps even by members of his own family."

"We were told," Arbuthnot said, "to watch matters here, keep an eye on the locals. That we might learn of some attempt to bring private interests into the operation and ownership of the mines—interests that would sell these critical materials to the highest bidder. Sir Gerard had already ingratiated himself with the family."

Sir Gerard nodded his thanks for this bit of recognition.

"And I sent word," the Phoenix said, "that we had received indications that something important would take place at Castle Crawsbey during the Dowager Duchess of Faughstrayne's party this weekend. And what happens?"

The two men looked sheepish.

"Clues as big as lorries go rolling under your noses, only to be forgotten. Let us begin at the beginning, shall we? Before the poison had done its worst. The time element. Sir Gerard, your first report to me indicated that you entered the Library just past midnight, read for some amount of time, and your reading was disturbed when you heard a woman scream."

"What?" Arbuthnot exclaimed indignantly. "You never mentioned a scream to me!" He paused, then added, "Er, did you?"

"No," the Phoenix answered before Sir Gerard could frame a reply.

"In fact, he would later say he heard a splash. Scream, splash—which is it?"

Sir Gerard ducked his head.

"A sultry July night, the windows of the place open to admit any little breeze, and our man hears what no one else admits to hearing—screams and splashes."

"I . . . I . . ."

"You failed to look at your watch. Or a mantle clock. Or a

hall clock. A female screamed, and you, a trained spy, took no note of the time. Constable Nettle, called from his bed—his bed, one would suppose, since he did answer the phone—and dressed and rode a bicycle all the way to the fountain."

"Wait—Gerard didn't make that call himself. We don't know where Nettle was that evening."

"Excellent point, Reggie. To continue. Later it is reported that the body was discovered at approximately one o'clock. But a great deal has happened in one hour, wouldn't you say? Someone has whistled, someone has smoked a cheap cigar, a couple appears near a fountain, Gerard becomes immersed in a book, the first victim—as yet," he bit out, "unidentified by either of you—becomes immersed beneath a rather large piece of statuary, the butler is summoned, a conversation is held with Lady Amelia, and a constable bicycles all the way from Market Winsome."

"Or wherever," Arbuthnot added, feeling sympathy for Sir Gerard.

"Yes. But there are other matters. Da Silva. The Order of the Apothecary? A Maltese Order, but having nothing to do with the Knights?"

"I never believed that," Sir Gerard said.

"I should hope not. He lied to you, you know, and you didn't bat an eye."

"About Lady Amelia and the sash?"

"No," the Phoenix said in disgust. "Will you try very hard to be logical about that woman? But I digress. Da Silva told you that he 'recognized the admiral by his uniform.'"

"But Admiral Brandon—or whatever his real name may be—wasn't wearing his uniform," Arbuthnot said slowly. "He was wearing a dark suit."

"Perhaps he changed," Sir Gerard said.

"Into a dress uniform? Hardly something more comfy. No. Besides, I saw the uniform hanging in the admiral's room the next morning. After the pomade had been cleaned from it, someone pressed it and left there, and he obviously had not been back to his apartment after it had been returned."

"Reggie," the Phoenix said, "I'm afraid your abilities were impaired early on. You've been lied to as well, almost from the start."

"From the start? No, sir, really—at first—"

"One of the first people you spoke to was the late 'doctor'?"

"Why do you say it like that?" Sir Gerard said. "I've known Squiffy for years."

"Then perhaps you've noticed a rather high mortality rate in Market Winsome and its environs?" the Phoenix said. "I exclude, of course, this highly fatal weekend from the statistics, and yet I'm sure you see my point?"

Sir Gerard opened his mouth to protest, and snapped it shut again.

"I suspect he worked with them, Sir Gerard, but found it hard to continue to deceive you."

"No one should die pinned down in a koi pond beneath a rather poorly rendered likeness of Sir Francis Drake," Hawksmoor said bitterly.

"On that, we are agreed," said the Phoenix. "By the way, did you stop to think that one can't tell, looking at a statue, which of Lord Admiral Nelson's eyes was blind? And yet anyone who would mention that, and then use the term 'embraced by a statue' of the one-armed hero of Trafalgar—"

"I never said such a thing!"

"No, someone else did." He turned to the other man. "Reggie, you were told, long before an autopsy had been performed, that the 'Admiral' had no water in his lungs.

How would it be possible to determine the contents of a dead man's lungs without opening his chest?"

"It wouldn't be," Arbuthnot said quietly. "Frobisher's not—he wasn't a real doctor?"

"No. Easier to get away with false credentials in the hinterlands, I suppose. However, my own tests have confirmed that the 'Admiral' was indeed killed by curare. Perhaps Mr. Frobisher's knowledge of the household, or his experiences in South America, or his connection to the conspirators led him to make a correct diagnosis. But he was no more a doctor than that boor at dinner was an American."

"Not an American!" Sir Gerard said.

"Think, Sir Gerard, think. Someone played to your known prejudices."

"You're right," he said after a moment. "He fit the stereotype a little too well, didn't he? And he singled me out. Good Lord—now I think back on it, his handling of his silverware—"

"Indeed. More about him later. But let us continue. Going through that first evening—"

"Egad, my cigarettes! That first evening, while I waited for Nettle to arrive, I left my cigarettes in the Library. Do you suppose that's when they were poisoned?"

"I suspect you were given at least a small dose before that," the Phoenix said.

Arbuthnot reflected that the Phoenix was not revered for his tact.

"You missed Lewis's odd appearance," the Phoenix continued, "although surely such an amateurish disguise would have been caught by an expert in espionage under other circumstances. More distressing, of course, that there was another gentleman present, someone who has gone unnamed in your reports."

"That can't be . . ."

The Phoenix smiled. " 'A minor aristocrat, with as little wit as chin,' I believe you said, who sat to the left of Lady Amelia."

Sir Gerard was silent.

"Well?"

"Ballingsley. Rupert, Lord Ballingsley. Local man. He left directly after the Dowager Duchess suggested cards. No one wanted to play, but he was terrified of being bullied into a game—lost a hundred pounds to her the last time they played bridge."

"Fortunately for you, dear boy, we've cleared him of suspicion. In this matter, anyway."

"Thank God for small favours."

"But now we come to the problem of the materials you found near the fountain, Hawksmoor. You haven't done a blasted thing about them."

"The beads and the feather dart and the—"

"Cigarette ends, yes. I have them here. They are important, perhaps, because Cooper has learned from the head gardener at Castle Crawsbey that although little is taken care of as it should be, the area around the fountain was swept and raked late that afternoon."

"So anything found there was left that evening," Arbuthnot said.

"Yes. Come over to the table, gentlemen. The light is better." When they were seated, he brought out a small tray which held the remnants of nine cigarettes. "What is the first thing you notice?"

"Dark red lipstick on some of them," Arbuthnot said, noting that Sir Gerard was blushing again.

"Yes, all the cigarettes of that brand have lipstick marks on them. A woman, one presumes. The others have no lipstick on them."

"A man?" Arbuthnot asked. "Sir Gerard saw a man and a woman."

"But some of the women in the household use cigarette holders," Sir Gerard said.

"Excellent!" the Phoenix said.

"Of the men in the party," Sir Gerard said, "Benfleet and I are the only cigarette smokers—although he refused my offer of a cigarette in the Library yesterday."

"Interesting."

Sir Gerard nodded. "We smoke the same brand. As does Nettle. Da Silva smokes horrid, cheap cheroots; the supposed Admiral also smoked cigars. Whitchell-Twitchell . . ."

"Ah! That was clumsy, wasn't it? He could not recall his own name."

"No one knows what to call him even now. Was he an American?"

"In the Henley Regatta? Be serious. He really is an actor, although what that forgives him, I'm sure I don't know. One other thing—his father hasn't been seen anywhere near the South American mines, but Twitchell Turley, Sr. is also known as 'The Copper King' in the States. Keep an eye out for the possible return of that young man. By the way, did he smoke?"

"No, he wasn't a smoker. Let's see—don't know the servant's habits. Which leaves only Reggie, who smokes a pipe."

"And the women?" the Phoenix asked.

Sir Gerard sighed. "Lady Amelia smokes. The colour of

the lipstick on the cigarettes matches the shade she was wearing that night. I noticed it, because it clashed horribly with the rose dressing gown she was wearing. She smokes that brand."

"But she already admits to standing near the fountain, talking to Da Silva?"

"Yes," he said, brightening. "Yes, she does."

"And the other women?"

"The Duchess and the Countess use cigarette holders. The late Consuela smoked without a holder. The Duchess smokes my brand, but I'm not sure about the others. I'll admit I didn't notice. As for Cecily—" he paused and smiled. "Hard to imagine her having any vices."

"Other than lying prodigiously," the Phoenix said dryly.

To Arbuthnot's amazement, Sir Gerard's smile widened. "Other than that."

"Whose lighter was in the Admiral's pocket?"

"The Dowager Duchess's, I'm afraid. Saw her using matches. Matches! I'm surprised she remembers how to strike one."

The Phoenix reached into a drawer and removed a magnifying glass.

"Take this, Reggie. Examine the ends of the cigarettes without lipstick."

After doing so, Arbuthnot said, "Some are slightly compressed on the ends, as if they had been in a holder. Some are not."

"Suggesting?"

"That perhaps three people stood waiting by the fountain for a time, or stood talking together."

The Phoenix put the tray and glass away, saying, "How much more we would know, if we had seen these in place—before the helpful constable gathered them without marking their positions."

"He's been a severe trial to my patience, sir."

"Understandably. Now. The dart." He produced it.

"Red feathers, not yellow!" Sir Gerard exclaimed. "So Lady Amelia—"

"May or may not have shown you all her plumage."

"Or her true colors," Reggie added, "when she showed you that basket in the wardrobe."

"Quite. But you are not alone in being misled, Sir Gerard. For now we come to the so-called-admiral's attaché case."

A clock chimed. The Phoenix frowned. "I'm afraid I'll have to make quicker work of this than I'd like, gentlemen. You've already been away from the castle far too long. I'm concerned about the safety of anyone there who may not be a part of the scheme. We're keeping an eye on things, but my team can only do so much—as you've seen.

"But as I was saying—Reggie, I'm afraid you were already the cerebral equivalent of a zombie by the time you found the case. Let's start with the photos. Tell me what you thought you saw."

Arbuthnot once again felt himself grow red with embarrassment.

"It's all right, Reggie. Sir Gerard is hardly in a position to lord it over you later."

"Too true," Sir Gerard admitted.

Arbuthnot swallowed hard. "I could swear—sir, I really don't like to say it, but I could swear that I saw an image of Queen Victoria."

"Yes?"

When he didn't speak, Hawksmoor prompted, "Fit to romp through Winsome St. John?"

"Certainly not! It was what she was doing, and with whom. She was with——" His voice dropped to a whisper. "Zachary Taylor."

"Zachary Taylor? Who in blue blazes is Zachary Taylor?"

"Was," the Phoenix said. "An American president. He died in 1850, after a mere sixteen months in office. What is it you believed she was doing with President Taylor, Reggie?"

"Offering him a prodigious amount of iced cherries and ice milk."

Hawksmoor grinned. "Is this some sort of new police slang for——"

"No!" The Phoenix and Arbuthnot shouted in unison.

"Taylor died after downing large amounts of each at an American Independence Day celebration," the Phoenix said. "The cornerstone for the Washington Monument was laid at that celebration—hence the cherries, I suppose. In any case, it was a hot July day, and the president overindulged. He died of acute gastroenteritis within five days. There are those who believe the American Civil War became inevitable from that day, but I am inclined to disagree."

"And what has this to do with Queen Victoria?" Hawksmoor asked.

"Prince Albert's death," Arbuthnot mumbled.

"What?"

"Stomach problems."

"Ah!" the Phoenix said. "So that was it."

"I see now that it was utterly absurd——"

"Yes, most certainly absurd," the Phoenix said gently. "You were quite out of your head, I'm afraid."

Sir Gerard looked between them. "Will someone explain——"

"Prince Albert died in 1861 of a stomach ailment. He

had hidden his condition from Queen Victoria, and a great deal of conjecture about the nature of his ailment followed. At one point, the Queen believed the shock of a scandal in connection with her son the Prince of Wales—"

"Bertie?"

"Albert Edward. Yes."

"Will there ever be a more scandalous Prince of Wales?"

"Do not tempt fate. We are speaking of Victoria. She believed that had hastened Prince Albert's death. The idiots who served as his doctors probably had more to do with it, with a false diagnosis of typhoid, and it was even rumoured at one point to be poison. Absurd, in part because Prince Albert knew of his condition. I recently read a paper that made a good argument that the Prince had stomach cancer. In any case, Reggie, you do realize the silliness of this now? For one thing, that's neither Queen Victoria nor Zachary Taylor—I suspect Consuela and Whitchell were allowed to play dress up for the parts."

"I suppose photography was a bit less advanced in Taylor's day."

"Yes. But let us move on—"

"Why on earth would they even try to purport such a thing?" Sir Gerard asked.

"My dear Sir Gerard, a falling out between Englishmen and Americans is the dream of many who are friends to neither country. This attempt is crude, but combined with the drug given both of you, it served to convince Reggie that we had a great deal to hide from our allies."

"Really, H—I mean, sir, we shall do fine with or without them."

"Perhaps," the Phoenix said quietly, then reached for an envelope that lay on the table. He trailed his fingers across its travel-stained surface. The return address, Arbuthnot saw, was in Palestine.

"Perhaps, but then again, perhaps not."

"You've given me a chill," Hawksmoor said uneasily. "What do you foretell?"

"Hawksmoor, I am no fortuneteller, but I suspect the day will come when these two countries have such fellow feeling, the American national anthem will be played at Buckingham Palace."

Sir Gerard's jaw dropped in disbelief. "What a sad day that will be!"

"Yes," said the Phoenix, closing his eyes. "Yes, it will."

"The attaché case, sir," Arbuthnot prompted, not liking this mood. "What else did I miss?"

"Oh, the money, my dear Arbuthnot. The money."

"Nearly one thousand pounds—anything else I should have noted?"

"What condition is it in?"

"Uniform bundles."

"Suggesting?"

"That it comes from a bank," Hawksmoor replied.

"Yes. Note the bands around the pound notes—small bills, which, taken from these banded bundles, will soon be hard to trace. These all came from one Southampton bank office."

"So," Arbuthnot said, "the pound notes are not collected from various individuals, or they'd be loose or folded, or come from a number of offices."

"They are being paid to the people on the list," said Sir Gerard. "They aren't payments from them, they are payments to them. For what?"

"A little hush money?" the Chief Inspector said.

"Perhaps," the Phoenix said. "Hawksmoor, I believe the note next to your name indicates your identity as one of my operatives is known by at least one person at the castle. Under the circumstances, you are, of course, free to withdraw—"

"Not bloody likely."

"Good man."

"Sir," Arbuthnot said, "Da Silva—'flat refusal'—if he's refusing to be paid off?"

"He is in grave danger. Yes."

"And if the weekend party is made up of a number of individuals who are not to reveal the whereabouts of the Duke," Hawksmoor said, "or not to give out the identity of those who plan to take over operations in Brazil and Argentina, and our discovering the case has put a stop to payments—then perhaps someone is killing off the competition, making sure that his or her own share is the largest."

"If that is the case, I'm sure more funds will be brought to the castle, and soon," the Phoenix said.

"We had better hurry back then," Arbuthnot said.

"Remember your roles, gentlemen."

"I suppose we should continue to act a bit potty."

"Certainly," Sir Gerard said with a smile. "I perceive I shall either need to give up smoking or behave as if I'm 'attics to let,' as dear mater used to say."

"Use caution. You have been seen going off together in the cab, and at least one person suspects or knows of Sir Gerard's involvement. We must find where the Duke is being kept before he is either killed or forced to give them too much information." He walked to a cupboard and removed two small jars of honey. These did not bear the Phoenix label, just the number 863.

"Look after each other. If one of you begins to show signs of further poisoning, then slip a teaspoon of this antidote into a hot cup of tea. That should do the trick."

"Where did you learn of this antidote?" Sir Gerard asked.

"The same place I learned of the poison. While traveling in South America, in search of the highest quality cocaine. It was perfectly legal then, you know."

"Yes, sir."

"Here's Cooper, come to take you back. Be a good fellow, Sir Gerard, and take this jar of arthritis-relieving honey to him."

He detained Arbuthnot for a moment more. "I never told you, Reggie, but your father was one of my Irregulars."

"Yours, sir? Truly?"

"Yes. He was one of the best, until one of my enemies tried this same brain poison on him."

"This same one?" Reggie had, for the first time, a frighteningly accurate vision of his father's torment.

"The very same. I didn't go to South America looking for cocaine. I went to find the ingredients for this antidote, eight-sixty-three. That's how many experiments I conducted, trying to find the correct formula. I was too late, though. By the time I had developed it, irreparable damage had been done to your father's great mind. But he would have been so proud of you, Reggie. So terribly proud."

"Thank you, sir. I never knew. It—it means a great deal to me to know the story."

As they drove back through Winsome-Under-Ware, Arbuthnot found himself softly humming a sea shanty. For the first time in his life, it was not maddening or painful to think of the song.

When Sir Gerard objected, he began singing it aloud:

"Put him to bed with the captain's daughter—"

"That was another name for the cat-o'-nine-tails, you know," Sir Gerard grumbled.

Arbuthnot kept singing. Sir Gerard laughed and joined in.

"Put him to bed with the captain's daughter, put him to bed with the captain's daughter—earlye in the morning!"

"Don't be stomping on the floor of me cab!" shouted Cooper, as they reached the chorus.

THIRTEEN

Peril at Castle Crawsbey

by Sarah Smith

"YOU may be wondering why I called you here together,"
Sir Gerard said.

Thunder walked up and down the leads of the house.
White light muttered across the fields. Sir Gerard
Hawksmoor stood in front of the fireplace, leaning against
it to rest his back and leg and, with his hands in his pockets,
surveyed the assembled guests—such of them that survived.
The women had taken the comfortable leather library chairs:
blonde Cecily, aristocratic Lady Amelia, the Dowager
Duchess, and the Countess Boronskaya. Against the
latter's pneumatic bosom, the emerald Order of the Fish
winked greenly, setting off the green-and-black of the lady's
Romanov tattoo, patriotism for a disappeared country. The
little lithe foreigner, Enrique Da Silva, sat at the Countess's
elbow, his dark eyes upturned towards her face. The solicitor
Roderick Benfleet hovered near the Dowager Duchess.
Hawksmoor noted disapprovingly that the knees of Benfleet's

suit bagged. Constable Archie Nettle guarded the door, and Jeavons, aided by Mrs. Ledbed, moved quietly around the room, setting out sliced almond cake, sandwiches, raspberries, and clotted cream.

The atmosphere of the room was as charged as the clouds outside. The Dowager Duchess knotted her thin elegant hands; Benfleet bit his lips. Only Reggie Arbuthnot seemed to be enjoying himself, humming softly, "What shall we do with a drunken sailor?" For Arbuthnot, sea shanties were now nothing but pleasant reminders of his father's heroism.

If only it were that easy, Sir Gerard thought grimly. Too clearly, Arbuthnot didn't remember everything yet—he was filling his pipe. Sir Gerard caught his friend's eye and shook his head.

"Nearly forgot," Arbuthnot muttered. "Not my usual self yet, am I?"

"The Phoenix," Sir Gerard said. "The Phoenix is the center of all this." He held up the brooch. "Not this pretty object, but another Phoenix." From the drawer of the library table he drew out an elaborately printed certificate. The stylized bird rising from a bed of flames was only too familiar; but overprinted on it were the words, in dark crude type, "Fünf Milliarde Deutschmarks."

"Five *billion* marks?" Cecily said.

"In America you would say five trillion," Sir Gerard said. "But there is little difference between the two. This note, which would have represented a fortune before the war, would not pay for this delicious tea Mrs. Ledbed is serving us—even if such a tea could be found in Germany."

"Before the War I have German securities," Countess Boronskaya said glumly. "Now, pouf, it is collapsed."

"Precisely," said Sir Gerald. "The German economy is in ruins. The Deutschmark is worth nothing. German business, German trade, cannot proceed for want of ready cash. Germany cannot afford to dig coal and be paid in its own currency. France and Belgium have taken over the Ruhr and are mining German coal and selling it to themselves, at their own price. This souvenir was taken from the pocket of a dead German spy in London; the possession of such a note has become a secret signal among them."

He passed the overprinted note around; Cecily looked curiously at the angular-winged black bird.

"The young Duke," he continued, "was secretly engaged in acquiring Brazilian treasures for England. But the treasures were hardly archaeological. Brazil has something more valuable to Germany—and to England—than gold. It has iron and coal; in short," said Sir Gerard, "it has steel. The great question that the Duke was negotiating was whether the great natural resources of Brazil would be perverted to the Huns' devious uses, or whether they would be preserved for England and the English."

"Brazilians?" Enrique Da Silva murmured, but no one paid attention.

"I knew it," said Benfleet. "I was doing the right thing after all."

"The Library is full of books on geology and, unlike the set of Sir Walter Scott, they have been read. The young Duke was—I hope is still—a metallurgist of no mean accomplishments. I fear we will not find him here, but imprisoned in some laboratory in Minas Gerais, forced to toil for his Hun masters—if, indeed, he still lives."

"Germans, who could tell?" the Countess said to herself. "Germans, they have not imagination to be ruined."

"Don't suppose any of those German chappies could be here, do you?" said Arbuthnot.

"Precisely!" Sir Gerard whipped out a magnifying glass from the library table drawer and advanced, limping, towards Countess Boronskaya's pneumatic and decorated bosom. "The clue was in plain sight," he said, focusing the magnifying glass. The Countess screamed and covered her tattoo with well-manicured hands. "As I thought, Countess! Your tattoo is not the Romanov double eagle; it is merely a clumsy attempt to cover up the German eagle!"

"*Moi*? A traitor? Nevaire! It is that the hand of the tattooer trembled at the thought of our Little Father's fate." The Countess burst into tears.

Enrique Da Silva passed her his handkerchief. "She, I can vouch for her! She is no traitor!"

"And you, Señor Da Silva, who will vouch for you? This house party has been as full of traitors as—as—" Sir Gerard paused to consider metaphors, decided he was distracting himself, and continued. "Consider the so-called Whitchell Brandon, actually Twitchell Turley, representing American mining interests. And his companion the false Admiral. Consuela Imelda Berthold de Cordova, who flaunted her allegiances in her very name. The Phoenix brooch is set not in platinum, but in steel, and the 'gold' statue was plated over another sample of steel—a steel of remarkable purity and quality. Benfleet was fooled into bringing it to the meeting."

Benfleet cringed. "But the Gorblec cult—the Maltecs—"

"You have clearly never had trouble sleeping," Sir Gerard said with the authority of the insomniac, "or added Maltex to your hot milk."

Benfleet groaned, and then looked around him with the

horror of a man fairly sure one should not groan aloud in country houses.

"But my stepfather," Cecily said in distress, "where's my stepfather, the real Admiral? Are you saying that he was involved in a scheme to export Brazilian steel to Germany? If so, you've got to fight me, Sir Gerry. You may be looking for traitors, but I'm worried about him; he's disappeared. And my brother—no one has heard anything from Whitchell for days." She looked up at Hawksmoor with the blue pugnacity of a welterweight violet.

"Are you sure he is not here?" said Sir Gerard.

"Daddy is a master of disguise, of course—" Cecily looked thoughtfully around her. "Daddy?"

"Nonsense." The Dowager Duchess stood. "Sit down, girl, Gerry doesn't know what he's saying." She tamped a cigarette into her long ivory holder and looked around her with a weary impatience. Benfleet, Sir Gerard, and Jeavons all sprang to give her a light. "How little you know of the depths of the human heart, Gerry. If this is all he knows, Amelia, he isn't worthy of you. True, the Germans have interested themselves in the Brazilian mines. But you have no idea what has been going on here, and I can assure you, neither the false Admiral nor Consuela is a traitor."

"Mother, do not," said Lady Amelia, her pale aristocratic face turning even paler.

"I must. No matter what it costs, what happened to Dudley must be revealed. Swear to me," said the Duchess, "swear to me all of you, you will tell no one, for what I am about to say touches the deepest secrets of the state."

"Of course not." "Right-oh." "Absolutely not!" Everyone looked narrowly at each other, wondering who would be the first to tell.

"My dearest Oswald was recruited into the Great Game at Cambridge, long before the war—and not only into the Great Game, but into the Very Highest Circles. This brooch," the Duchess said, taking it from Sir Gerard's hand, "this brooch, Sir Gerard, once belonged to the Queen." Hawksmoor remembered the astonishing photographs he had seen of Victoria. At the Imperial throat, as she served Albert the fatal cream tea, had there not been pinned a brooch of a familiar shape—? "Yes. She Herself fought the good fight against the Hun, no matter the cost, and Her late Majesty was Herself the leader of the Phoenicians, a post my husband succeeded to."

"The Phoenicians," Benfleet said, anxious to show off his learning. "They were explorers."

"Yes, Mr. Benfleet," said the Dowager Duchess patiently. "Explorers. Jason and the Argonauts, Sir Francis Drake, Sir Martin Frobisher . . . Buccaneers when necessary. Did you not think it peculiar that the family retains so much Elizabethan decor in an eighteenth-century house, built with the proceeds of—"

"Coal," said Arbuthnot. "Rutfordshire coal!"

"Geology," said Sir Gerard. "Why did I not think of it?"

"It is true that my marriage was not valid when my children were born. My husband had of course confessed the existence of his previous liaison, and of the son who had proceeded from it, but neither of us believed that his 'marriage' to her, performed by a dwarf Disraeli impersonator, had the force of law."

Thunder rumbled closer over the gardens.

"To my husband's horror, just before his 'mistress' succumbed to an overdose of Old Daniel Boone, she confessed to my husband that their marriage was valid. Her son was the heir. The Dukedom would go not to Dudley, but to—an American. Whitchell Crawsbey," the Duchess said sadly, "would be Duke of Faughstrayne. It was not right, it was not euphonious, but it was, alas, too true."

A near crack of thunder made them all jump. "Garn!" Mrs. Ledbed exclaimed involuntarily.

"The effect on my son Dudley was deplorable. Since he would not succeed to the Dukedom, Dudley went to Brazil and indulged not only his talents for geology and metallurgy, but other of his special interests. In Brazil, although by day he was Dudley Crawsbey, metallurgist and explorer—by night, he became—Consuela, the Darling of Bahia Beach."

"Consuela?" Arbuthnot exclaimed, horrified, thinking of that sensual, lithe—steady, man.

"Meanwhile," the Dowager Duchess continued, "the war came. Whitchell Brandon, as he was still known, formed the Lafayette Espadrille—"

"Escadrille, Your Grace," Jeavons murmured apologetically.

"Do not venture to correct me, Jeavons. Though I regretted his status, Whitchell was an inventor, a true son of the family. Whitchell realized that, though the Hun were alert to an invasion of their shores by boat, an invasion by naval infantry would come as a surprise. He created a revolutionary inflatable rubber boot and himself led an all-volunteer American invasion. Operation Drunken Sailor—from the motion of the men in the boots, you know."

"What happened?" asked Benfleet.

The former Daisy Digby gave him a look that eloquently combined desolation, patriotism, and annoyance.

"But my brother is at Annapolis!" Cecily gasped.

"We will deal with your brother at Annapolis presently,

Cecily. After your mother's death, your father and I had promptly regulated our union." The Duchess produced from the library table drawer a massive parchment. "Here is the proof."

"This is indeed signed by the Very Highest Authority!" Arbuthnot examined the document, which was decorated with a massive wax seal and much red tape, into which had somehow got entangled a teacup marked *Property of Buckingham Palace, Do Not Remove.* "But I do not understand, Your Grace—the Duke's signature is dated after his death."

"We will deal with that presently. You will perceive that, by virtue of the same document from the Very Highest Authority, Dudley and Amelia's status had been made proper as well. As Whitchell Brandon was dead—"

"You mean my brother who's studying at Annapolis now?" Cecily said.

The Dowager Duchess gave her a look that could have frozen live fish. "—Dudley became my husband's heir."

"You mean Consuela?"

"That was a difficulty," the Duchess admitted. "However, it could be dealt with. Dudley apparently became the Duke after my husband's accident in the hunting field; but in fact my husband had not died."

"Not died?" gasped Lady Amelia.

"My dear Oswald's whole life was needed for his secret work; he could no longer live a double life as Duke of Faughstrayne. I did my part by pretending to murder him myself." The former Daisy Digby took a beat, as if waiting for applause, then recollected herself and continued. "When one is being vilified in every London drawing room for having murdered one's husband, even the most censorious will not believe the husband in question is still alive."

"Mother," said Lady Amelia.

"It was my duty, my dear. My Queen inspired me."

"But—you didn't tell me?" Lady Amelia quavered.

"Your father spent the latter part of the war in disguise as a Belgian refugee, and succeeded in infiltrating the headquarters of the Imperial Vegetable Marrow Growers' Association, then considered the second most dangerous organisation in London. He was so effective that, even after the end of the war, it was considered advisable that the Enemy believe him dead, else they would assassinate him. He is alive to this day."

Benfleet, thinking of five years' worth of wills, bequests, and inheritances, put his head down on his hands and groaned aloud again. This time no one noticed, not even Benfleet; they were too busy bending their minds around certain knotty questions of gender.

"Ah," Arbuthnot said, "Consuela—"

The Duchess continued imperturbably. "And ever since the unfortunate affair of Duchess Hortensia and King Charles, the Dukes of Faughstrayne have had the unique right to name whatever successor to the Dukedom they please, if there is no living son of the family. My husband could name his heir."

"My brother's not dead!" Cecily objected.

"Isn't he, Lady Cecily? During the last days of the war, on assignment in Washington, my husband arranged to meet his only surviving child by his first wife—you, Lady Cecily. Washington is a dangerous city; with the prudence common to those who have spent many years in the Great Game, Oswald sent another man in his place, and spied on the meeting. What was his astonishment to see that his man was met by—Whitchell."

"At least she's not lying about that, he's at Annapolis."

"Someone is at Annapolis, Lady Cecily. Or should I say—Lewis?"

Cecily looked helplessly up at the Duchess. "But I—I just played Lewis to—"

"The false Whitchell poisoned my husband's man at dinner and pitched him into the Potomac, and then coolly went home, changed out of his suit into a stunning dinner frock, took the lifts out of his shoes, and became—you, Lady Cecily."

Cecily stared at the Duchess. "You must be mad! My brother is over six feet tall!"

"Like my dear Oswald, like indeed poor Dudley—Consuela—you have made yourself a perfect character actor, a most essential attribute for a master—or mistress—of disguise. My dear Oswald has personally seen you act a three-day beard."

"This is insane," Cecily said, crossing her arms uneasily. Thunder rumbled closer; a lightning stroke illuminated the formal gardens and the fountain. Cecily stood up and looked out the window as if wondering whether she could escape this madhouse; Constable Nettle moved closer to the window, and away from the door.

"Whitchell was dead," the Duchess continued. "Dudley—Consuela—was no longer fit to serve in the House of Lords, for, ahem, any number of reasons." Through the room passed, like a mental haze, a momentary thoughtful silence such as might ensue after someone has said *Don't think of a hat made of bananas.* "And, as she admitted, she was having too much fun. She had resigned any claim to the Dukedom." The Dowager Duchess took another wax-bedecked parchment out of the library table drawer. "At this country-house party, my dearest Oswald and I had planned to gather family and friends to discuss our choice for the next Duke, or Duchess, of Faughstrayne, when Oswald should be gathered more definitively to his ancestors."

"Do you mean," said Lady Amelia, "that I could be—?"

"Wait a second," Cecily said. "Even if Whitchell's dead, which he's not, what about me? Does age count? Which of us two is older, Lady Amelia, you or me? I'm twenty-five and was born on the twelfth of May."

"I also am twenty-five and was born on the twelfth of May. That is my birthday," Lady Amelia added with the air of someone who had been deprived of much in her life and did not intend to be deprived of this.

"Lady Cecily, you will never become Duchess of Faughstrayne!" the Dowager Duchess exclaimed. "Your goal was to murder the Duke. You knew the Duke would be here this weekend. As Lewis, you planned to bash in his head with the garden urn, tie him to the statue of Neptune, and push the statue and the body into the fountain pool, where the koi, carp, and orfe would complicate the process of identification. As I had been suspected of murdering my dear Oswald for the past five years, no one would suspect you had murdered him this weekend. Instead, the body would be supposed to be that of a stranger, a man who had impersonated the true Admiral Brandon."

"Then I could be—" Lady Amelia thought out loud.

"You yourself had hired him," the Duchess said. "He was an actor. To a," she paused and drew on her cigarette in momentary agitation, "to a fellow professional, the signs were obvious. You played the first part of your plan to perfection. As Lewis, you gave Jeavons a message for the Duke, saying that you needed to talk with him about Dudley, and asked the Duke to meet you at the fountain at midnight. In the dark, you saw a shadow of the proper height and build,

swung and connected. Using the scarf of the Order of the
Apothecary to implicate your innocent sister, you attached
the body to the statue of Neptune and pushed it over, crushing the body beneath."

"But the fish did not touch the face," Arbuthnot put in
eagerly if somewhat late, "because of the make-up. I wondered why the Admiral retained his ruddy complexion after
a night in the water."

"But you overreached yourself by hiring a man of the
same height and build as my dear Oswald. The false Admiral, having drunk heavily through the evening, went into the
gardens to clear his head, and a malign fate led him to dunk
his head in the fountain where you were waiting to murder
your father. A crushing blow, then a prick in the shoulder
with the sharp end of a blowpipe dart, again to implicate
your sister, and the false Admiral could offer no resistance."

"Of course!" said Arbuthnot. "The brown 'make-up' in
Lewis's room was actually curare."

"Gerry!" Cecily cried. "You don't believe all this?"

"When Lady Cecily came to Market Winsome—'for the
first time'—to identify the body as her father, of course she
expected to see a stranger. If she were innocent, she would
have recognized as 'Lewis' that the false Admiral was not her
father, and when she saw him again as 'Cecily' she would
not have fainted. But she did faint, genuinely—not because
she did not recognise him, but because she did. She had
murdered the wrong man."

"She's the murderer!" Cecily pointed at the Duchess.
"She murdered her husband five years ago. And it wasn't
just knowing about Whitchell that drove Duddikins to
Brazil, it was you, Duchess. He was terrified of you. Yes, I
knew about 'Consuela'—I met Duddikins in Minas Gerais

when my father was investing in silver mines. We used to go shopping together. 'Consuela' called herself the Phoenix too, in honor of her rebirth in Brazil, and I heard a lot about you folks. Especially you, Daisy Digby. You can get all hoity-toity about my mother being an actress, but the Duke married her and my mother didn't murder him. You ought to count yourself lucky you're not her daughter, Amelia."

"What?" said Lady Amelia.

"You're an orphan, you're not a Crawsbey at all. The Duke wanted a daughter but Daisy wanted to keep her figure. Isn't it funny you're the one she likes? 'Consuela' found out and was going to tell you, let you get out from under Mommy Dearest's thumb."

"Mother," gasped Lady Amelia. "Is this true?"

"She killed her only child," Cecily said passionately. "Killed her own son, my friend Duddy, to make sure he didn't tell! She was going to keep you here and unmarried, just so she wouldn't have to leave the castle—and you bet I would have thrown her out if I became Duchess." Cecily took Lady Amelia's shoulders and turned her so she faced the glass doors of the library shelves. "Look at you, girl! You don't look like either of them. Forget this Duchessing; you can do what you like."

For a long moment Lady Amelia stared at her reflection in the glass. What gazed back at her was the very essence of British upper-class womanhood, spinster version: a pale woman in a twin set, her long hair bound up in a neat braid, watching her youth fade away. Entirely proper for the daughter of such an old family. Orphans, on the other hand, are entrepreneurs. And so are duchesses. Between one second and another Lady Amelia made her decision. She looked once back at her mother, and once at Sir Gerard. "Gerry," she said. "There should be scissors in that drawer. Give me them, won't you?" As she spoke she was pulling the pins out of her hair and shaking out her braid. She looked over at Archie Nettle, and she glowed. "I know what I want," she said, and took the scissors, and sheared through her hair with one quick stroke. "Archie. Will you have me?"

Archie Nettle held out his arms to her, and she walked across the room into them, leaving her long pale hair on the floor like a shed skin. "You'll like him, Mother," she said from the shelter of his arms. "Or you won't. But if Papa's still alive and you both back me for the Duchess sweepstakes, you'll take Archie too."

The Duchess looked from her adopted daughter, now bob-haired and determined and completely transformed, to Cecily, and back to Lady Amelia and Constable Nettle—tall, stalwart, handsome, and no more intellectually challenged than many in the Upper House. "Between your brother's murderer and a representative of the Law," she murmured, "my dear, I find it ridiculously easy to choose." Constable Nettle momentarily looked confused, as though he were not quite sure this was approval, but Amelia nodded, satisfied.

"Now, Mother," she said. "What about Papa? Is he alive?"

"Ask her to prove it," Cecily said sulkily. "If she's accusing me of murdering Duddikins, she can say anything."

"With your permission," Jeavons said, "Your Grace, milady, milady," nodding at the Duchess, Lady Amelia, and Cecily, "I believe I can settle that."

"How, call in Sherlock Holmes?" Cecily asked. Sir Gerard and Arbuthnot looked at each other uneasily.

"I believe that won't be necessary, milady," Jeavons said.

Cecily screamed, for before their eyes, the Duchess's perfect butler was transforming himself. The admirably wooden

face took on animation; the pale fish-egg eyes began to spark
with the fire of a massive intelligence; the nose became nobly
aquiline, and even the jaw seemed more angular.

"Papa?" said Lady Amelia.

"Daddy!" Cecily exclaimed.

"Garn!" said Mrs. Ledbed.

"Whatwhatwhatwhatwhat?" Arbuthnot sputtered, and
agitatedly stirred a teaspoonful of Phoenix Honey, Special
#863 into his tea, in case he was still hallucinating. "But
you are—the Phoenix!"

"Dearest Oswald," the Duchess said contentedly.

"The man you know as the Phoenix," the Duke said
solemnly, "is not I, but the most wicked man in London."

"But you were the Phoenix—" Arbuthnot stammered.
For there the man was, the same man he had seen this afternoon, the same man who had freed him from the nightmare
of his father's madness—

"Was that Moriarty?" Arbuthnot guessed.

"Not Moriarty."

"Consuela?" Cecily said.

"Queen Victoria?"

"Is everybody named Phoenix?" Benfleet asked plaintively.

Arbuthnot held up the honey jar thoughtfully, then
poured the entire contents into his tea.

"Let us call him by another of his names," said the Duke.
"Edward Lestrada. Or—Admiral Cornelius Brandon."

"Daddy?" Cecily said. "Daddy is the Phoenix?"

A great crack of thunder sounded just outside the windows; loose windowpanes rattled as the rain blew against
them.

"The man you know as Cornelius Brandon," the Duke
said, "and you, Arbuthnot, have met as the Phoenix, I have

the misfortune to call my brother—my identical twin brother. I am three minutes older than he, and from earliest infancy he has resented my very existence. By accident of three minutes' precedence, I was the Duke of Faughstrayne; he was no one. From my university years, I dedicated myself to government service, while in the guise of a private detective, he became equally dedicated to chaos, anarchy, and destruction. Who made the Metropolitan Police Force look like a home for village idiots? He did. Who repeatedly took the law into his own hands? None other. Who was intimately familiar with all the worst criminal elements in London— and, I ask you, why was he familiar with them?"

"You don't mean *Sh—he himself*—" Hawksmoor gasped.

The Duke held up one hand. "We do not speak his name in this house."

"But," said Enrique Da Silva, "if you are—"

"But *you* never left your rooms," said the Countess. "And you had the great fat stomach—me, I have read—"

"Slander," the Duke said, sucking in his stomach, "all slander. And 'never left my flat,' 'a misogynist'? Hardly. He was jealous of my success—of my happy family life."

"Lives," Cecily muttered under her breath.

Arbuthnot's head was churning. He gulped his still-hot tea, which, because of the amount of honey he had stirred into it, had taken on the consistency of Earl Grey–flavoured fudge.

"So jealous, in fact," the Duke continued, "that he must have the same happy family life as I. The Reichenbach Falls? Pushing Moriarty over the edge? Not likely. They divided the world between them. My brother left England to Moriarty, said he didn't like the climate. I shall never forgive him for that. We caught Moriarty in the end, though not before he'd done great mischief. You knew him, Arbuthnot, as Froggie Nelson-Whyte."

"But Froggie was innocent—" Arbuthnot's head pounded and his ears were buzzing. Shouldn't have drunk that tea so fast, he thought; his throat burned; but in spite of the tea, his mouth was dry.

"My brother made his headquarters in Washington, D.C.," the Duke continued. "Taking over the identity of one of his arch-enemies. And when your mother, Cecily, got into her spot of trouble over here, it was 'Brandon' who welcomed her in America, looked after her, and—"

"Oh, Daddy!" Cecily cried. "Daddy can't be a traitor! I won't believe it!"

"Alas, my brother is true to no cause but his own. For many years he has been an agent of the Evil Hun Empire— more than an agent, one of their controlling minds. In the guise of aiding the unfortunate and bringing the evildoer to justice, he has committed more crimes than the Ripper. At his door may be laid many of the disasters of recent years, the sinking of the *Lusitania,* the assassinations of noble families—" the Duke nodded briefly but compassionately in the Countess's direction.

The Duchess nodded in agreement. "Wonder Bread," she added.

"Garn!" said Mrs. Ledbed.

"Darling Louisa," the Duchess murmured, "you must get yourself a better set of lines."

"Can't shay anything elsh," Mrs. Ledbed muttered back, "my makeup teethsh keep shlipping."

"Dental glue's in the library table drawer," the Duchess whispered understandingly; such mishaps frequently occurred among masters of disguise.

"He has interested himself in the Hun's success in Brazil," the Duke continued. "I understand that he has been promised the Order of Bloody-Mindedness, Pour le Mérité, and the governorship of an important German colony. Perhaps," the Duke said significantly, "the United States."

Cecily shuddered. "Never!"

"It is not your fault, my dear, he has misled many keen minds before yours. That doctor chappie of his, the one who wrote his 'cases,' started out decently enough; by the time my brother'd got through with him he couldn't remember which limb he'd been shot in or his own name—" The Duke's eye fell, as if accidentally, on Arbuthnot.

"But I thought—" Cecily was nothing if not up on her detectives. "*He* was retired—Suffolk Downs—raising bees—"

"Those bees," said the Duke in a voice of doom. "The most deadly of his plans. They are killer bees, my dear, and their honey drives men mad."

But I am not mad, Reggie Arbuthnot thought. All these other people are mad. Evil Empires! Transvestite Dukes with bananas on their heads! Masters of disguise! Daughters who can't recognize their own fathers! *Butlers!* But I am not mad. His head was pounding and flashes of light were dancing before his eyes. "Ahahahahaha," he chuckled, though it came out like a scream. "The butler did it. I see it all now! *The butler murdered everyone! Get him!*" He dropped to the floor, scrabbled towards the scissors, grabbed them like a dagger, and launched himself towards the Duke.

"Stop him!" the Duchess screamed. Lady Amelia grabbed at Arbuthnot's ankles, Cecily hung onto his arm, but neither of the women was a match for the superhuman strength of the insane Arbuthnot. Constable Nettle tackled him and was driven back with a slash across his cheek. The Duke upended the library table, trying to drive the Chief Inspector back.

"Reggie," Hawksmoor pleaded, and Arbuthnot kicked him in his bad leg. "What will we do with a drunken sailor," Arbuthnot sang merrily, a feral light in his eyes, "what shall we do with a drunken sailor, carve him up in pieces!" The drawer of the library table fell open, scattering pens, pencils, compromising photographs, the original manuscript of Harriette Wilson's *Memoirs,* various communications from the Very Highest Authority, a letter from a well-known sweepstakes saying that Mr. Arthur Jeavons might have won a million pounds, and quite a number of the Duchess's hairpins. Arbuthnot's foot slipped on a pen, but still he pressed the Duke back, stabbing at the oak tabletop, feinting to one side and the other, so that the Duke, if he had not been a Duke, would have been in the process of being chased around the table.

"Your Grace," said Enrique Da Silva, "give me your cigarette holder."

"What can you do with a cigarette holder?" the Duchess said, but handed over the long ivory wand, still with her cigarette burning in it.

"The best a man can do, Your Grace—fight! *En garde,* you villain!"

What the cigarette holder lacked in strength and flexibility—more or less everything—it made up in surprise. Arbuthnot exclaimed as the tip of the Duchess's cigarette burned the back of his neck. He spun around to find himself confronting a whirling dervish, stabbing with a lighted weapon at his face, his eyes. He rushed at the little Argentinian, but hitting Da Silva was like trying to sew a button on a rooster. "Katerina!" Da Silva shouted. "Your necklace!" She tossed it and Da Silva whirled the Order of the Fish over his head like a bolo, whacking Arbuthnot about the head and shoulders. Hawksmoor, still writhing on the floor, tackled Arbuthnot by the ankles just as Mrs. Ledbed threw her makeup teeth at the insane Chief Inspector, clipping him nastily above the ear. The Duke pushed the table over onto Arbuthnot, forcing him to the floor, and stood on the table while Lady Amelia and Cecily bound Arbuthnot's wrists and ankles securely. "That should do him," said Cecily, gagging him with the Order of the Apothecary. Da Silva surveyed the writhing but helpless Arbuthnot. With the tip of his weapon, he slashed three strokes of cigarette ash onto the front of his adversary's best white shirt,

S

and added a small, precise D. "What can you do with a cigarette holder," he murmured, "what can you do with a cigarette holder . . . Me, I have always wanted to do that."

"So," said the Duke. "Is everything explained?"

"Frobisher's death?" Hawksmoor suggested, painfully getting to his feet and favoring his injured leg.

"What Maisie saw in my room?" added Lady Amelia.

"What we saw in the secret passage," Cecily put in.

"All shall be explained. But first," the Duchess said, "let us have tea."

"Without honey," said Hawksmoor grimly, regarding his old friend writhing on the floor.

"Mad!" shouted Arbuthnot indistinctly through his gag, "M'd! Mfffl!"

The Duchess frowned as she realized there was a difficult question of etiquette to be surmounted. Jeavons was the Duke; Mrs. Ledbed, the trusted operative Louisa Ferncliff; who would serve tea?

"Let us serve ourselves," the Duke suggested, daring to flirt with democracy.

"My dearest," the Duchess smiled at him, "you think of everything."

"What a weird story!" Cecily sighed as she helped herself to plum cake. "Duddikins, and evil twins, and mines, and murders. I don't know about you, but I need something in my tea. How about I find us some of that whiskey from the sideboard?"

"My darling Cecily, how good of you."

"Some brandy too?" Benfleet suggested weakly.

"Wodka?"

Cecily left and closed the door behind her. For a few moments nothing was heard in the Library but the clink of spoons, the faint crisp sounds of cucumber sandwiches being bit into, and the thump of Arbuthnot's enraged heels against the floor. "Mfffl! Mffly!" he shouted through the gag.

"Oy," Constable Nettle said suddenly, and Lady Amelia directed towards him the first of what promised to be many quelling and instructive glances. "I mean—Cecily—didn't want to mention it while she was here, of course—but—did she murder the chap the Duke sent to meet Whitchell, or didn't she?"

Enrique Da Silva ran for the door. "Locked!" he exclaimed. "Cecily, she has locked us in!"

"Do you smell smoke?"

*   *   *

AND, from the formal gardens overlooking Castle Crawsbey, the Phoenix laughed. Lightning crashed over the rooftops of the great building, showing Cecily making her escape out the front door, the fire she had set beginning to take hold in the west wing, and the new, deliberately misinstalled lightning rod on the roof. "None shall escape," the Phoenix exulted. And the lightning cracked again, and the flash illuminated the face of the only person whom no one had suspected, whom the Duke himself had banished from this house of doom—the housemaid, Maisie.

For the Phoenix, too, was a master of disguise.

FOURTEEN

Bon Voyage

by Edward Marston

THE novelty of the situation spread an understandable panic. None of them had ever before been locked in a library while a thunderstorm raged outside, a fire was roaring nearby and, worst of all, the cucumber sandwiches they were eating had a faint tang of curare. There was further cause for alarm. An avalanche of soot fell down the chimney, the bust of Admiral Rodney that stood on a pedestal in the corner suddenly keeled drunkenly over and crashed into the Ming vase, shattering it beyond recall, and Reggie Arbuthnot, trussed up like a Christmas turkey, bearing the mark of scorched initials on the front of his best white shirt, trying in vain to bite his way through the gag in his mouth, twitched so violently on the floor that his trouser legs worked their way up to his knees, revealing, for all to see, the telltale brand of a phoenix on both shins.

The false teeth discarded by Mrs. Ledbed began to chatter with sheer terror.

"We'll all be burned alive!" yelled Roderick Benfleet.

"Hold me, Archie!" implored Amelia, who, shorn of her title, did not wish to be deprived of her lover as well. "Let's die in each other's arms."

"Yes, my darling," said Nettle, embracing her with alacrity and taking the opportunity to touch parts of her anatomy that he had only ever glimpsed before in advertisements for ladies' underwear. "Closer, Amelia, closer."

"Can't we escape through the window?" cried Enrique Da Silva, running across to it with the sinewy grace of a panther. "How does it open?"

"Don't be a fool," said the Duke, rushing to stop him from tugging at the latch. "Look at those flames outside, man! Open that window and we're doomed."

"We're doomed if we stay here," howled the Countess, so frightened by the turn of events that, in the space of a single sentence, she shed her Russian accent, acquired and lost a German one, then reverted, when extremity stripped her disguise completely away, to the Welsh lilt she had inherited as a girl in the Rhondda Valley. Realizing that she had exposed herself as a triple agent, she put her hands to her face. "Vladivostock! Gott in Himmel! Iesu Mawr!"

"Oswald," observed the Duchess, remaining icily calm in the crisis, "this tea tastes of gravy browning. I shall have to speak to Cook."

"We're going to be cooked ourselves!" shouted Benfleet.

"Caught like rabbits in a snare," added Mrs. Ledbed, aging by the second without the help of her make-up kit. "We've been thoroughly duped."

"How do we get out of this place?" asked Da Silva.

"Send for the butler, of course," said the Duchess, reaching for the bell.

"There is no butler, my dear," the Duke reminded her. "Jeavons was merely a convenient camouflage for me. It was only because I was so disgusted by what the butler saw that I shed that particular role."

Benfleet was gibbering wildly. "What are we going to do?"

"Find a new solicitor, for a start," replied the Duke sternly. "Pull yourself together, man. What's happened to the bulldog spirit of a true Englishman?"

"I've lost it. I don't want to end up as a hot dog!"

"Be quiet, you sniveling hound!" chided the Duchess. "Consider yourself well and truly dismissed, Mr. Benfleet."

"We'll all be dismissed when that fire gets in here," said Benfleet, pointing to the clouds of smoke coming from under the door. "There's no escape."

The Duke struck a pose. "There's always a means of escape for a Faughstrayne."

"I fail to see it," said Mrs. Ledbed, recovering her composure. "I think that we should perish without fear. We're in a magnificent library, after all. Why don't we each select our favorite book and read aloud a passage from it?"

"What a droll suggestion," said the Duchess, putting her pince-nez in position. "Oswald, would you please pass me my illustrated copy of Rabelais?"

"*Vanity Fair* would be my choice," confessed Amelia.

Mrs. Ledbed peered at the shelves. "I don't suppose you have Foxe's *Book of Martyrs,* do you? They die the most wonderfully gruesome deaths in that. It will take our minds off our own predicament."

Nettle looked sheepish. "I'm an H. G. Wells man myself."

"What!" exclaimed the Duchess, shaken to her albeit acquired aristocratic roots. "You dare to mention the name of that evil revolutionary under my roof! It's unforgivable.

Amelia," she went on, wagging a finger. "You may not be my daughter but I speak to you like a mother. Do not prostitute yourself by marrying a man who reads H. G. Wells."

"I'm not going to be able to marry anyone," sighed Amelia.

"What's your choice, Mr. Benfleet?" asked Mrs. Ledbed.

"I can't read at a time like this!" howled Benfleet.

"No," agreed the Countess, abandoning her Russian and German accents for the pleasing cadences of the Rhondda. "Let's sing a few Welsh hymns instead."

Da Silva stood to attention. "I prefer my country's national anthem."

"Wait!" ordered Sir Gerard Hawksmoor, speaking for the first time. "I think that I may have solved the problem that confronts us all. Fire, hysteria, claustrophobia. I met them all before in the trenches and I did not flinch. Nor will I buckle now. I, ladies and gentlemen," he continued, rising to his full height, "have given serious thought to Mrs. Ledbed's suggestion and deem it to be admirable. My choice will be the collected works of Sir Walter Scott."

"Dear God!" protested the Duke. "He's going to bore us to death."

Benfleet quailed. "Is he going to read the whole lot of them?"

"No," said Sir Gerard, standing before the volumes like a conjurer about to pull a white rabbit from a hat. "I wondered why nobody had ever taken one of these novels from its shelf and the answer is simple." He tugged at *The Heart of Midlothian* and it refused to budge. "They are not real books at all but fake covers. Indeed, none of these shelves contain a volume that can be removed. Do you know what that means?"

"Yes," said Benfleet, remembering that he was supposed

to be a lawyer. "Whoever sold these books to the family should be prosecuted for fraud."

"This is not the work of a bookseller, Benfleet," said Sir Gerard, taking a firm grip on *Quentin Durward,* "but the art of a cabinet maker. Behold, my friends." He pulled hard and the shelves rotated on hinges to reveal a gaping cavity. "As I thought. These old places are honeycombed with passages."

Mrs. Ledbed darted forward to kiss him. "Well done, Sir Gerard!"

"We're free!" blubbered Benfleet, rushing to the hole in the wall. "We're free."

"Women and children first," insisted Sir Gerard, holding him back. He distributed a courteous smile among the ladies who were present. "When you are ready . . ."

The Countess was through the secret door like a greyhound out of the slips. Amelia was close behind her and Mrs. Ledbed, showing a remarkable turn of speed, was the next to race past the bogus collected works of Sir Walter Scott. The Duchess made a more dignified exit, pausing to take a last look around the library and wondering if she should try to salvage the bust of Admiral Rodney. Abandoning the gallant sailor to the encroaching flames, she cleared her throat and stepped into the safety of the passageway.

"Splendid work, Gerry," said the Duke, shaking the hand of their saviour. "Not a reading man myself so I'd never have guessed there was this ingenious device here."

He made his escape, followed by Benfleet and Da Silva, who, robbed of the chance to sing his national anthem, resorted to a recitation of "The Boy Stood On the Burning Deck" in faultless Spanish. Archie Nettle was the next in line.

"I can't help liking H. G. Wells," he said. "He makes me laugh."

"Get out, man!" snapped Sir Gerard, pushing him through the secret door. "Anyone who reads H. G. Wells should be horse-whipped!" He was about to leave the Library himself when he heard the drumming of heels on the floor and looked back to see the bound and gagged Reggie Arbuthnot wearing a hole in the carpet with his frenzied feet. "Sorry, old chap. Almost forgot you."

Scooping up the squirming detective, Sir Gerard flung him over his shoulder with the fluency of a man who is used to rescuing helpless captives from burning buildings, then retrieved the book about the ancient topography of Salisbury Plain that he had been reading earlier. Flames were now starting to bite their way hungrily through the door, and the intense heat made the windows explode into a thousand shards. The imminent danger did not prevent Sir Gerard from confiding something to his old friend.

"Anyone who reads the Marquis de Sade should be horse-whipped as well," he whispered. "It adds immeasurably to the pleasure."

LADY Cecily had watched the drama unfolding from beneath the sheltering branches of a chestnut tree. She chortled with glee and congratulated herself on the skill with which she had started the inferno, a legacy of her time in the Girl Scouts where she had won her Fire Lighting Badge at the first attempt, even though she incinerated the Girl Scouts hut, singed the uniforms of everyone present, and left third-degree burns all over the peeping tom who had been peering through the keyhole at the time. Now she had destroyed a whole dynasty and left herself as the only surviving member of the Faughstrayne family. She clapped her hands in delight.

"It's like Bonfire Night!" she declared.

"Yes," said Maisie, standing beside her. "Except that we didn't burn a mere effigy of Guy Fawkes. Our fuel was human. We fried the devils alive!"

A last flash of lightning dazzled their eyes; then the downpour increased to such a torrent that the flames rising from the west wing were extinguished with a deafening sizzle. Lady Cecily gave a smile of satisfaction.

"No phoenix will arise from those ashes," she said.

"I am the only true Phoenix," announced Maisie. "Remember that."

Lady Cecily turned to look at the remarkable young woman at her side. In a house that had been full of masters and mistresses of disguise, Maisie was supreme. No drugs, pigments, wigs, false mustaches, or elaborate make-up were needed. Nature had endowed her with the most perfect disguise of all. She was what she appeared to be. Maisie looked, talked, walked, felt, and tasted like an innocent young Irish girl from the Lower Orders. Instead of having to pose as an upstairs maid, she was one, a put-upon domestic with the unmistakable aura of a menial. What was not so evident to the naked eye, however, was the razor-sharp brain, the iron determination, and the heart that beat with vengeful fury.

"What about my reward?" asked Lady Cecily.

"Service to the Cause should be enough reward in itself," replied Maisie.

"I was promised money as well."

"You shall have it in the form of gold doubloons from a sunken treasure ship. Each one is worth hundreds of pounds. Come," said Maisie as the rain suddenly stopped, "let's go to the fountain, where I hid the booty. And we must toast our success. After all, we have something to celebrate, Lady Cecily."

"My acquisition of Crawsbey Castle!"

"There's been a far greater achievement than that to-night."

Smiling a secret smile, Maisie led the way through the soggy grass towards the fountain. The west wing was now no more than a smoky ruin. Chilled by the rain, a magnum of champagne awaited them. Maisie picked it up with the dexterity of a gymnast reaching for an Indian club.

"I'll open this," she said. "Pass me those glasses behind you, please."

"Where?" asked Lady Cecily, turning her back.

"On the parapet."

"I don't see any glasses."

Lady Cecily groped about in search of champagne flutes. It was a fatal mistake. Before she knew what was happening, a magnum of champagne was smashed across the back of her head as if it were the bow of an ocean-going vessel.

"I name this ship The Wreck of the Faughstraynes!" shouted Maisie, launching her into the fountain with such a powerful shove that Cecily nose-dived into the water and, with a glancing blow from her shoulders, dislodged Nelson from his plinth so that he fell into the fountain and removed the two remaining prongs from Neptune's trident. "I haven't forgotten your reward, Lady Cecily," she continued, tossing gold doubloons into the water. "There you are—three coins in a fountain."

As they sank down past the sightless eyes of Lady Cecily, the coins swiftly lost their gold patina and were revealed in their true colors as nothing more than Irish pennies. The mocking voice of Maisie echoed across the terrace.

"Dublin doubloons doubling as real doubloons. Give my regards to Neptune."

THE tunnel beneath Castle Crawsbey seemed to be endless. Guided by a mysterious light that illumined their way, the fugitives from the burning Library followed a tortuous route that took them past a disused tin mine, the skeletal remains of a Lost Tribe of Aborigines, and a derelict station that was built in the bizarre hope of connecting with the London Underground. The subterranean passage also contained aromatic evidence of what happened when one of the chains was pulled in the castle bathrooms. Holding their breath, they hurried on. When they emerged into the fresh air, they gasped with relief. Benfleet fell to his knees to offer up a prayer of thanks, the Countess burst into a song about the Bells of Aberdovey out of sheer joy, and Da Silva executed a series of lithe movements, with an imaginary cape, copied from a bullfighter he had once admired. Amelia was eyeing her lover with a mixture of affection and suspicion.

"Who is H. G. Wells?" she asked warily.

"I believe him to be a genius," said Nettle proudly.

"I believe him to be a bounder!" said the Duke.

"And I believe him to be intent on destroying our civilization!" added the Duchess, raising a haughty eyebrow. "Deplorable fellow! He should be sent to the galleys and lashed to the oars."

Benfleet was a stickler for detail. "We don't have galleys anymore, I'm afraid."

"Then we should build some. Oswald, use your influence with the Navy."

The Duke shrugged ducally. "I don't have any influence with the Navy, my dear."

"Then acquire some."

It was Sir Gerard Hawksmoor who, once again, brought logic to bear on their plight. After dumping Reggie Arbuthnot on the ground like a sack of coal, he gazed around. They were in the middle of a forest, miles from anywhere.

"What we need to acquire is a map of the area," he observed. "Does anyone have the slightest clue where we are?"

"It reminds me of Argentina," decided Da Silva.

"It reminds me of Robin Hood," said Mrs. Ledbed.

"Or *The Wind in the Willows*," noted Amelia.

"Or the enchanted wood in *Hansel and Gretel*," said the Countess.

"It reminds me of a forest," said Benfleet, ever the realist.

"Can nobody tell us where we are?" demanded the Duchess.

"We are safe, my dear," murmured the Duke, touching her fondly on the left buttock, his favorite, for the first time in seventeen years. "That, surely, is all that matters."

"Look," said Sir Gerard, pointing to Arbuthnot. "I do believe that Reggie is trying to tell us something."

All heads turned to the horizontal Chief Inspector. Unable to do more than twitch and roll, he was nevertheless using his keen analytical brain for the benefit of them all. As he wriggled to and fro, kicking away with his toes, it became clear that he was giving them a pictorial message. A shape was soon etched in the soft turf.

"It's an arrow!" remarked Sir Gerard. "Reggie knows where we are."

Arbuthnot shook his head as vigourously as he could and pleaded with his eyes.

The Duke was an observant man. "I think he wants us to untie him."

"But he tried to kill you," said Da Silva.

"Only because he thought that the Duke was the Phoenix," said Mrs. Ledbed. "We all saw those brands on his legs. No wonder he went berserk. He wanted to avenge himself on the organisation that marked him for life."

"I'm only a pretend Phoenix," confessed the Duke.

"Do you hear that, Reggie?" called Sir Gerard into his friend's ear. "You attacked the wrong man. If we let you up, will you promise to behave?" Arbuthnot nodded again. "What's the general feeling?" asked Sir Gerard, turning to the others. "Shall we vote?"

The Duchess was outraged. "That's taking democracy too far!" she snorted.

"I fought for female suffrage," said Mrs. Ledbed. "Untie him."

"No," said the Countess. "Remove his gag first."

"Ask him if he's calmed down now," suggested Da Silva.

"Ask him if he can guarantee my safety," said the Duke.

"Ask him what he thinks of H. G. Wells," said Nettle.

"Archie!" cried Amelia reproachfully.

"It was the Chief Inspector who loaned me *The War of the Worlds*."

"Then leave him tied up in perpetuity!" decreed the Duchess.

But the compassionate Sir Gerard had already given the casting vote. Untying the gag, he popped a peppermint into the mouth of the guardian of the law to take away the taste of the fabric. Then he hoisted him into a vertical position and used the knife that he always kept concealed in his tobacco pouch to cut through the man's bonds. Reggie

Arbuthnot was free at last. Letting out a roar of anger, he spat the peppermint a good thirty yards then shook himself so violently that they all backed away in fear. His index finger then followed the direction of the arrow.

"That way!" he affirmed.

"How can you be so sure?" wondered Sir Gerard.

"Because I've been here before. Take a closer look at that oak, Gerry," he went on, indicating the noblest tree in the forest. Do you see something carved into it?"

"Why, yes," said Sir Gerard, crossing to stare at a heart that had been crudely gouged into the bark. "It says G LOVES S."

Benfleet was scandalized. "Gilbert loves Sullivan! Upon my word!"

"No, you legal lunatic!" snapped Arbuthnot. "Googoo loves Sofa. They were pet names for two young lovers who once met in the shade of this tree. I refuse to say how and why I was christened as Googoo and everlasting fidelity to the lady in question means that the origin of her nickname, too, will remain shrouded from your eyes. Suffice it to say," he told them, pointing yet again, "that the one safe way out of the forest is in this direction."

They followed him in single file, like natives on safari, picking their way through the trunks of oak, ash, elm, willow, and the occasional incongruous palm tree. Arbuthnot was as good as his word. Taking the route he had once trodden with his beloved Sophie, he brought them to the edge of the forest and out on to a narrow road. The deserted location produced a touch of exasperation in the Duchess's voice.

"How on earth do we get back to the castle from here?" she asked.

"By taxi," said Arbuthnot with quiet confidence.

"There are no taxis in this wilderness."

"That, with respect, is where you are wrong."

And with a flick of his fingers, the Chief Inspector accomplished a small miracle. Around a bend, as if waiting for the summons, came Edwin Cooper in his taxi. The driver turned a cynical eye on the passengers.

"Think I'm taking the whole lot of you?" he asked. "Not bleeding likely!"

MAISIE entered Castle Crawsbey with the arrogant strut of an army of occupation. The west wing might have been completely destroyed but the main part of the building had been untouched by the fire. She took possession of her new home. Dismissed by Jeavons, the make-believe butler, she had crept away with her tail between her legs. Metaphorically, it was now waving in the air. The final conquest had at last been achieved. Maisie was confident that every living member of the Faughstrayne family had been dispatched to his or her grave, including the treacherous Lady Cecily who had sold the others out for a few fake doubloons. Maisie was exhilarated. Her own family would be proud of her.

When she worked there as an upstairs maid, she had tiptoed tentatively around, afraid to enter a room until she was bidden and behaving with the submissive politeness of an underling at all times. That time had gone. She sailed along corridors, burst into bedchambers, and even played a few shots in the billiard room. Elevated into the peerage, she could do anything she wished. The rest of the staff at Castle Crawsbey had fled when the fire started. Nobody was there to challenge Maisie or to stop her from pouring herself a glass of the Duchess's special port, kept by her bedside for the

sorts of emergencies that elderly aristocratic ladies sometimes encounter in the middle of the night. The port sent
the fire of victory surging through Maisie's veins.

There was one last thing to do. Making her way to the
top of the house, she let herself out on to the flat roof and
strolled to the flagpole. Down came the Union Jack to be
replaced by a flag of a very different color. Maisie was just
about to haul it aloft when she spotted something that made
her gurgle in astonishment. On the road, far below her,
approaching the castle with painful slowness, was a taxi that
was so heavily laden that it coughed and spluttered every
inch of the way. How many bodies were packed inside the
vehicle, Maisie could not see. What she could make out,
however, was the figure of a Russian Countess, standing on
one running board, the shape of an Argentinian, balanced
on the other running board, and, clinging to the roof of the
taxi as if his life depended on it, a young police officer who
had chosen that moment to defend his preference for the
works of H. G. Wells and who was shouting about his reading habits at the top of his not inconsiderable voice.

Maisie recovered quickly. There was still work for her
to do.

"THIS'LL cost you!" warned Edwin Cooper, as his taxi
emitted a series of small explosions. "D'you hear that? My
gaskets have blown."

"You should have had them removed with your tonsils,"
said the Duchess airily.

"This taxi is only licensed to hold four, you know."

"I'm only holding one," said the Duke with a chuckle,
his arms encircling the waist of his wife, who was perched

on his knee. "I've never enjoyed a taxi ride so much in all my born days."

"What about my cylinder head?" wailed Cooper.

"Please, Edwin!" reprimanded Sir Gerard. "We'll not have that kind of talk in front of the ladies. Keep your mind on the road ahead."

"This is police business, remember," added Arbuthnot. "The fate of the British Empire may lie in your unworthy hands."

Cooper snorted. "All I'm worried about is my big end."

"Then discuss it with your doctor," advised Mrs. Ledbed. "I don't think that this is the appropriate place to reveal your medical problems."

"What about Archie?" said Amelia with alarm. "I hate the thought of him being up there on the roof. What if he falls off?"

"Then he'll take H. G. Wells with him," replied the Duke, "Good riddance to both of them, I say. We want no Bolsheviks over here."

"Raise your minds to higher objectives," said Sir Gerard, composing his features into the fearless look he had perfected in the trenches. "We are on a mission."

"Quite right, Gerry," agreed Arbuthnot. "We must kill the Phoenix."

Amelia shuddered. "As long as we don't kill Archie in the process!"

"It's the best thing that could happen to you, Amelia," said the Duchess. "If the man's mind has been corrupted by H. G. Wells, imagine what his body would be like."

"Oh, I do! All the time!"

"Excuse me," whispered Benfleet, unused to the close proximity of women and sweating profusely as a result. "If

you must sit on my lap, Mrs. Ledbed, could you please
remove the set of knives that are digging into me?"

"They are not knives, Mr. Benfleet," retorted Mrs. Ledbed.
"I am wearing a whale-boned corset and I will certainly not
remove it for your convenience, either here or anywhere else,
for that matter. Suffer in silence, man."

"That's what I am doing!"

The taxi rolled uncertainly on. The harassed driver continued to complain, Amelia continued to worry about her
constable, the Duke enjoyed re-acquainting himself with
parts of the Duchess that he had not caressed since his wed-
ding night, and Benfleet, while suffering in silence, vowed
to start a Society for the Abolition of Whale-Bone Corsets.
Something then happened to concentrate all their minds. A
distant explosion was heard, followed by a whistling sound
that culminated in a series of loud crashes as a heavy object
bounced past them on the road.

"Crikey!" yelled Cooper. "That was a cannonball."

AFTER rolling the second iron ball across to the cannon,
Maisie loaded it with an effort into the still smoking barrel.
Grateful that she always carried a supply of gunpowder with
her for just such contingencies, she tipped it into the hole,
inserted a taper, then lit it with a match. As the flame
burned its way slowly down, she used all her strength to
manoeuvre the cannon around until it pointed at the taxi.
Maisie then stepped back to avoid the recoil and inserted a
finger in each ear.

"B_O_O_O_O_O_O_O_M!"

The cannonball shot out of the barrel and explored the

heavens before starting its downward path. Maisie could see nothing through the smoky haze left behind. What she heard, however, was a massive explosion as the cannonball hit its target, reducing the taxi to a mass of tangled metal. Maisie started to cheer. The smoke then cleared and the noise died in her throat. What she could now see was that the taxi might have been destroyed but that its occupants had had the sense to get out of it first.

They were still alive, running towards the castle. The Phoenix was in danger.

IT was Reggie Arbuthnot who discovered the dead body in the fountain. Peering into the water, he saw that Lady Cecily was embracing the statue of Nelson with the passion of a latter-day Lady Hamilton, so much so that the Admiral's single eye was glowing like the beam of a lighthouse. The others gathered round the fountain and stared in horror.

"That's the second C. B. to go in the drink," noted Sir Gerard.

"And we can guess why," said Arbuthnot, looking at the shattered fragments of the magnum of champagne. "Thinking that she'd killed us all, she celebrated by drinking this whole bottle and became so tiddly that—like many intoxicated women—she fell into the arms of a sailor. Unfortunately, this sailor, the good Admiral Nelson, was under water. It's a classic case of involuntary suicide."

"I beg to differ, Reggie," said Sir Gerard, who had examined the circumstantial evidence more carefully. "Even inebriated women do not smash themselves over the head with a bottle before diving into a fountain and reducing Neptune's trident to state where it is all dent and no tri. Look at those scalp wounds. Someone hit Lady Cecily from behind and pushed her into the water."

"The Phoenix," decided Nettle.

"Good thinking, Archie."

"It was the Phoenix who fired those cannonballs at us."

"Then we must apprehend her," said Sir Gerard. "Maisie is the master criminal."

The Duke grimaced. "And to think that I engaged her as an upstairs maid."

"Good domestics are so hard to find these days," remarked the Duchess.

"I want Maisie behind bars," said Arbuthnot, grinding his teeth.

"I want her to explain about the turquoise beads," said Da Silva.

"And the missing negatives," said Mrs. Ledbed.

"And the list of names," said the Countess.

"And who killed Squiffy Frobisher," said Sir Gerard.

"And what she saw in my room," said Amelia.

"I just want her to pay for my taxi," cried Cooper, close to tears. "You expect some hazards on the road but you don't allow for hostile cannonballs. She's put me out of business. I want compensation."

"I want answers," said Benfleet.

"Then let's get them," announced Sir Gerard. "Surround the castle and close in."

EVEN in a building as full of hiding places as Castle Craws-bey, the Phoenix knew that they would find her eventually, so she adopted her perfect disguise once more. When the ring of searchers closed in on her, she was cleaning Amelia's bedroom with a dustpan and brush. Maisie looked up in surprise.

"Mother McCrea!" she exclaimed. "What are you all doing here?"

"We could ask you the same thing," said Arbuthnot.

"I'm just doing my job, sir."

"But I dismissed you, Maisie," said the Duke.

"It was Jeavons, the butler, who did that. And he doesn't exist anymore so I reapplied for my former post. You'll need me, after all," she argued. "Someone must clean up that mess in the west wing."

"But you caused it," challenged Sir Gerard.

"Me, sir?" she asked innocently. "I'm just a simple Irish girl from Dublin."

"Who destroyed my taxi!" yelled Cooper. "Is that what they teach you in the convent? How to fire cannonballs at harmless motorists?"

"And how to kill someone with a magnum of champagne?" said Nettle.

Arbuthnot folded his arms. "You've a lot of explaining to do, Maisie."

"Then I suggest you all make yourselves comfortable while I do it," she said.

And before they could stop her, she tossed the dustpan and brush aside and produced a pistol from beneath her white apron, firing a bullet into the ceiling to prove that it was loaded. An impromptu snowstorm of plaster fell on the room.

"Sit down!" barked Maisie, and they rushed to obey. "That's better," she said in her sweet Irish brogue. "You might as well know that you're looking at the person who killed Squiffy Frobisher for offences against the Cause. I take no prisoners. Before I execute you, I think that you're entitled to know what your crimes are. It'll make you sleep easier in your graves."

"Oswald!" said the Duchess sharply, turning to her husband. "I don't know which agency you recruited this young lady from but I can assure you that it's the last time we hire any servants from them."

"It's the last time you'll need any servants," said Maisie. "Now, let's begin at the beginning. Have any of you ever been to Dublin?" There was dead silence. She looked around the blank faces. "Someone must have visited Dublin."

"I think that H. G. Wells went there once," said Nettle helpfully.

"Then he will doubtless have come across Phoenix Park. And if he did that, he would have heard about the notorious Phoenix Park murders. That is what lies behind all that's happened here at Castle Crawsbey," explained Maisie. "On May 6, 1882, a date that is burned into my memory, gallant Irish assassins killed Lord Frederick Cavendish and his deputy, Mr. T. H. Burke, two men appointed by the British government to keep my people in subjection. There were fierce reprisals."

"I remember now," said Sir Gerard. "The assassinations were the work of some crazed Fenians who called themselves the Invincibles. We rounded the devils up."

"Not all of them," continued Maisie. "My father escaped and he was pursued by British agents for the next twenty years. They finally caught up with him Argentina, in the year that I was born. Do you know the names of those British agents?"

"I think that you're about to tell us," said the Duke, wriggling uncomfortably.

"One was Bernard Benfleet."

"My father!" cried the lawyer.

"Another was Nigel Nettle."

"My uncle!" gasped the Constable.

"A third was Andrew Arbuthnot."

"My cousin," gulped the Chief Inspector. "He always claimed to be a carpet salesman."

"Last came Fred Ferncliff."

"My husband!" groaned the abandoned wife. "He told me that he was going on holiday in South America and I never saw him again."

"It was no holiday, Mrs. Ledbed," said Maisie. "He was part of an execution squad. My father, Liam, had fled to Argentina, where he was making an honest living as naval rating. He was betrayed by a close friend, Juan Domingo Da Silva!"

"My brother!" admitted the Argentinian.

"Those names are engraved on my soul. Benfleet, Nettle, Arbuthnot, Ledbed, and Da Silva. Those men were responsible for the death of my father, Liam Liffey. As a result, anyone who bears those foul names must die."

"That lets us out, my dear," said the Duke to his wife. "May we leave, Maisie?"

"No," replied the upstairs maid, aiming the pistol directly at him. "Because the name of Faughstrayne also comes into the reckoning. When my father was captured, he had been drinking in a Buenos Aires nightclub. An exotic dancer, in the pay of the British, got him so drunk that he was easily overpowered. The name of that dancer, I can now reveal, was none other than the famous transvestite, Dudley Faughstrayne, also known as Consuela."

"Our son!" chorused the Duke and the Duchess.

"Now you see why your names are on the death list as well."

"You've got nothing on me," argued the Countess. "I can see why you have to get rid of all the others but I'm just a down-to-earth, common-or-garden, innocuous Welsh spy. Let me go and I won't say a word about this."

Maisie was scornful. "You're in it up to your neck, Countess. I was the one who discovered you in this very room in a compromising position with Jeavons."

"Is this true, Oswald?" demanded the Duchess.

"I was a butler, then, my dear," he said earnestly. "Different roles, different rules. The Countess offered me her body in lieu of a tip."

"It means that she's tainted along with you," said Maisie.

"What about me?" asked Sir Gerard. "I'm not tainted."

Cooper was restive. "And what about my bleeding taxi?"

"You won't be needing a taxi where you're going, Mr. Cooper. As for you, Sir Gerard," said Maisie, "I have some bad news. When Liam Liffey was betrayed and arrested, they were not sure how best to kill him. An exiled English diplomat gave them the answer. His name was Harold Hawksmoor."

"My stepfather!" confessed the amateur sleuth.

"It was Hawksmoor who pointed out that my father was an inebriated seaman. 'What shall we do with the drunken sailor'?" he asked. "Why—'put him in a longboat till he's sober'." So that's what they did. They set him adrift in an open boat in the middle of the ocean. What a hideous way to die! When his body was found and the truth came out, my mother raised me to get revenge on everyone involved. Since it all started with the Phoenix Park murders, I took the name of the Phoenix."

"There are still some loose ends left hanging," Amelia pointed out.

"Forget about those. It's time to go."

Holding the pistol on them, Maisie ushered the entire group up on to the roof. There, to their consternation, they saw the Irish flag flying over a noble English pile. Maisie strode to the edge of the parapet and gazed down.

"It will be a quicker death than they allowed my father," she said. "Who's going to be first? Mrs. Ledbed? Sir Gerard? Chief Inspector?"

Cooper was irate. "I'm not jumping off there till you pay me for my taxi."

"Spare us, Maisie," implored the Countess. "We meant no harm."

Others began to beg for mercy and Benfleet even fell to his knees but Sir Gerard and Arbuthnot remained silent. They were trying to work out a means of escape. While they racked their brains in vain, however, it was Nettle who took decisive action. He slipped a hand under the flap of his jacket to remove an object that he always kept, in defiance of police regulations, in his back pocket.

"Right," said Maisie. "Age before beauty. We'll start with the Duke."

The Duke was unafraid. "It is a far, far better thing that I do now than I managed to achieve in bed with the Countess."

As the brave nobleman moved forward, Nettle seized his opportunity. Hurling the object at Maisie, he caught her in the middle of the forehead and sent her backward over the edge of the parapet. The Phoenix had been outwitted. After turning somersaults in the air, she landed with a loud splash in the fountain and expired beside her victim. Everyone rushed to congratulate the resourceful constable who was now reclaiming from the ground the book that had saved their lives. Amelia hugged her future husband. Cooper asked for his autograph. Arbuthnot promised to promote him. Nettle gave a bashful grin. He held up *The History of Mr. Polly.*

"I never go anywhere without a copy of H. G. Wells," he confessed.

So ended the flight of the Phoenix. Archie Nettle, the unlikely hero, married Amelia and lived happily ever after. The Duke and Duchess rebuilt the castle and turned it into an aristocratic theme park. Mrs. Ledbed, seized by an impulse of irresistible passion, proposed to Reggie Arbuthnot, who was too much of a gentleman to refuse. Recovering quickly from the irrevocable loss of his beloved Amelia, Sir Gerard Hawksmoor made a major contribution to Anglo-Celtic relations by marrying the Russian-German-Welsh spy, Countess Boronskaya.

Enrique da Silva returned to his native Argentina to plot the invasion of the Falkland Islands. Edwin Cooper bought himself a new taxi with the insurance money and bored his passengers with the tale of how he helped to capture the Phoenix. The only person who did not find happiness was Roderick Benfleet, the lawyer, who became an itinerant herb gatherer and was often seen flitting around the Faughstrayne estate, issuing writs and subpoenas to parsley, sage, rosemary, and thyme, while singing a medley of sea shanties, one of which adorns this curious tale. Bon voyage, shipmates!

MEET THE CREW OF
The Sunken Sailor

Simon Brett, who keeps his pond clear of inconvenient corpses, is the author of the Charles Paris and Mrs. Pargeter mysteries. The fourth of his Fethering series, *Murder in the Museum*, was published in 2003. Brett is president of the Detection Club, under whose aegis *The Floating Admiral* was published.

Jan Burke has a pantry stocked with Phoenix Honey, Special #863, for those occasions when guests suffer from brain fever. Her long-running series with reporter Irene Kelly includes the Edgar-winning *Bones*. Her latest novel, a stand-alone thriller, is *Nine*. Her website can be found at www.janburke.com.

Although born in England, Dorothy Cannell now resides in Illinois and so rarely confronts a butler in his dressing gown. She has published a dozen mystery novels and won an Agatha Award for her short story "The Family Jewels." Her latest book is *The Importance of Being Ernestine*.

Currently shopping for a tutti-frutti hat, Margaret Coel is the *New York Times* bestselling author of the Wind River mystery novels set among the Arapahos in Wyoming. *The Spirit Woman* was named the winner of the Colorado Book Award and the Willa Cather Award for best novel on the west and was the finalist for the Western Writers of America Spur Award. The latest novel in the series, *Killing Raven*, was published in 2003.

For more about the mystery series, the Wind River reservation, and the author, visit www.margaretcoel.com.

Ever ready to be summoned by the Home Office, *Deborah Crombie* was a Macavity winner and Edgar and Agatha nominee for *Dreaming of the Bones* and an Agatha nominee for *A Share in Death*. Her latest book in the Duncan Kincaid/Gemma James series is *Now May You Weep*.

Eileen Dreyer and her evil twin Kathleen Korbel have published between them 26 novels and 7 short stories. Her current novel *With a Vengeance,* for which she studied to be a medic on a SWAT team, is now out from St. Martin's Press. A trauma nurse by training and incurable researcher by inclination, she can be found in St. Louis with her husband and two children. She has animals, but prefers to protect them from the glare of the limelight.

Never resorting to Miss Pinkerton's Rectifying Beauty Preparation, *Carolyn Hart* has written 34 mysteries, including the Agatha Award–winning Death on Demand series and the Henrie O series. Her newest title is *Engaged to Die*. She also has a stand-alone novel, *Letter From Home,* published by Berkley Prime Crime.

Edward Marston, who travels with a ready copy of H. G. Wells, has written plays, short stories, and more than 30 historical mysteries. He is the author of the Domesday Books, set in Norman England; the Nicholas Bracewell series, featuring an Elizabethan theater company; and the Redmayne mysteries about a young architect who is helping to rebuild London after the Great Fire of 1666. He writes nautical mysteries under the name of Conrad Allen and golf mysteries as Keith Miles. Latest titles are *The Vagabond Clown* (Marston);

Murder on the Marmora (Allen). A former chairman of the British Crime Writers Association, Edward Marston was the Guest of Honor at Malice Domestic XIV.

When not prowling the streets of Market Winsome, *Francine Mathews* writes spy thrillers (as herself) and a series of mysteries featuring Jane Austen (as Stephanie Barron). Her books include *The Secret Agent*. Her website may be found at www.francinemathews.com.

Although *Sharan Newman* normally writes about the Middle Ages, she also has a passion for the time when people knew how to use a fish fork and why you can't use finger bowls unless you have a butler and servers. Her family makes fun of this and they will eat the whole meal with the salad fork, just to annoy her. Therefore, she is very grateful for the chance to spend some time in the civilized (?) company of this tale.

The most recent book in the medieval Catherine LeVendeur series is *The Outcast Dove* (2003). For further information on the series and how people survived before fish forks (but not finger bowls) see her website at www.hevanet.com/sharan/Levendeur.html

Anne Perry is relieved not to be a guest at Castle Crawsbey. She received the Edgar Award for her story "Heroes," which serves as the basis of her series set in World War I. Her two Victorian series feature Superintendent Thomas Pitt and his inquisitive wife Charlotte and private inquiry agent William Monk and nurse Hester Latterly Monk. Her latest books include *The Rising Tide* and *No Graves As Yet*.

Although *Alexandra Ripley* does not have as many disguises as Mrs. Ledbed, she is overjoyed to have contributed a chapter to this masterpiece. Her favorite reading is the murder mystery, and she tried many times to write one . . . but always failed. She had to settle for successful historical novels, including the sequel to *You Know What.*

Walter Satterthwait was raised by wolverines in New Mexico, which has no wolverines. His many novels include the Agatha Award–nominated *Escapade, Masquerade, Wilde West,* and *Miss Lizzie.* His website may be found at www.satterthwait.com.

Sarah Smith denies any association with the Imperial Vegetable Marrow Growers' Association and writes novels set at the turn of the twentieth century. They include *The Vanished Child, The Knowledge of Water,* and *A Citizen of the Country.*

Carolyn Wheat usually avoids stowing blowpipes in her closet and has won the Agatha, Anthony, Macavity, and Shamus awards for her work. *Tales Out of School,* her short story collection, was nominated for an Anthony as Best Anthology. She teaches creative writing at UC–San Diego and has published a how-to book, *How to Write Killer Fiction.*